THE ROOM WITH
EIGHT WINDOWS

Also by Jane A. Adams from Severn House

THE ROOM WITH EIGHT WINDOWS

Jane A. Adams

SEVERN
HOUSE

First world edition published in Great Britain and the USA in 2023
by Severn House, an imprint of Canongate Books Ltd,
14 High Street, Edinburgh EH1 1TE.

Trade paperback edition first published in Great Britain and the USA in 2024
by Severn House, an imprint of Canongate Books Ltd.

severnhouse.com

British Library Cataloguing-in-Publication Data
A CIP catalogue record for this title is available from the British Library.

ISBN-13: 978-1-4483-1110-1 (cased)
ISBN-13: 978-1-4483-1171-2 (trade paper)
ISBN-13: 978-1-4483-1111-8 (e-book)

Typeset by Palimpsest Book Production Ltd., Falkirk, Stirlingshire, Scotland.

Praise for Jane A. Adams

"A dense and atmospheric plot with plenty of surprises, authentic historical details, and intriguing characters . . . make this one a good pick for fans of British historical mysteries"
Booklist on *The Girl in the Yellow Dress*

"Lovers of tweedy English murder mysteries will find much to like"
Publishers Weekly on *The Girl in the Yellow Dress*

"A cautionary tale . . . about the perils of getting what you wish for"
Kirkus Reviews on *Bright Young Things*

"Complex characters and an intricate plot . . . Adams effortlessly conveys the police procedures, business practices, and social mores of the period . . . Fans of golden age mysteries will be delighted"
Publishers Weekly Starred Review of *Old Sins*

"Vivid . . . well-constructed . . . will appeal to the **Downton Abbey** crowd"
Booklist on *The Good Wife*

"Appealing characters . . . Fans of historical police procedurals will be satisfied"
Publishers Weekly on *The Good Wife*

"Fast-paced fun"
Kirkus Reviews on *The Good Wife*

About the author

Jane A. Adams was born in Leicestershire and still lives there – even though it is too far from the sea. She teaches creative writing and writing skills, mentors other writers for various arts organizations and is a Fellow of the Royal Society of Arts and a Royal Literary Fund Associate Fellow. Her first book, *The Greenway*, was shortlisted for the CWA John Creasey Award and for the Author's Club Best First Novel Award. When not writing she can often be found drawing racing dodos and armoured hares and the occasional octopus.

As well as the Henry Johnstone series, Adams is the author of the highly acclaimed Naomi Blake and Rina Martin mystery series.

For Katie, and November.

PROLOGUE

December, 1930

For two days now he had heard footsteps when none should be possible, someone walking – and it sounded, because the old house was filled with odd echoes, as though it was coming from above. His investigations had shown him that there was nothing above him but ceiling and then a void and then the roof. He could hear the patter of pigeon claws and the occasional crow on the tiles, but this was different. These were human steps. He could find no entry into an attic space and sometimes the sound seemed to be coming from behind the walls – he would wake up startled by its closeness.

If he hadn't already thought that he was losing his mind, this might have convinced him, but Henry Johnstone was possessed of far too logical a brain to consider such simple explanations. Though he had to admit it had disturbed him.

But this time was different. These steps were definitely on the stairs leading to his room and definitely belonged to someone who was trying to be silent and not quite succeeding. Henry pulled the plug from the wash bowl and let the water gurgle down, certain that this sudden rush would cause the usual clanking groan and protest of the ageing plumbing and that whoever was on the stairs would think he was oblivious. The same sounds would cover any noise that Henry might make. He pulled on his pyjamas and slipped from the bathroom into the bedroom, a curious and uncomfortable place with eight curving windows. The room was built into a corner section of the house that curved to form something resembling a tower attached to this rather dull, grey house. It was as though the architect had wanted one exuberant detail while the rest was tediously utilitarian.

Silent on bare feet, Henry moved to the fireplace and

equipped himself with a poker. He had no idea what or who he might be up against and that worried him greatly. The operation on his left shoulder had done something to ease the pain but very little to improve mobility, and so to all intents and purposes he had one good arm. If he swung this poker in anger he would have to make the first blow count; he doubted he'd have time for a second.

Beside the fireplace was a desk, and on the other side of the desk was a gap. When the bedroom door was opened it did so against the desk, leaving room for Henry to stand in this space, invisible to whoever entered the room, and hope that would give him some advantage.

You're riding your luck here, he told himself, and wished he had one of his brother-in-law's guns with him. Albert had quite a nice collection. More than that he wished that Mickey Hitchens, for a long time his sergeant and now promoted to inspector, was at his side. Mickey's solid, square presence and his strength would have been reassuring just now.

As it was, ex-Detective Chief Inspector Henry Johnstone was not at full strength – far from it in fact – and he was on his own.

He heard the footsteps reach the top of the stairs and then whoever it was paused on the tiny landing. Henry fancied that he could hear them breathing but realized it was probably his own attempt to control his breath that was so loud in his ears. And then the handle turned, the door crashed open and the man hurtled into the room.

Henry knew he had one chance at this. He slammed the door shut and came out swinging. The poker made a satisfying crunch as it hit the man's face and he made a satisfying yell. He turned towards his attacker and Henry realized that he had a knife, and then realized that he had been cut as the man surged forward. Not, thankfully, the arm that held the poker but the other that swung limp at his side, little more than useless.

This time Henry used the poker to jab, like the point of a sword, and caught the man beneath the chin. His assailant had backed off enough that the poker did not penetrate the soft triangle of flesh and muscle beneath the chin, but it was evidently enough of a shock that the man decided to run rather than continue the fight. Henry managed another blow as the man was forced to stop to open the door. He was not a big man, Henry thought; wiry and tough but not heavily muscled. His third blow hit the man obliquely across shoulder and neck. He yelped again and then took off downstairs.

Henry crossed to the window and stood for a moment trying to catch his breath, and also to see if he could view the means of the man's exit, but it was still dark outside and the sky thickly clouded. No visible moon, no lights, no headlights from a getaway car. The pain in his left shoulder was now intense and his left arm was bleeding and dripping on to the floor. He grabbed a towel from the bathroom and wrapped it around his wounded arm, tying it in place with strips from the edge of the towel cut with his pocketknife. Only then did he notice that something must have fallen from his assailant's pockets as they fought.

Awkwardly, Henry bent to retrieve a penknife, a few coins and a matchbook. He opened it. Inside the cover an address had been written in an unskilful hand.

He managed to dress, knowing that the man was likely to come back with reinforcements and he had to get out.

Henry struggled into his overcoat, went downstairs to the library and then through to the little study where the telephone was still working. He debated whether or not he should call the police. He hesitated . . . Not so long ago he would have been calling upon colleagues to assist him. Now he was just a hapless victim. Somehow he could not bring himself to play that role and deal with the judgement and the questions and the process of law that had not so long ago been his to implement.

Leaving had been hard enough. This would be like rubbing salt into an already inflamed wound.

Instead, and knowing that it was foolish, he dialled another number and then, understanding that he should not remain at the house, he began to walk, or rather to stagger, to the door, his aim being to walk down the drive and towards the road where he could remain in the shadow of the hedge and hope that the only headlights that picked him out would be hers.

ONE

Five years previously, the body of a man subsequently identified as Sidney Carpenter was found on the pavement in a quiet suburban street in St John's Wood in London. High hedges surrounded most of the houses, with their little front gardens and imposing redbrick facades. It was not an area where murders were commonplace, and certainly they did not generally turn up in the middle of a cold afternoon, just a few weeks before Christmas.

There was little vehicular traffic along this obscure residential road and not a great deal of pedestrian traffic either, so the body may have lain there quite some time before it was discovered, positioned as it was behind a parked car and so out of sight to the casual observer. It was found by two children returning from school; their shouts attracted the attention of parents and servants, also collecting children. Within minutes the police had been summoned, several of the residents in the street being affluent enough to afford telephones. Curious children were ushered away and guard was kept by a middle-aged widow, Mrs Hamblin, deemed old and sensible enough not to become distressed at the sight of a dead man, and a gardener borrowed from a neighbour's house.

The police arrived, as did the police surgeon. Death was pronounced, the obvious cause being a major stab wound to the chest.

Mickey Hitchens remembered it well. Detective Chief Inspector Henry Johnstone from Central Office at Scotland Yard was summoned and had brought Mickey, his then sergeant, with him. But the oddest thing about the case was when the widow, Mrs Hamblin, who had been keeping watch, commented that she was surprised that none of the Deans had come out to see what the fuss was about. She was referring, Henry discovered, to the family who lived closest to where the body had been discovered. A husband and wife and her brother, who lodged with them.

'Might the menfolk not be out at work?' Mickey asked. 'Mrs Deans might therefore be nervous to come out.'

'Angela Deans isn't nervous about anything,' Mrs Hamblin declared. 'And I know they're all at home, they're just getting over a bout of flu. Laid them all up for two weeks it has.'

Curious, and a little anxious in case the body on the street might only be part of the story, Henry had one of the constables knock at the door and, on receiving no answer, go round the back. The back door was unlocked and the constable let himself in. There was nobody inside but there clearly had been recently. In the kitchen an empty kettle was set on the trivet beside the stove, the teapot next to it filled with cold tea. On the dining room table sat the remains of half-eaten lunches. There was no mess, no disruption, no sign of anything violent having happened within the house. There was simply nobody there.

'It's like the *Mary Celeste*,' Mickey commented when he too went to look around. Like the *Mary Celeste*, the residents never did turn up. The murder of Sidney Carpenter also remained unsolved.

And like all unfinished business it occasionally nagged, though Sidney Carpenter had been a toerag of a man and was generally considered unmissed and unmourned. His wife had certainly been relieved, Mickey had noted, and of course she was suspected but she had a solid alibi. As for the Deans, relatives were interviewed, neighbours questioned, societies and associations they had belonged to investigated, but no one could shed any light on why the family seemed to have left home in the middle of a meal and neither hide nor hair of them had been seen since.

From time to time the file was fetched out again and re-examined by either Mickey or Henry, and on one occasion by a colleague as Henry wondered if they might have missed something significant, but the dead remained dead and the missing remained missing and that was that for five long years.

So why, Mickey Hitchens now wondered as he stood, perplexed, in the room Henry was last known to have inhabited before going missing, had his old boss, his friend, his now very absent friend, written the name of a murdered man on the edge of a blotter?

Mickey Hitchens was now an inspector and had a sergeant of his own, albeit one of several who had occupied the position of bagman and general factotum in the last few months. Mickey, as the newest of his rank in Central Office, and the most recent to have been elevated to the rank of inspector, had naturally fallen into the role of mentor to the newly qualified.

He hadn't minded. He knew this was the way it was, but he had become slightly resentful of the fact that he would just get used to a person before they were purloined by some senior inspector, or sent back to their own constabulary or, on one occasion, demoted within two weeks of their promotion for drunkenness on duty. He was a little tired of repeating the same little informative speeches over and over again.

His latest protégé rejoiced in the name of Bexley Tibbs and, to be fair, he was not the slowest, most arrogant or otherwise irritating of the batch. Mickey could not recall a time in his own career when he had assured any of the inspectors he had worked with that his own promotion to inspector was just a hop, skip and a jump away. Or questioned their expertise. Or had to be told a dozen times not to step in that very obvious pool of blood, or turned up so hungover as to be incapable. All this and more Mickey had encountered among the batch of new sergeants he had recently supervised. At least Tibbs did seem to be willing to learn and also seemed to have a reasonable number of functioning brain cells.

'So,' Mickey said. 'Stop and look. Take your time. What strikes you about the scene?'

They had paused in the doorway and Mickey had not mentioned the name written on the blotter that rested on the desk close to the door. He felt impatient; what he really wanted to do was get into the room and work the scene, especially as this time his involvement was intensely personal. But he knew he had to do it by the book, especially with an inexperienced officer. If something really had happened to Henry Johnstone, then this last known location needed to be examined properly and thoroughly.

Tibbs, a skinny, sandy-haired fellow with large grey eyes and nervous hands that fluttered and were never still, shuffled his feet and studied the room. 'Um, not many personal possessions,' he said, 'unless he took things with him, but there are pyjamas on the bed and the wardrobe door is open and there are clothes still inside, so . . .'

'So it would seem he has not packed,' Mickey confirmed.

He watched as Tibbs turned his attention to the desk and reached as though to open a drawer. 'Wait a moment, lad,' Mickey said. 'Remember we're looking with our eyes first and our hands after. We'll be fingerprinting in here so we don't want random dabs to deal with as well.'

Bexley Tibbs nodded. He swallowed nervously, the Adam's apple bobbing in his throat. He really did need feeding up, Mickey thought. It was hard to see how the fellow held together, there was so little meat on the bones.

'Blotter on the desk,' Tibbs said. 'It has some ink on it, maybe from letters he wrote. So we should look at that. And there's a name.' He squinted and leaned forward to see better.

'For goodness' sake, put your spectacles on, lad,' Mickey told him.

Tibbs flushed an even deeper pink. He fumbled in his jacket pocket then produced a pair of wire-framed spectacles and hooked them over his ears. 'Sidney Carpenter,' he read. 'Does that name mean anything to you, Inspector?'

Mickey knew that the question had been asked more in hope than expectation and it pleased him to surprise Sergeant Tibbs by saying, 'Actually, yes, it does. Mr Sidney Carpenter got himself murdered five years or more ago. In fact, it would have been five years this past November. Stabbed in the chest in a street in leafy St John's Wood and Inspector Johnstone and I were initially called to the scene. Whoever did the deed was never tracked down and there was little evidence.'

Bexley Tibbs frowned as though trying to call something to mind. 'Was that when that family went missing too?' he asked. 'Walked away from the dinner table and were never seen again?'

'Lunch,' Mickey said. 'They seemed to have left their midday meal unfinished.' He was slightly surprised that Tibbs should remember, but only slightly. The peculiarity of the incident meant it had gained somewhat legendary status, particularly among the lower ranks. He had heard some of the theories about the disappearances, everything from white slavers to the Deans being Russian spies and the possibility of a multiple murderer who had cleaned up very effectively after himself in the house and yet left a dead body on the pavement. 'That will be the one,' he said. 'The big question is why should Detective Chief Inspector Johnstone have written it here?' No longer detective chief inspector, Mickey reminded himself. Not since this past September. It was still a hard fact to take in.

He could feel Bexley Tibbs staring at him as though in expectation of an answer. Mickey took a cautious couple of steps into the room and then another look around.

'It's an odd sort of room,' Tibbs said.

Mickey agreed. Two of the walls were set at right angles to one another in standard fashion, the sort of formation you might reasonably expect from a room. What would have been walls three and four had been replaced by a great arc, a bay of more than a semicircle that housed eight tall, narrow windows affording views of sea and white cliffs and somewhat overgrown garden. On the floor immediately below, Mickey knew, was the apse-like end of an impressive library, this bay an addition to a long and broad rectangular room. It was the library that Henry had been concerned with. He had, somewhat reluctantly according to Henry's sister Cynthia, taken on the job of cataloguing and inventorying the books and papers of the late Sir Eamon Barry, who had died a few months before. The house would eventually be sold along with its contents, Barry's son not only having little interest in it but not having the financial wherewithal to keep it on. Experts would be coming in to value the furnishings and the silver had already departed to the auction house, along with the two cars that had once occupied the carriage house. Sir Eamon had been a keen bibliophile and his son was reluctant to let anyone make an offer on the library until he had some idea of the actual contents, and also until he had ensured that his father's paperwork had been sorted and archived. There were several universities interested in his research and his collections, but in later years he had not kept either in good order.

Mickey found it hard to think of Henry working here. But at least it meant that Henry was working at something. The last time he had seen his friend, some six weeks ago in late October, Henry had looked frail and old and tired and, worst of all, despairing. Mickey had despaired too, wondering if the old Henry would ever return and had not been lost forever. Now that faded, weakened Henry had also completely disappeared, and Mickey felt utterly bereft and very worried indeed.

'So what else do you see?' Mickey asked quietly.

'No photographs, not even a travel clock beside the bed, no books and yet you tell me he liked reading.' He glanced around again. 'No dressing gown or slippers,' he added.

Mickey raised an eyebrow but a swift check confirmed that this was the case. 'There is a small bathroom through that door – it could be that his dressing gown is in there,' he said. 'Go check, but try not to touch anything.'

He watched Tibbs cross the room, treading carefully as though the floor might be hot or sharp or unstable. He was not a graceful man, Mickey thought. When Henry Johnstone moved it was with feline precision. Mickey himself was like a bulldozer, square and powerful and something of an immovable object. Tibbs in contrast always managed to look as though he was walking along a slack line without a balance pole.

'Dressing gown behind the door and slippers beside the bath.' Tibbs sounded vaguely disappointed as he emerged from the bathroom, but Mickey was frowning. 'Is that significant?' Tibbs asked, but looked as though he couldn't possibly imagine how it could be.

'Inspector Johnstone suffered from the cold,' Mickey said, reminding himself again that Henry had not been an inspector for almost three months now. 'And his pyjamas are still on the bed . . . Which makes no sense if he went for a bath and took the dressing gown and slippers with him.' He shook his head, wondering if he was grasping at facts that could not even be classified as straws.

Tibbs was quick to pick up his thought process. 'So a man that felt the cold would take his nightwear and his dressing gown and his slippers into the bathroom with him and the moment he was dry would dress in his nightclothes, wrap himself in his dressing gown and put his slippers on,' he said. He nodded as though this satisfied him and then said, 'I wonder if his overcoat is missing.'

Mickey smiled. That was a good question. 'Then look in the wardrobe. It's long and black and of heavy wool with a deep red lining. And there will be a scarf wrapped around the coat hanger and probably gloves in the pocket.'

'The coat is not there,' Tibbs informed him.

So he had gone out somewhere, Mickey thought, and if he'd had the chance to put on his overcoat, he had presumably gone of his own volition. That was promising, wasn't it? Mickey watched Tibbs as he turned and glanced back towards the bed and then stiffened.

'What is it, lad?'

'The rug beside the bed,' Tibbs said, indicating the floor on the far side of the bed. 'I think it's been kicked out of position and . . .' He glanced at Mickey and then bent down as though to verify something with a closer look. 'I think there is blood on the floor, Inspector. I'm pretty sure that's blood.'

Tibbs moved aside so that Mickey could get a closer look. Several large spots, confined to a space about the size of Mickey's hand, red brown in colour, stained the boards. This room was not carpeted. In fact, it had the look of a space that was little used and had been hastily prepared for Henry's residence, furniture moved in from elsewhere in the house and a large rug placed to cover the floor on one side of the bed, this smaller runner on the other. There had been no fire in the grate for several days and the room was chilly, especially close to the windows. This was not a room that Henry would have enjoyed inhabiting, Mickey thought. He could imagine it being beautiful in the summer when the sun would stream through these tall windows, days when the sea would sparkle and the cliffs become almost blindingly white. Today, however, the sea tumbled and churned as dark grey as the sky and even the white cliffs looked dowdy. The light through the windows was restricted as though filtered through layers of muslin and Mickey, glancing at the windows, wondered when they had last been thoroughly cleaned. He thought about opening one to increase the illumination but the strong wind outside put him off; it would make the room even colder for one thing, and for another was likely to blow everything about.

Mickey glanced around and pointed to the bedside lamp on the other side of the bed. 'See if the flex will reach across to this side of the bed,' he instructed Tibbs, and Tibbs moved quickly to comply. Leaning across the bed, he managed to angle the lamp so that it cast some extra light on the floor and Mickey inspected the stain more closely. Whatever it was, it was thoroughly dry and did not look new. Did it predate Henry's presence here?

'Inspector?' Tibbs sounded worried again. 'I think there may also be blood on the pyjama sleeve.'

Mickey took a closer look. Blood stained the cuff and had soaked back along the left sleeve. The stains on the floor might have a different source but this, Mickey would bet his pay packet, was definitely blood.

'I'll need my kit,' Mickey said, 'and we'll need to take these with us to get the stains analysed. He halted Tibbs before he went to fetch the murder bag from where Mickey had left it by the door. 'No, hold up, lad, we need to speak to Mr Barry first. See if he or the daily maid can shed any light on this business, and then I need to speak to Central Office. The suspicion of blood in the room should be enough for us to get the investigation started properly.'

Tibbs nodded. He wriggled back across the bed and sat the light back on the bedside table. Mickey straightened up and took a last look around the room. This would need examining properly, as would the main library below, and the stairs that led from the servants' quarters through a small door into the study that adjoined the library. A further flight of stairs led from the library up to this room. The rest of the house was closed off. A daily maid came in to cook meals for Henry and make sure that shopping was done and any cleaning and washing taken care of. This would have been a lonely place, Mickey thought, especially for someone as tired and despairing as Henry had been. But then it was Henry's way to search out the quiet and isolated when he needed time to heal. Or at least that was Mickey's experience, and also what Cynthia had hoped when she told Mickey she had suggested Henry take this job.

No, Mickey thought, when she had *manoeuvred* the situation so that there was a job for Henry to take. He wondered if it was actually Mr Barry who was paying for Henry's services or if somehow Cynthia had contrived to do so. Speaking to her on the telephone, he had realized just how anxious she was and he was now equally anxious to get this investigation on to a formal footing and then go and see Henry's sister and have a proper chat. And maybe borrow her car.

Tibbs recovered Mickey's bag and they went back down the stairs, into the library and thence through to the study, where the owner of the house was waiting impatiently for them. Mark Barry was not a tall man but he was well built, broad shouldered and handsome in a rough kind of way, Mickey thought. The kind of handsome that would not last: the signs of a man who drank heavily were already evident on his face and the grey-blue eyes, though intelligent and piercing, had no sympathy in them. He did not wait for Mickey to speak.

'You see, completely vanished. Left his clothes behind but Lord alone knows where he's gone. I have to say I had expected better.'

'There is blood,' Mickey interrupted him coldly. 'It is possible that Detective Chief Inspector . . . Mr Johnstone has met with misadventure. It is possible that there has been foul play.'

'In this house? My God, as though I don't have enough problems. I have a valuer coming in two weeks to look at the library and representatives from Durham and Cambridge to come and examine my father's research. I can't have the police—'

'We will attempt to keep the investigation discreet,' Mickey said harshly. 'But a man is missing and there is evidence of blood in the room he last occupied. An investigation will take place, Mr Barry, and it will be easier if you cooperate. I would hate to have to force the issue and apply to the chief constable of this county—'

'The chief constable was a friend of my father's. I'm sure he'll be understanding of my position.'

Of course he was, Mickey thought. 'The chief constable is

also a very good friend of Mr and Mrs Garrett-Smyth, and his brother is a close business associate of Mr Garrett-Smyth,' Mickey told him. 'Mrs Garrett-Smyth, as you know, is the sister of the missing man. I'm sure the chief constable would urge you to cooperate. And, as I say, we will be as discreet as possible.'

Barry threw up his hands. 'For God's sake,' he said. 'Well then, you'll have to take care of it, I have business elsewhere. I can't be wasting time on something like this. I've not even seen the man since I engaged his services. And now I wish to God I'd never seen him at all.'

Mickey bristled, but he managed to keep his temper and said evenly, 'I will need to speak to anyone who has been in touch with Mr Johnstone. I believe you have a daily maid come in?'

'Yes, yes. I've written her details down for you. Anything else, any other queries, you can address through my solicitor. His card is on the desk. I take it I can trust you with the keys. I'm assuming you won't need to unlock the rest of the house.'

'We will definitely need to search the rest of the house,' Mickey told him firmly.

'Oh, for goodness' sake.' Barry fetched a bunch of keys out of his pocket and cast them on to the desk. 'These unlock this part of the house and the rear door. You will find everything else you need in the key cupboard in the kitchen. And now, if there is nothing else . . .?' He was already reaching for his coat, laid out on the small sofa that occupied one corner of the room.

'And where will you be, should I need to speak to you?' Mickey asked.

'Travelling. I will be travelling. I will be in Scotland. It is December, after all. My wife's family have their estate up there and I will be spending Christmas and New Year with them. Speak to my solicitor if you need any assistance. If he deems it necessary, he will speak to me, and if I deem it necessary, I will send my response to you.'

Mickey made no further comment, knowing that the effort of keeping his temper might be too much if he did. Had Henry been here, he might have been protecting the man from a well-deserved bloody nose by now, Mickey told himself. Henry could not abide arrogance, especially the kind of arrogance backed solely by an accident of birth. He was aware of Tibbs staring at Mr Barry's departing back, his eyes widened and his mouth slack. He'd probably had little to do with such high and mighty gentry, Mickey thought, Tibbs having served his time as a uniformed constable in Limehouse and Whitechapel, as had Mickey and Henry for that matter. Their cases since then had brought them into contact with all states and classes of person, murder being no respecter of money or rank.

'Well, that's him out of the way,' Mickey said, rubbing his hands in satisfaction. There was a telephone on the desk and he picked up the receiver to see if it was still connected. It was. 'And now we can make use of his facilities to call our bosses in Scotland Yard and get this investigation under way. Though I'm guessing, my lad, that it will be just the two of us involved in this unless things get really sticky, and then we might be able to call on the local constabulary for help.' Strings had already been pulled – largely thanks to Cynthia and her husband – to encourage the Brighton and Hove police to formally ask for assistance, something which would not usually have happened unless there had been definite suggestions of murder in the shape of a very dead body. Being rich and having influential connections definitely helped at times like this, Mickey thought, and though that kind of toadying generally irked him, he was grateful for it on this occasion.

'You think it really is a murder investigation?' Tibbs asked.

He had, Mickey knew, been surprised that they had even been called in.

'I'm thinking we don't know at this point,' Mickey told him. 'But I think there are circumstances suspicious enough for us to want to eliminate that possibility.' And frankly, Mickey thought, if Central Office wouldn't cooperate and give him leave to continue with the enquiry, then he'd simply have to take some time off and do it himself. Henry would have done the same had their roles been reversed and Mickey was not about to let his friend down.

TWO

S ergeant Bexley Tibbs looked somewhat terrified as he stood on the doorstep of Cynthia's house, Mickey thought. He looked as though he was about to suggest they went round to the tradesman's entrance, and when the maid opened the door he took two steps back as though he really wanted to run away. Mickey remembered how uneasy he had felt the first time he had visited Cynthia, not here at her Bournemouth house but at the vast pile they had owned in Piccadilly. Before the Wall Street crash and the fallout from Albert Garrett-Smyth's overinvestment in the futures markets had hit their fortunes, they had owned major property in the capital. That they still had money and property and social standing was due in large part to Cynthia's own wisdom and quiet manoeuvrings in the background.

Mickey felt some sympathy for the young sergeant; that first visit to Cynthia's house had been daunting, Mickey remembered, even though he'd been with Henry. But he was now a frequent and, he knew, welcome visitor.

'The mistress is waiting for you,' the maid servant told them, 'and Cook said to tell you that she's making apple crumble specially, seeing as you've come to dinner. With custard.'

'Well, bless her kind heart,' Mickey said. 'Tell her that is much appreciated.'

He could feel Tibbs staring at him, the big grey eyes practically boring into his skull. If anything Tibbs' eyes grew even larger when they were shown into Cynthia's sitting room and Mickey was engulfed in a warm hug and a cloud of silk and perfume.

'It's so good to see you,' Cynthia said. 'I feel as though everything will be sorted out now you are here.'

'We're going to do our very best, you know that,' Mickey told her. 'And this here is my new associate, Sergeant Bexley

Tibbs. I've spoken to Central Ofice and they have granted us permission to do a proper investigation, now the preliminary look has cast up some real evidence. Mr Barry has been good enough to surrender the keys to his house and the number of his solicitor, should we need to get in contact with him. I have to admit he was not best pleased at the idea of big-booted police officers trampling around his estate.'

'Obnoxious little man,' Cynthia said. 'If I'd known him better I would never have got involved, and never suggested Henry should go and do that work for him. His father was a lovely man. Sometimes the apple falls very far from the tree.'

'And rolls down the road and into a ditch,' Mickey agreed. 'When did you last have contact with Sir Eamon?'

'Goodness, now you're asking. Sir Eamon died about eight months ago. I don't think I'd seen him since the summer before, so well over a year. We used to bump into one another regularly, but then he fell ill, dropped his committees and didn't seem inclined to attend social gatherings.' She frowned as though this suddenly troubled her. 'Why do you ask?'

'Because the house is in a terribly neglected state,' Mickey said. 'I can't see that Henry would have been comfortable there. It's cold and damp and the kitchen is no longer worthy of the name. I'm sorry, my dear, but I'm sure you'd not want me to lie about it.'

'Oh, Mickey.' She could not keep the distress from her face or voice and Mickey felt a prick of guilt, for all that he knew he could not dissemble. 'I arranged this business thinking it would be good for him. I've misjudged this badly, haven't I?'

He leaned over and patted her hand. 'What you did was with the best of intentions,' he said. 'If the big lummox couldn't take it upon himself to walk away, well, that's his fault, not yours.'

She nodded, but Mickey could see that she was punishing herself.

Tea arrived, and cakes and tiny sandwiches. 'It's a while until dinner,' Cynthia said, gathering herself and remembering her role as hostess. 'And of course you'll be famished. Help yourself, Sergeant Tibbs,' she said, and then, when the young man looked alarmed, she piled a little plate with cake and sandwiches and Mickey made certain that a table was set beside Tibbs' chair so that he didn't have to manage conversation, note-taking and holding a cup and saucer all at the same time.

Not that Mickey expected him to contribute much to the conversation, but he did know that Tibbs seemed happier when he took notes and was unsurprised when the notebook and pencil appeared on the young man's lap. He noticed Cynthia trying to hide a smile. He was very relieved that she could still find things to smile at; she was obviously deeply upset at her brother's disappearance.

'Wherever he's gone, he's taken his overcoat,' Mickey told her.

'That's a blessing. But you say he's left his other things behind?'

Mickey had spoken to her briefly on the phone after he had finished with his superiors at Scotland Yard.

'As close as we can tell, he doesn't appear to have taken anything else with him, though I couldn't find his journal and neither was there a book on his bedside table, as Tibbs here noted, and that would be unusual for Henry.'

'And it would be a natural thing for him to slip both of those items into his coat pocket,' Cynthia observed. 'He probably wouldn't even think about it.'

'You're probably right, though I was hoping he might have left his notebook behind,' Mickey confessed. 'To know what his thoughts had been immediately before he left, that would have been a useful thing. It was getting too dark for us to do a proper examination of the room. The illumination was bad, just two little lamps, one on the desk and one beside the bed. The impression I got was that the room had been prepared hastily for Henry's arrival but with little real thought as to his comforts. Tomorrow in the daylight we will see what is what, but you should know, Cynthia, that we found a stain on the floor that might be blood and also on his pyjama sleeve. Not much blood, and the stain on the floor might be older and have been there when Henry first arrived. The one on the sleeve might have an innocent explanation, but it might be significant.'

Tibbs had made a strange little sound as though he wanted

to protest at Mickey's further frankness, and Mickey and Cynthia both turned their gaze on the nervous young man.

'It's all right, Sergeant Tibbs. Mickey knows me well enough to understand that I need information, good or bad. My chief worry was that my brother might have been in such despair that . . .' She shook her head. 'He was not in a good state, Mickey. Leaving the police force was the last straw for him. I thought the cataloguing of the library and the papers might occupy his mind, stimulate his curiosity, and frankly nothing I could do here was helping him. He was restless and he was exhausted and bored, but he couldn't seem to summon the energy to do anything about it.'

'And it was a good thought,' Mickey told her. 'If anything was designed to excite Henry's imagination and give him some kind of quiet purpose, it would be a library like that. You did the right thing, Cynthia. I don't think either of us realized just how far he had sunk. I should have said something the last time I met with him. I've never seen him in such a funk, not since the war. But he survived that and he will survive this. We just need to find out where he's gone and why.'

'Sir, do you think it has something to do with that name he wrote?' Sergeant Tibbs asked.

'Name?' Cynthia asked.

'Do you remember that strange business of the murdered man, Sidney Carpenter, found on the pavement in St John's Wood, outside the house where that family disappeared? The Deans family. Just over five years ago. Puzzled the blazes out of us, it did, and we never did get to the bottom of it. Well, for some reason Henry had written Sidney's name on the edge of his blotter. Had he mentioned anything to you?'

'I remember it vaguely. Chiefly because it was such a strange thing. But no, he's not mentioned it recently. Why on earth would he think of it now?'

'I don't know. But tomorrow we will go back and inspect the room thoroughly, tear the whole house apart if we have to. Henry left that house in a hurry, so clearly he did not have time to leave behind clear intelligence of what he was up to. But he would have left something for me, I know it. He would expect me to understand. We worked together for too long for him to have shut me out of his thoughts now.' He realized as he said it that he was implying that Henry would have confided in him rather than Cynthia and that he might well have hurt her feelings. He would not do that for the world, and began to apologize, but Cynthia cut him off.

'I hope you're right,' she said. 'He had reached the stage where he would not even confide in me. He seemed to be chasing the same thoughts round and round in circles and I could not help him break out of those circles. To be truthful, we became frustrated with one another and that hurts me a great deal, Mickey. I can't help but feel that there might have been more I could have done. But if the implication is that Henry was investigating something then honestly I'm heartened by that. Even if whatever he was investigating turns out to be a wild goose chase, the fact he has perhaps found enthusiasm for something is a start.'

Anything is better than the idea he might have thrown himself off a cliff and into the sea, Mickey thought. And that's what Cynthia was afraid of.

THREE

'Do you often stay with the Garrett-Smyths?' Tibbs asked as they made their way back along the coast road the following morning.

'I do,' Mickey told him. 'Cynthia is a lovely woman and I get on well with her husband too. He and I share an interest in microscopes, though young Melissa usually has to make up his slides for him. He's a little cack-handed, it has to be said. The boys are away at school just now and Cyril is almost sixteen, so quite the young man. Both are keen on cricket but I've taken them to the football from time to time.'

'But Mrs Smyth, she and Mr Johnstone are not from . . .' He hesitated, and Mickey guessed what he wanted to know.

'Not from money, no. Both are the children of a country doctor, though their father had been a brute and their parents were dead by the time Cynthia was fifteen, not much older than her daughter Melissa is now. She and Henry had to fend for themselves. Cynthia married well,' Mickey conceded. She had been working for Albert's father as his secretary when they met. Albert had fallen for her, assumed that Cynthia would be flattered and become the latest in a long line of his temporary amours. In that, as his father had warned he would be, he was disappointed.

'Isn't this all a little unusual?' Tibbs asked.

'Unusual, yes, but Cynthia has a good head on her shoulders and both Albert and his old man recognized that.' Garrett-Smyth senior had also recognized that his son had failed to inherit his business acumen and would need a subtle, guiding hand, so he had made no objection when the relationship had deepened and Albert had spoken to his father about proposing marriage. After all, his father had also come from humble beginnings. There were a few snide remarks, of course, and some representatives of the old money would still not countenance her in their drawing rooms. But Cynthia could hold her own in most situations. Mickey respected that.

'I take it you were comfortable enough last night and that you slept well,' Mickey said.

'Oh yes, I did, that room was—'

Mickey laughed, unable to help himself. Tibbs' expression was close to ecstatic. Albert had not been home the previous evening, though Mickey had seen him at breakfast and they'd had a good chinwag. Tibbs, somewhat intimidated, had been practically silent throughout. Dinner the previous night had been an intimate affair of Cynthia, Mickey, Bexley Tibbs and Melissa, Cynthia's middle child. She was now fourteen and looking very grown-up and very much like her mother, though her hair was a little darker and she still wore it long. Melissa and Henry had a very fond relationship and she had questioned Mickey acutely about what he had found and what he thought might have happened to her uncle. She was as forthright as her mother and Mickey realized that Tibbs had been very disturbed by this, not just by the questions but by the fact that such a young girl should be allowed to speak so openly at the dinner table. He guessed that Tibbs' upbringing had been more formal than this, being the son of a nonconformist clergyman.

Mickey had expected Malina Beaney to be present at dinner. She was Cynthia's secretary and general factotum – and, Mickey suspected, was also quietly helping with the business side of things, Cynthia being an unobtrusive but executive partner in her husband's affairs these days. She was away at a family funeral, Mickey had been informed. He was sorry to have missed her, knowing that she and Henry got along well. It was possible she might have drawn him out and therefore been able to advise Mickey.

And now here they were, in Cynthia's car, driving back to what Mickey was already thinking of as a crime scene, though he wasn't yet sure what crime might have been committed. He comforted himself that the amount of blood, if that's what it was, didn't seem of sufficient quantity to suggest major violence. He was also comforted by the fact that Henry had been in good enough shape to have dressed himself warmly before he left. Somehow the overcoat had become a symbol of Henry's well-being. It had been a gift from Cynthia some years before and much abused by its owner, often splattered with mud, scratched by thorns, drenched with rain and snow and worse. A concerted attack with a clothes brush usually brought it back to a proper state, and it had protected Henry from the worst that his professional life could throw at him.

'First of all, we're going to speak to Sadie Bevans and see what she has to say for herself,' he told Tibbs. Sadie Bevans was the maid of all work who had been coming in to prepare a meal for Henry in the evenings and to ensure that he had provisions to get his own breakfast and lunch, which probably meant he hadn't bothered, Mickey thought. Henry was fairly hopeless at remembering he was hungry, especially when he was dejected, and Mickey had usually been the one who reminded him his body needed fuel. He could not but help wonder if this lack of someone to remind him of his basic human needs might have contributed to Henry's failure of health. Mickey had taken up his new position as inspector in early May and Henry seemed completely unable to settle after that. New sergeants came and went, usually very quickly, as Henry's temper with what he saw as their ineptitude had grown so volatile that their superintendent had eventually intervened. It then came out that Henry was in a great deal of pain. An injury to his shoulder sustained the previous year had not healed as well as it might, and by late August surgery had been inevitable to remove fragments of bone that had been causing major irritation and infection. After that his leaving of the police force had also seemed inevitable. After surgery he had gone to stay with Cynthia to recuperate. But recuperation did not seem to have happened.

Physically he was at least in less pain, though he had been warned that the shoulder would never be as mobile as before and that he must take care. Mickey had last seen him six weeks previously in late October – he had been pale but was at least gaining a little weight. He had clearly been depressed and had confided in Mickey that he had no idea what to do with his life now. From time to time during his career, when the blue mood had hit, he had talked about leaving the police force, about leaving behind the sordid, tragic, disheartening round of witnessing and investigating the worst that human beings could do to one another. Even bringing the perpetrators to justice did not always compensate, Mickey was aware, for the sense of inevitability; one case might be solved, another would appear on the board.

'Would he have had a conversation with her if she only came in to bring a meal and his shopping?' Tibbs asked.

Sunk in his reverie, it took Mickey a moment to realize he meant the maid. 'Henry would have been polite. Beyond that I couldn't say. But it's my experience that servants are observant and she must at least be ticked off our list. She is likely the only person who had anything like daily contact with him. If she was doing his shopping he wouldn't even have needed to go out to buy food, and believe me, Henry Johnstone is not the kind of man who would simply pop down to the local for a pint.'

Tibbs nodded wisely. 'This is a very nice car,' he said enviously. 'Is it a nice car to drive?'

Mickey glanced at him, bursting into laughter at the obvious hint. 'Well, perhaps that's something you'll have to find out, my lad,' he said.

Sadie Bevans was little more than a child, barely out of school and still living at home with her parents and siblings in a two-up, two-down terraced house about a mile from the Barry house. She was obviously nervous at being confronted by two Metropolitan Police detectives. Her mother, exuding an atmosphere of fierce protectiveness, arms folded across her bosom, stood close by and Mickey immediately realized he must placate the mother first before he'd get any sense out of the daughter.

'This must all have been very upsetting,' he said. 'I hope Mr Barry has dealt fairly with your daughter. It's hardly her fault that his guest is no longer present at the house.'

As Mickey had presumed, having met Mr Barry, this was a major bone of contention. 'Refused to pay he has, saying there was nothing for her to do, therefore she should not have gone in. A full week's pay she's lost. Where's the justice in that? I don't imagine you'll be chasing *him* for the money even though he's cheated her.'

'I'm afraid that's not in my remit,' Mickey told her. 'But if you tell me how much is owed I will see if there's something that can be done. I can have a word with Mr Barry's solicitor when next I speak to him.' *And failing that, I can maybe get Cynthia to help out*, Mickey thought to himself. The loss of a week's wages, even if that was a pittance, would still be a hard blow to a household like this one.

He turned his attention to the daughter. 'Did you see much of Mr Johnstone?'

She shook her head. 'Usually only when I took his meal up. The kitchen was always cold, so I made sure there was a fire in his room and I took the tray up there. Mr Johnstone seemed to feel the cold something awful and there's nothing you can do to get that room warm. I found him some mornings asleep in the study on that hard little sofa. I always set a fire in there for him, even though Mr Barry had said it wasn't necessary.' She cast a glance at her mother as though looking for approval.

'That was very thoughtful of you,' Mickey said, and earned a brief nod from Mrs Bevans.

'And him recovering from that shoulder hurt. It didn't seem right.'

She hesitated and again glanced at her mother, who nodded as though telling her to go on. 'I'd appreciate it if you didn't tell Mr Barry,' Sadie continued, 'but I let myself into the main house through the main door and fetched some more blankets. I know where they're kept because Mum worked there when the house had a full staff, under the old Mr Barry. He was such a good man, he would not have put a guest in that awful room.'

'Now, now, Sadie. It's not our place to criticize,' her mother said, but Mickey sensed that she was very proud of her daughter's compassion and had done a lot of her own criticism when there had been no outsider to hear it.

'I'm sure Mr Johnstone was grateful,' Mickey told her. 'He did feel the cold and recovering from surgery made it worse for him. To be honest,' he added, lowering his voice a little as though taking them into his confidence, 'I am surprised he stayed. He had been recuperating with his sister who lives just along the coast and I'm certain he could have borrowed her car and come in daily.'

Sadie leaned forward and mirrored Mickey's tone. 'He mentioned his sister. Several times he did, and how he was considering going back to stay with her. Then . . . then I'm afraid, sir, I happened to mention that I wouldn't get paid if he went. Sir, I feel awful about that, but I think he might have stayed because of what I said.'

Mickey nodded. Knowing Henry, he probably had. 'Did he have any visitors?' *And was he actually eating his meals?* Mickey also wanted to ask, but that seemed too personal a thing to question this young woman about.

'Not that I *saw*, but one day I went in and the coffee pot in the kitchen had been used and there were two cups in the sink. So I think someone must have gone to see him.'

'You have no sense of who it might have been?'

Sadie Bevans looked embarrassed and glanced at her mother again.

'Go on,' her mother said. 'It's not gossip if it's going to help someone.'

'I think it might have been a lady,' she said. 'There was lipstick on one of the cups. I'm not suggesting she went upstairs or anything, just that he made coffee for her in the kitchen. I'm sure it was, you know, respectable.'

Knowing Henry it almost certainly was, Mickey thought. 'Could you describe the shade of the lipstick?' he asked. Cynthia wore pinks and roses but nothing too dark, though if Cynthia had called on her brother she would have surely mentioned it.

'It was quite red, not overly bright, but definitely red not pink or coral. It was a nice colour and there was just a trace on the cup. Some ladies, when they drink, they leave an imprint of the whole lip.'

She sounded, Mickey thought, quite put off by that.

Mickey thanked her, then looked at Tibbs to see if the younger man had anything to add, observing that Tibbs had been making copious notes of the conversation.

'Did you understand what Mr Johnstone was doing in the library?' Tibbs asked.

'Oh yes, he told me about it. He was listing the books that were on the shelves and organizing them so that the subjects were the same, history with history and religion with religion and that kind of thing, and then placing them in order of when they were published and then writing everything in a big ledger. I asked him if he weren't tempted to read some of them and he said that at another time he might have done, but at that moment it was taking all his energy just to take them from the shelves and see how they needed placing. I think the gentleman was very tired,' she added quietly. And then, 'I did like him; I hope nothing bad has happened to him. He was always very polite and kind. Sometimes he was a little . . . as though his head wasn't there, as though he was thinking about other things, but he was always very nice and very grateful for what I was doing.'

As though his head wasn't there, Mickey thought. Henry's head hadn't really 'been there' for months. He had done his job well enough, but Henry Johnstone could have done his job with his eyes closed, his ears plugged and half asleep.

'I'm sure he was very grateful,' Mickey said sincerely.

'Are you a friend of his, as well as being a policeman?' she asked rather shyly.

'I am. He was a policeman too, you knew that? A detective chief inspector.'

She nodded. 'He said he had to leave because he was hurt and you have to be fit to be a policeman. He seemed sad about it.'

'He was my inspector when I was still a sergeant. We were good friends.'

'I thought you might have been. He mentioned someone called Mickey – is that you?'

Mickey could see that Sadie's mother was a little disapproving of her daughter asking these questions, as though she was over-stepping some invisible mark.

'Yes, I'm Mickey Hitchens,' he told her. 'You say he mentioned me?'

She nodded. 'Twice he said "I wish Mickey was here" and

I said was that a friend and he said yes, a very good one. And then the day before he . . . went off like he did, he said to tell you that his book was in the desk drawer in the study and that if you came looking for him I should tell you that.'

'If I came looking for him. So you think he meant to go somewhere?'

She looked away and then looked down, and Mickey suddenly realized that this was difficult for her, that going away did not necessarily mean just leaving. 'What did you think he meant?' he asked gently.

'It's not for me to say, is it, sir? But I do know he was very unhappy; I told my mum that he was very unhappy. I was worried about him. And when I went that day and he wasn't there, and then I went back in the morning and his meal hadn't been touched, I thought . . .'

'Now then, Sadie, we don't need your imaginings,' her mother said firmly. She looked meaningfully at Mickey, who nodded and did not push any further.

'Did you go up to his room, in case he was there?' Tibbs asked. 'In case he was ill, I mean.'

'Of course I did. And I saw that his things were still there so I thought he might come back. And the wardrobe door was open and I could see he'd taken his big overcoat. But when he didn't come back I didn't know what to do. In the end I went to see Mrs Heather – she's the old housekeeper from the big house and she got a message to Mr Barry.'

And he had called Cynthia to find out where Henry was, Mickey thought, but by that time five days had passed and Mickey had been up in Yorkshire and unable to return in a hurry, and so it had been seven days since Henry had left the house. Too long, far too long.

Mrs Bevans followed them out of the house wanting, Mickey assumed, to have a private word.

'The gentleman was in the disturbed state of mind I think,' she said. 'I had no fear that he would be harmful, or dangerous, you understand, or I would have stopped Sadie from going up to the house. He just seemed very sad. The kind of sadness that, well, you know. As his friend you must have thought about it. And if he'd gone into the water in that heavy coat of his . . . Well, it can take a long time for a body to surface and this time of year it can be taken right out to sea first if the tides catch it. I don't mean to be . . . I know I sound a little blunt, sir, but it's possible. And often those that go into the water are not seen again. I just wanted to say that.'

'Thank you,' Mickey said, knowing that the thoughts were well meant. 'I must confess that both his sister and I had been concerned, but you know, the more I look at this the more I think Henry suddenly got an idea in his head and went off chasing it.'

He could not help but note that her look was pitying, full of sympathy for what she saw as his misplaced optimism.

As they drove away, Tibbs observed, 'It would have been better if we'd been able to come here sooner. As it is, any trail will be very cold by now.'

'It will, but we are already one step further on.'

'We are?'

Mickey smiled. 'Young Sadie said that Henry had left his book for me in the desk drawer in the study. That will be his journal.'

'Ah, the volume you hoped would be in his room. You think he'd have told you in that what was going through his head, where he's gone maybe?'

'We can but hope,' Mickey said.

Mickey's first instinct on reaching the Barry house was to go into the study and find the journal, but first he wanted to ensure that Henry's room was treated to the same in-depth search he would have employed in any other investigation. 'You should be methodical,' he told Tibbs, 'so let's see how good you are at the finding and developing of fingerprints and the taking of photographs. Any article that can be easily packed can go with us. For the rest, clear photographs will have to suffice. Remember, black powder on the lighter surfaces or on the glass. If you need the grey, you'll have to grind it fresh and mix only what you need. It sucks the moisture from the air and in a room like this will be clogging in no time at all.'

'The light in here isn't good,' Tibbs said.

'Do what you can. Set the camera on a steady surface and

use a longer exposure, bracket the exposure like I showed you.'

Down in the study, the desk drawer was locked. Henry would have left the key somewhere that Mickey would be sure to find, but which would not be obvious to a casual observer. It was not in any of the other drawers or the containers on the desk that housed paperclips, pen nibs and the like. Mickey eventually tracked it down on one of the shelves, wedged between two volumes of Wisden, the cricketing almanac. Henry had no real interest in cricket but he must have known that Mickey would notice the presence of these books in Barry's library.

'Now let's see what you have left for me,' Mickey said, unlocking the drawer. Henry's journal, a small book with a somewhat stained brown cover, together with his favourite pen, lay in solitary splendour. If the overcoat had been a positive sign, Mickey thought, the fact that Henry had deliberately left this pen behind said the opposite. He picked it up, noting the inscription and the name, Alfred Green, that was not Henry's but represented one of the men lost in the Great War, a man who had been friend to both of them. He was relieved that Henry's cigarette case was not there; that too had belonged to their comrade who had fallen in the trenches. Dented and polished smooth by its owners' hands, the case generally lived in Henry's jacket pocket alongside a lighter that had been another present from Cynthia.

'Why leave the pen behind?' Mickey wondered, and then reminded himself of just how close Henry had been to the young man who had died. It would have broken Henry's heart to have lost any of these memento mori, but particularly this one. The pen was used daily and had been ever since it had come into Henry's possession back in 1917. Alfie had lent it to Henry and then never returned to retrieve it. He had died that day and lain for another three in no man's land before Henry had retrieved the body. Mickey had his own precious objects that he would be loath to part with.

He looked quickly through the journal, noting that the final entry was made on the day before Henry had disappeared, and read it.

Since Malina visited I have seen no one but young Sadie Bevans, and I am keenly aware that the isolation has not been good for me. Perhaps I am imagining things. Perhaps the strain is proving too much. Perhaps . . . many things. I wish fervently that my faithful Mickey was with me. His good sense would straighten out my thinking and help me to divine what is the product of an overwrought imagination and what is solid reality.

But I have heard the footsteps again and twice now I have seen the car drive by, twice more come briefly into the drive as though whoever was in the vehicle planned to come directly to the house. Lord knows there's no other destination once you leave the road. On the first occasion they must have seen Sadie Bevans arriving with my supper and I could make out little apart from the bulk and length of the vehicle in the fading light.

The second time was the morning after Malina visited. So, three days past. I heard the engine as it rounded the bend. It sounded powerful; there was no straining at the steepness of the hill and no downshift of the gears when they came upon the bend. I had gone to the library window, hoping for a better view, thinking perhaps that I might have a visitor – though I had no idea who might visit me here. No, truth to tell, I thought for an instant that the car might be Albert's Lagonda – the engine had that same throatiness and that same smoothness as it ascended. I was reminded of this spring when we all went to watch Albert race at Brooklands in the open event. It seems that my presence at the window was a mistake. The car appeared, turned in through the gate and then someone must have glimpsed me, standing by the window on the library floor, because just as quickly it reversed, turned, and headed back down the hill.

I must confess that this disturbed me. Had they come to rob the place, in the mistaken assumption that there was still something here worth the trouble of thieving? If so, then they would have been severely disappointed.

There are books. And there are more books. There is

little else. And what common thief would have access to an automobile of that fierce quality?

Am I safe here? That's a question I cannot answer. Should I leave? I believe so . . . but curiosity, the like of which I have not felt in weeks, urges me to remain. To see this played out. This feels to me like the beginning of an investigation when, for all that you know that wrong has been done and some severe injury or even death dealt out, there is still that moment of . . . I hesitate to call it excitement; the word seems crass and insensitive. And yet, that is what it is. That sense of excited purpose, I suppose, and anything, anything that breaks through the numbness I have felt and the despair I have endured has to be welcomed, even though in my gut I know that this is not a safe place to be.

I wish that Mickey were here. He could at least be relied upon to talk some sense into this brain of mine.

I will do as I have done each night for the past week and lock my journal in the desk for him to find, should he come looking. Should something happen. That, I feel, is all that I can do.

'Oh, Henry,' Mickey said. 'This is a rum do. Just what sort of a pickle have you got yourself into?'

FOUR

Mickey returned to the library. A desk had been set out for Henry to work at and the ledger that Sadie had mentioned lay open. Henry had no real knowledge of the Dewey Decimal System. Instead, he appeared to have divided the library into broad categories, then alphabetical order by author's name, and was working his way through the inventory. Rough scraps of paper showed that he had first made lists of the books as he had come across them, then crosschecked them with dates and details of publication, moved any that had been mis-shelved and finally made the entries in the ledger. He had left space at the end of each column for any he might have missed on the first sweep and headed these additions as 'addendum'. The books in the columns were numbered and if the book was written into the addendum then a letter had been added together with a number that showed where it should have been within the ledger. Mickey could almost feel Henry's impatience at having to spoil his neat entries with something as disorganized as an addendum. He could also guess at the man's irritation that the library should be in such a state in the first place. It had clearly been a well-organized and well-studied collection at one time but presumably as the senior owner, Sir Eamon Barry, had aged he had not been quite so meticulous.

Henry did not seem to have started work on Sir Eamon's papers and when Mickey opened a few of the drawers in the big cabinets beneath the shelves he could guess why. There were loose papers everywhere, together with journals, published material, random press cuttings and ephemera from theatre trips and train journeys. Where could you begin with this? Mickey wondered. At least with books you could see what they were about and what fitted with what.

He glanced at his brass pocket watch, worn smooth and old and shiny with age – it had belonged to Mickey's father. It told him that it was one in the afternoon, though the dark sky outside suggested a different story. Heavy grey clouds threatened equally heavy rain and Mickey was deeply grateful that Cynthia had loaned him her car.

He switched on the lights and took another look around the room, noting that the illumination did little to lift the gloom. This felt and looked like an abandoned place, Mickey thought. The old man had probably loved this room but now he had gone and there was no one to care for it and not even his ghost remained. Soon it would be stripped out and the house either demolished or sold, or both, and the last remnants gone. Had this ever been a happy place? Mickey wondered. Sir Eamon Barry's son certainly seemed to have no affection for it and, while everyone seemed to say that the elder had been a good man, had his son felt the benefits of that? It didn't always follow, Mickey thought. Some men could be street angels and house devils.

He went back up the stairs to see how Sergeant Bexley Tibbs was getting on and was pleased to note that the young man had worked methodically around the room, first taking photographs and then applying himself with the various grades of fingerprint powder.

'I have found the prints of three distinct individuals,' Tibbs told Mickey. 'I identified them as different individuals by the categories you taught me about. The most prevalent I'm guessing must be Detective Chief Inspector Johnstone's. His prints have tight whorls, with a distinctive closed end on what I believe is an index finger. There is a corresponding thumb print on the front of the mirror, as though he grasped the edge to tilt it,' Tibbs explained.

Mickey did not bother to correct the use of Henry's rank. He too continued to think of him as an inspector rather than as a civilian. He inspected Tibbs' work and agreed with his conclusion.

'These are on the bedside table, the desk and in the bathroom, and so it seems reasonable to assume they are his.'

Mickey nodded encouragingly. 'And the other two sets?'

'Inspector Johnstone has a predominance of whorls that are very distinctive. The other two are predominantly arches.'

'And what makes you think that there are two different people?' Mickey asked. 'It might be the same person but touching objects with different fingers.'

'Both are on the door. One is smaller than the other, more likely a woman's hand. I would think belonging to Sadie Bevans, perhaps? Besides, I have two distinct right thumbs.'

Mickey nodded. 'That would settle the matter,' he agreed.

'But there is another matter, Inspector. I have found more blood. Not pooled on the floor but splashed on the walls, here and here.'

He pointed and Mickey's gut tightened. He went over to look at the spatter Tibbs had identified. It was hard to see against the brown, time-darkened wallpaper, but the young man was right, Mickey thought. 'There is more here,' he said, pointing to a few small dots and specks higher up the wall. 'So likely someone got hit and the assailant lifted the now bloodied weapon for another go. The blood was cast from the weapon and on to the wall.' Hopefully, he thought, Henry was the assailant and not the victim here, though Henry was still not back to full strength and that troubled Mickey deeply.

'Look at the fire irons,' he instructed Tibbs. 'If it's Henry that struck the blow then he'd trust me to be looking for the weapon and would have placed it back, tidy like.'

Tibbs looked doubtful but did as he was bid. 'There's blood on the poker,' he said. 'I'll develop the prints.'

'Good, well, that's coming back to Scotland Yard with us. And we'll take strips of the wallpaper from the walls. You have a sharp knife?'

Again, Tibbs looked doubtful. 'That will ruin the paper, sir.'

'And your objection to that is what? We are collecting evidence, Sergeant. That's our one concern here. If you slice either side of the stain and then slide your knife beneath, you should lift the strip intact.'

Still with a dubious look upon his face, Tibbs set about the task. Mickey knelt and studied the floor. At one time there must have been a large, square carpet in the space, he thought. The boards beyond where it had stretched had been stained a very dark brown but Mickey could just discern more drops of blood, as though someone injured had shed them as they hurried away. He tracked them into the hall and down on to the stairs, cursing the lack of light.

He returned to the room and was satisfied to see that Tibbs had taken his samples and was carefully packing them into envelopes and tucking them into the murder bag.

'You'll find brown paper in that pocket at the side,' Mickey said. 'Wrap that loosely around the poker and then rest it across the top of the bag. And now we need samples of what might be blood from the boards, so we'll need scrapings from the floor.'

'Will we be driving back?' Tibbs asked eagerly.

'That we will,' Mickey agreed. 'And no doubt you would like to try your hand,' he said. Cynthia had recently acquired a Model A Ford. It was a nippy little thing, capable of up to sixty miles an hour on a straight, flat road, and although still only four cylinders it had a nice, smooth stroke and easy acceleration. Mickey was enjoying the experience.

'Do you think Mr Garrett-Smyth would mind?' Tibbs asked.

'I don't think he should have a say in the matter seeing as the car is not his,' Mickey said. 'It belongs to Cynthia and I'm sure she won't mind in the least.'

He could see Tibbs absorbing this information but not quite believing it. In Tibbs' world women did not own cars; their possessions became their husband's on marriage, did they not, so the thought was an absurd one. *The young man has a lot to learn*, Mickey thought, *and a lot to unlearn.*

'Before we go, I want to examine the rest of the house,' he said. 'I doubt Henry ventured far. He'd have no reason to, but best to check.'

He fetched the keys from the butler's pantry and unlocked the door at the end of a long corridor that separated the servants' quarters from the family rooms.

'We'll start at the top,' Mickey said. 'The attic rooms will likely be where the personal servants lived, the valet perhaps and the ladies' maids. Then we'll work our way down.'

On the top landing they discovered that there was also a door through to the other side of the house and this was not locked so, Mickey thought, anybody that wanted to gain entry could have done so from the back stairs. Was that relevant?

Young Sadie Bevans had mentioned unlocking the main door on the ground floor and coming through that way when she had come in to get the blankets for Henry. He wondered where she had taken them from and assumed there must be a main linen closet somewhere, perhaps close to wherever the housekeeper's room was situated. The layout of the house was odd, he thought, the kitchens being in the same block as the library, the room with eight windows and the study. The flight of stairs from the servants' quarters in the attic seem to lead down one storey and then join, by means of a short landing, the doorway through into that part of the house. Then they continued down into the kitchen and other utility areas. So the servants could gain access from the kitchen to the top floor of the house and thence down to the rooms where they might be summoned by Sir Eamon Barry or whatever women had lived here without coming through that main door and disturbing their employers.

Mickey realized he had no idea of what the household had been like before Sir Eamon had died. Perhaps he should speak to the housekeeper. Was it even information he needed? Probably not, but he would almost certainly chase it up anyway. Mickey knew himself to be something of a completist in this regard, a habit that had probably rubbed off from Henry but one which had previously stood him in good stead.

The second entrance into the main residence was on the ground floor and that was how he and Tibbs had just entered. This door, Mickey speculated, was probably used by the butler and housekeeper, as senior members of staff, and possibly the footmen as their duties would mostly be confined to that lower floor. Mickey led the way up the central staircase and then up the narrow flight that led to the attic rooms. A small landing with two doors opening off it took them into the servants' quarters: two rooms, one leading off the other, two beds in each, locks on the inside of the main doors.

'So,' Mickey speculated. 'Two ladies' maids perhaps, with space for visitors' servants? Or perhaps the parlour maids . . . the kitchen staff would either sleep downstairs, I think, or come in daily. Of course, we've no idea if the household even had live-in servants any more, not if the older Mr Barry lived alone.'

'Do Miss Garrett-Smyth's servants live in rooms like this?' Tibbs asked a little warily.

'Indeed they do not,' Mickey told him sharply. 'Cynthia treats her staff well.' He looked around the small, sparse rooms, seeing what Tibbs was seeing: the peeling paint and narrow beds and tiny fireplaces. There was no comfort here and, it seemed, nothing useful to see.

Cynthia's staff were indeed better treated. She had endured enough cold and hunger and lack of care in her younger days, as had Henry, to never inflict that kind of pain on others. When they had sold off the London house and their various other properties, they had done their best to ensure those servants they could not take with them had found positions elsewhere and ensured they had three months' pay to tide them over. The household was very much slimmed down now. Cook had gone with Cynthia, as had Josie, who called herself a parlour maid but who answered the door, took the mail to be posted and filled the position a butler or footman might hold in a bigger establishment. Agency maids came in for a few hours a week to help with dusting and cleaning and any heavy work.

Nanny, though she was no longer needed as such, had been kept on and helped out with Melissa's lessons, supplementing the tutor she shared with three other girls her age. Nanny was too old to have found another position easily and Cynthia regarded her as part of the family. Malina acted as secretary to Cynthia and assisted her with the accounts and daily administration of the house and, increasingly, so Cynthia had confided, Albert's business affairs. Both Cynthia and Malina were trained in the running of an office and their expertise had, Mickey knew, been invaluable in the past couple of years since Albert's professional world had been so badly shaken.

The financial crashes in London and on Wall Street had impacted him badly, Mickey knew, and his business had contracted dramatically, pulling back to the British-based manufactories that had been the core of their business when his father had first started out. The family were still very comfortably off, but much had changed. Mickey remembered the parties at Halloween and Christmas which Cynthia had organized and at which attendance had been viewed as essential, even by those whose old money and titles made them reluctant to invite Cynthia into their own drawing rooms.

He knew that Albert did not miss these affairs, and he wondered if Cynthia did. He wondered also just how many of those previous, fawning visitors had remained part of their social circle.

They had descended the narrow stairs and gone back through the discreet little door and on to the main landing. Had Henry been with him, Mickey and he would have divided the work, but Mickey did not yet know how reliable Tibbs' observations would be. The lad was clearly a good policeman to have got through his sergeant's exam so young, but as far as Mickey was concerned he was still in training as a detective.

They wandered slowly through bedrooms, dressing rooms and bathrooms, furnishings all clad in white dust sheets and now sullied by a fine layer of dust.

'No one's been in here for an age,' Tibbs commented. 'The dust hasn't been disturbed.'

Mickey nodded and they descended another level. Reception rooms on one side of the landing, what looked like a ladies' withdrawing room, the silk wallpaper on the walls decorated with painted butterflies and birds. It had once been a very pretty room, Mickey thought, but now there was evidence of damp coming in through the window frames and in one corner of the room, spotting the silk with black. An even heavier layer of dust coated the now grey dust covers and even the once bright carpet with a layer of grime.

'No one's used this room in years,' Tibbs said, sounding slightly awed.

'If they don't want places like this they should let them out to families,' Mickey said. 'Think how many could be given shelter in a house this size?'

Tibbs looked startled and Mickey reminded himself that Henry would tease him about what might be termed his Bolshevik ideas. He had grown so used to Henry's tacit agreement that he'd forgotten how shocking they might sound to someone else.

Tibbs opened his mouth as though to say something, but then seemed to decide to let it lie, though Mickey noticed that the music room, unloved and neglected, did seem to affect the younger man quite profoundly. The piano was not even covered down. The gramophone had been left with its lid open and sleeveless records scattered on a nearby ottoman. He watched as Tibbs pulled a large dust sheet from the sofa and draped it over the piano.

'Folk shouldn't be allowed nice things if they can't be bothered to take care of them,' Mickey commented, and Tibbs nodded.

'Play, do you?' Mickey asked.

'A little. We had a piano at home, though not like that one, of course. My mother used to play in the chapel and she gave lessons at home.' Tibbs smiled. 'I'm afraid I wasn't very good.'

They paused in the doorway and Tibbs said, 'So where did the old man live? This part of the house seems like it's been empty for years. The library and the study are well enough looked after and the kitchen is . . . adequate, I suppose. Though I'd not want to be using that stove, it's rusty as he— Heck. Have you seen it?'

Mickey nodded. 'I'm guessing that young Sadie or someone like her did the cooking at home and brought it over for Sir Eamon. She could have warmed up a plate of food over a pan of hot water on the gas hob rather than light the stove. This place has had no staff since Noah was a boy. But you make a good point. He must have slept somewhere. Taken a bath once in a while.' Though that would involve boiling several kettles just to get a tepid bath, Mickey thought, since there presently seemed no other means. 'It certainly wasn't up here, and I don't believe it was in that big, draughty room they put Henry in.'

It occurred to Mickey that as the house furnace would not have been lit, there would have been no hot water either should the old man – or indeed Henry – have wished to take a bath. It was most likely, he thought, that there would have been a copper in the laundry room that could have been lit to heat water for bathing, and for simple washing a kettle on the stove would have sufficed. Somehow that realization made the place seem even more cheerless and Henry's discomfort more acute. Water would have to be carried up from the kitchen to the top floor, Mickey thought, either by Henry himself or by the daily maid.

Cynthia, he thought, was going to be furious when she realized how badly her brother had been treated, how little hospitality he had been shown. He thought that he'd quite like to witness the inevitable explosion.

They descended once more to the ground floor and returned to the big door that Mickey had assumed separated the domestic quarters from the family residence. He soon realized he'd only been half correct. At the end of a short corridor he found the tall cupboard that housed the sheets and blankets and household linens that Sadie had referred to. The heavy doors had kept the contents fairly clean, but everything felt damp and chill and a faint, stale scent that made Mickey think of mildew clung to everything. *What a waste*, Mickey thought. All of this could have found a home elsewhere, done someone some good instead of being left to rot.

Beside the linen cupboard was a door that led into what he assumed had been the housekeeper's rooms. There was a bedroom, small sitting room with a decent-sized grate, an old-fashioned trivet with the pan she had probably used for her night-time cocoa still set beside it and a spirit kettle beside the hearth. It might once, he thought, have been a pleasant lodging.

'There's less dust here,' Tibbs said.

Mickey nodded. But still no sign that the old man might have slept here.

Back through the door, Mickey changed his mind about where the servants might have been housed. The attic rooms, he thought now, were probably the domain only of the female staff. Two rooms off the corridor leading to the kitchen, with three beds in each, suggested further servant accommodation, and a tin for celluloid collars suggested male inhabitants.

'So the men slept here,' Tibbs said, 'and the women went upstairs to the attic. The housekeeper probably locked the connecting door at night. Or the butler. Didn't Mr Barry say these were the butler's keys?'

Mickey nodded. 'So to ensure no hanky-panky between the staff,' he said. The butler's pantry, the silver probably long gone and presumably sold, turned out to be next in line, and adjacent to that was a room equipped in a similar manner to that of the housekeeper.

'Ah,' Mickey said. 'I think we've solved that mystery at least.'

No dust in this room. Clothes in the wardrobe, a small bathroom, the bed stripped of sheets but a stain on the mattress that suggested to Mickey that—

'He died in here, didn't he?' Tibbs asked. 'Given the evidence of that . . . I'd not have wanted to come and sleep down here.'

'No,' Mickey agreed, following his line of thinking that Henry might have considered sleeping in what would have been a smaller, warmer room as the one-time master of the house had done. He wondered if Cynthia had known how Sir Eamon Barry had lived in his final days and decided she probably had not. A cursory search turned up nothing of interest. Mickey, out of habit, checked for loose floorboards and rattled the poker up the chimney. That this did not produce a great fall of soot informed him that the chimneys at least were recently swept, at this end of the house anyway. Lord alone knew what debris and birds' nests might be blocking those in the rest of the house.

Following his example, Tibbs had been opening drawers and poking and prodding at anything that looked as though it ought to be poked or prodded. 'Check beneath the drawers, lad,' Mickey told him. 'You never know.'

'You think Dectective Chief Inspector Johnstone might have left something here?'

'I'm thinking I'll be happier if we make sure he did not,' Mickey said. 'It's unlikely,' he conceded, glancing over again at the stained mattress and thinking that Henry would be repulsed by it. By what it represented. And yet . . .

He crossed to the bed abruptly and began to examine it more closely. At first there was no sign of anything unusual, until Mickey felt down at the back of the mattress and his probing fingers discovered a place where the stitching was loose. 'Give me hand to turn this over.'

Tibbs looked askance at him but then moved to oblige. 'What's that?' he asked.

A small slit seemed to have been opened up in the seam where the side joined the top. Gingerly, Mickey felt inside and pulled something out that proved to be an old tobacco pouch. He carried it over to a chest of drawers and tipped the contents out on top. Five gold sovereigns sparkled against the brown varnish.

'Sir Eamon kept his money in the mattress?' Tibbs sounded astonished.

'Well, a little of it anyway,' Mickey said. 'Whatever Barry senior was thinking or not thinking when he stuffed his cash into his mattress is probably no concern of ours and nothing to do with Henry.' He dropped the coins back into the pouch and tucked it into his pocket. 'We should inform young Barry's solicitor,' he said. 'Or maybe just drop them into the nearest poor box where they can do some good.'

'That would be stealing,' Tibbs objected, but Mickey could hear that he quite liked the idea. No doubt, Mickey thought, the ill treatment of the rather lovely piano was still weighing on his sergeant's mind.

'I think we've seen enough,' Mickey said. 'We should be heading back to London, get our fingerprints checked and our samples tested, and a night at home would not come amiss.'

Tibbs nodded. 'But we will need to come back here to try and pick up his trail.'

'That we will.'

'And will we be staying with Mrs Garrett-Smyth?' he asked, his pale cheeks flushing a little as though embarrassed to be asking, Mickey noted.

'Indeed we will, young Tibbs,' he said. 'Though we've got a trail to follow in London first. I'd hoped to speak with Malina Beaney, Cynthia's general factotum, but *if* she's off at a funeral . . .'

'Then surely she'll not be gone too long.' He paused as though suddenly noting Mickey's emphasis. 'If?'

'She didn't tell Cynthia exactly where she was going and that's unusual. Cyn and I had a bit of a chat about it before you came down to breakfast this morning and we both wondered the same thing. Did Malina go after Henry? Apparently she received a phone call and then summoned a taxi as both Albert and Cynthia were out. She left them a note, but we do think her behaviour was a little odd.'

'Why would she do that? Why not tell his sister if she had heard from him?'

'Presumably because he requested that she did not. Malina and Henry are good friends – have been for a while. I know he talks to her about things he finds hard to talk to me or his sister about, so it's possible he might have confided something he didn't want to worry Cynthia with. And, of course, he wasn't able to get hold of me,' Mickey added a tad bitterly.

'Cyn told me that Malina had asked her family to put the word out. Eyes and ears everywhere, they have. It could be she went off to check something out.'

Tibbs was clearly puzzled. 'Eyes and ears everywhere?'

Of course, he wouldn't know, Mickey thought. 'Malina Beaney's from Gypsy stock, my lad.'

'Gypsies!' The disgust on Tibbs' face was not something he could hide.

Mickey raised an eyebrow. 'And if we're going to be working together, you'll drop that attitude,' he said sternly.

'Thieves and vagabonds, the lot of them. How can a decent woman like Mrs Garrett-Smyth have one of them living in her house?'

'I'd close your mouth now, Sergeant,' Mickey said, 'before I feel obliged to close it for you. Malina Beaney is one of the finest young women you are ever likely to meet. She earned her position in that household and, truth be told, a lot more beside. You'd not find anyone more loyal or more honest.'

Tibbs looked shocked; Mickey did not know if it was his words or his tone that had disturbed the young man more. 'I'm not telling you that all her kin are the same. There'll be good and bad, honest and cheats in all walks of life and all places, and I have no doubt some of them are, as you say, rogues and vagabonds. But you'll find the same in any place, in any walk of life. There's good and bad all over, lad, and don't you forget that. I've known men and women who occupy positions of the highest respectability and who have committed the most heinous of crimes and the most disgusting and despicable of acts against their fellow man. So you put your prejudices back in your pocket and leave them there. You'll deal with folk as you find them, not as you think they might be, or you and I will not last very long.'

Silently, Tibbs followed Mickey up the stairs to collect their belongings, and they took a long last look around the room with eight windows. Mickey glanced at his watch. 'We should find ourselves some lunch before we go,' he said. 'I spotted a little pub on the way that might do a bit of grub along with a beer.'

Tibbs seized what Mickey had intended to be an olive branch and nodded agreement. 'So how do you plan to find out where this Miss Beaney has gone?' he asked.

'Her brother works on the barges on the Thames; if he happens to be in the city then he might know. If he's not, we'll have to look elsewhere. One thing's for sure, if Malina is on Henry's trail then I feel a little happier about the matter.'

'But she's just a woman, what can she do?' Tibbs asked.

Mickey closed his eyes and sighed deeply. 'You have so much to learn,' he said. 'You can stick that particular prejudice in your pocket as well – we don't need it here and if Cynthia hears you say something of that sort in her house, you'll find yourself with your ears boxed and out on the streets.'

'I didn't mean . . . I mean . . .'

Mickey held up a hand to halt the flow of words and then touched a finger to his lips as a schoolteacher might with small children. 'Best hush before you say more, Sergeant. Least said, soonest mended.'

FIVE

They arrived back at Central Office quite late in the afternoon and Mickey sent Tibbs up to the topmost floor to the Criminal Records Office while he went to make their report to the senior officers. In truth there wasn't much to tell: Henry Johnstone was still missing, certainly nowhere in the house, and the stain on the floor had not been confirmed as blood yet. He seemed to have had a visitor. A woman, as there had been lipstick on the cup – as Sadie had told them – and Mickey was fairly convinced that this was Malina, but beyond that . . .

As he had expected, he was told that he could continue but that he couldn't be provided with any extra manpower unless his vague suspicions grew into something more solid.

He called Cynthia with an update and asked her more specifically about Henry's relationship with Malina.

'I had a talk with Melissa and Nanny this afternoon,' she told him, 'and they both agreed that they had become much closer. Mickey, you know how I feel about both of them – if their relationship should develop into something more, then it would be with my blessing. But I do feel a little aggrieved that neither of them had confided in me. If Henry was in trouble, if Malina knew that Henry was in trouble, why did they not tell me?'

'I think because he did not want to worry you further,' Mickey said. 'Forgive me for being blunt, my dear, but I think we know each other well enough. You told me yourself that you and Henry had been frustrating one another and that you had run out of things to say to him and ways to make anything better. Henry withdraws from conflict, you know that. Oh, not in the usual way of things when he's working – he's as bullish as any man when there's need. But from those he cares about and those he loves. He could have sent me a telegram and I would have come running, no matter what else was pressing on my mind or what other work I was doing. He could have told you and you would have been there at his side, but he is not the most sensible of men when it comes to asking for help. We both know that. Your dear brother, *my* dear friend, can be remarkably stupid on occasion.'

He heard Cynthia laugh and the relief in her voice. 'I can't disagree with you,' she said. 'Just find him, Mickey, and we can sort it out from there, whatever wild goose chase he's on.'

'You really think it is a wild goose chase?' Mickey asked.

'Mickey, when he left the police it was with a very heavy heart. Difficult as he found the job, he at least felt he was making some difference in the world. If he'd left simply because he'd had enough, and you and I both know that's not true, then it would have been a different matter. But to be forced out as he was because he was no longer fit enough . . . That was hard, Mickey. He felt he had failed. He felt useless. He was casting around for things to do, for jobs that he could apply for, even asked Albert if he could find some position for him in an office somewhere.'

Mickey barked laughter. 'I know Albert was always on at him to go and work in the company, but they both knew that neither was serious. Henry would have been climbing the walls within a month. What did Albert say?'

'Albert said that when he was fit enough to work he would find him a position, if that's what he still wanted. What else could he say? We both believed Henry would have forgotten all about it by then, he would have found his own way. When I heard that Sir Eamon's son needed help with his inventory of the library, I thought . . . Well, perhaps I was wrong.'

'Did you visit him at the house?'

'No, no, I did not. As you so perceptively noted, our relationship had grown fractious. I think we both needed a break. Sometimes, Mickey, I just wanted to shake him and he knew it. He was angry with himself and therefore angry with the world. There were some days when even Melissa found him difficult, and you know how close their friendship is. No, if she and Nanny are right and he had found solace in Malina's company, and she is now searching for him, then I can't be angry. I'm just disappointed that he didn't come to me. But none of that matters. I just want him home.'

It was good, Mickey thought, to be spending the night in his own place. His wife, Belle, an actress, had returned from the theatre and they had a late supper together. He had retrieved from the files all of the information he could find on Sidney Carpenter's death and the disappearance of the Deans family and brought that with him to study. Tomorrow he would go in search of Malina's brother, Kem Beaney.

'Do you think this will take you away from home for long?' Belle asked.

'I've no way of knowing. Henry's not exactly left a trail of breadcrumbs behind. I am worried about him, love. If he was irritable even with Cynthia and Melissa then he is definitely out of sorts. I remember how he was when we came back in 1918, how broken. Work gave him purpose then, but what does he have now?'

She took his hand. 'Family, friends, people who care about him. I think you're being too pessimistic about this, Mickey. I think something has occurred to him, something he could not previously solve. The fact that he wrote Carpenter's name on his blotter demonstrates that. He's come up with some new evidence or some new idea and he's doing what he does best – investigating. Of course he'd be worried in case he's wrong, so he doesn't want to include you, not until he's sure.'

'I think you could be right but I also think he's not up to it. Not physically, and even not mentally. When I talked to him last he could barely string two thoughts together.'

Belle nodded. 'I know, but there was nothing more you could have done. Well, this production finishes at the end of the week, as you know, and the pantomime season starts so I have some time off. Cynthia suggested I go down and stay with her.'

Mickey laughed. 'So the two of you will be together, poking your noses around, using your womanly intuition.'

She punched him none too gently on the upper arm and grinned broadly. 'It's stood you in good stead before,' she reminded him. 'Now you'd better get that reading done that you've brought home with you. I'm assuming you'll be off in the morning and wanting to brief this new sergeant of yours. What's he like anyway?'

Mickey sighed. 'As green as he is cabbage looking,' he said. 'But I'll knock him into shape.'

When Belle had gone up to bed, Mickey picked up Henry's journal and began to read. What he read was destined to cause him a restless night.

26 November

I heard the noises again as though someone was walking on the floor above. There is no floor above and the roof is tiled and steep so it would seem impossible that anyone had gained access to that section of roof – or could have remained up there if they had, given the storm that blew in from just after nine. Besides, the sound was not of someone scrabbling for purchase on slippery roof tiles, more like quiet but steady steps across a wooden floor. I thought about the possibility of an intruder in the attic and took my torch to investigate. However, the lighting in this section of the house is so poor that I could not find the hatch that might lead into the roof. I know that on the other side of the house the attic spaces had been given over to rooms for servants and storage, and mean and pitiful spaces they are too. I suppose at one time they might have been warm and cheerful, but I find it stretched my imagination to breaking to think that any room in this godforsaken place could ever have been warm, and as for cheerful . . .

Though I'm told that when Sir Eamon Barry was a younger man this was a pleasant enough spot, and Cynthia certainly seems to have been taken with the old man.

My sister's judgement generally being sound, I must assume she does not really know the son.

I was early to bed tonight. I had banked up the fire and closed the curtains tight, but I must confess that the only way I could stay warm was to crawl beneath the covers in my dressing gown.

These days I do not even have the energy to read. This account has taken three attempts to pin to the page.

27 November

I spoke to young Sadie when she brought my dinner and she tells me that she is unaware of any attic space above my room or indeed any hatch that might have led to one. She was clearly curious about the question, and to tell the truth I felt a little embarrassed at the idea that my mind could be fooling me and the footsteps are just the product of a dream. I told her I thought I heard a scrabbling, like rats or mice. Lord knows this place has enough of those. She tells me Sir Eamon was in the practice of putting poison in the library and setting traps on the lower floors. He apparently took great pleasure in hurling any unfortunate creatures he managed to catch from out of the upstairs window. I assume she meant one of the windows in this bleak old room. Not an idea that further endears this space to me.

I am assuming that the rodents were already dead before making their flight.

Sadie has promised to find the traps and bait them for me. I know, however, that it was not the rats I heard; I can distinguish the sound of a rat's claws and pattering feet from that of a man, however softly he treads.

Slowly, Mickey read on and then set the journal aside. Footsteps in the attic, a car whose driver seemed reluctant to be seen. And Henry's curiosity finally aroused. Mickey was both heartened and worried by that. What was his friend getting himself involved in, and whose blood had been spilled on the floor of that room with eight windows? Right now, Mickey could not guess, but his instincts told him that no good would come of any of this . . . and his anxiety was exacerbated by the knowledge that whatever Henry had done, wherever he had gone, Mickey was trailing a week behind.

SIX

Mickey knew where Kem Beaney usually lodged when he was back in London. Like many others that plied their trade on the river, he spent a few nights at one of the several hostels that provided cheap bed and board in the Docklands. The area was one to which Mickey had frequently been called in his early days in the police force when as a beat copper he had broken up fights, thrown troublemakers out of pubs and been thrown out in his turn. Arrested the girls whose vocation it was to get the sailors drunk so they'd be easier to relieve of their pay or, on occasion, an easier target for the men who controlled the girls. A few of the women had taken up the business on their own account, a dangerous decision as Mickey well knew, though some of them were as tough as the menfolk. Dressed up to the nines and armed to the teeth, Mickey would have thought twice about crossing them.

First light on a Tuesday morning though was a quiet time. He found Kem reading the newspaper and finishing his morning tea. The newspaper, Mickey noticed, was a few days out of date. As he put it down, a headline caught Mickey's eye. It announced that President Hoover was to embark on a job creation scheme to the tune of $150 million. *About time our government did the same*, Mickey thought.

'Sergeant Hitchens, what brings you here?' Kem automatically looked around for Henry Johnstone, then seemed to remember that Henry had left the force and said, 'Strange to see you without the big man. How's he finding civilian life?'

'Not so good as it turns out, and that's really what brings me here. I'm wondering if you know where your sister is? She told Cynthia she had family matters to attend to, a funeral in fact, but we both suspect that may not be the full truth.'

Kem's eyes narrowed. 'Why would Malina lie to Cynthia? She counts her a friend; we count her family.'

'And I know Cynthia feels the same. It's likely that Henry asked Malina not to tell his sister where she was going. The fact is, Kem, Henry is gone and we think that Malina is either searching for him, knows where he is or is even with him, but has been asked not to tell.'

'That sounds like a muddle. But there's no funeral, that's for sure – if someone had died I think I would have heard about it. So you'd best tell me what goes on, and how I can be helping.'

Quickly, Mickey gave him the facts as he knew them. That Kem had not heard from his sister was not in itself unusual. They wrote to one another, brief notes mostly on Kem's part and longer letters from his sister, which were left at regular drops along the river. Kem picked up his letters as he got to them. It was not unusual that he would catch up with a month's worth of news in one go. The last letters he had received had been a couple of weeks before and, as usual, had been chatty and full of the events that made up Malina's life. She had mentioned Henry, he said, that she was worried about his state of mind and was planning on going to see him.

'I was surprised he weren't at his sister's place,' Kem said, 'but Malina said he got work at a big house up the coast. Helping to organize some chap's library or summat. She seemed to think it was good that he was keeping his mind occupied but that she was still worried about him.'

Kem moved restlessly, his body suddenly awkward as though whatever was on his mind was expressing itself physically. 'You know she's sweet on him.'

Mickey nodded.

'Reckons he's sweet on her too but he's not much good at saying it. Last letter she wrote, Malina said she figured she ought to say it for him. Women do, you know, our women, if a man is being a bit slow.'

'A bit slow is certainly a description that applies to our Henry.' Mickey nodded. 'Good for her, it's about time someone told him what's what. But no sense of where she might be going or even that she might be going somewhere?'

Kem shook his head but he didn't look particularly concerned. They both knew that Malina was well able to look after herself. 'I'll put the word out, if that's what you want?'

'I'd be grateful, but emphasize that neither of them are in any trouble with anyone, we're just concerned about their welfare. I suspect Henry has a bee in his bonnet about an old case and when he's on the hunt he's not exactly in a frame of mind to be concerned about anyone or anything else. If I'm concerned about anything it's what he might be barging his way into.'

'She'll keep him straight,' Kem said. 'Just like you used to do. But I'll tell anyone that finds them that there are folk worried about them and they have no right to make people afraid. Sometimes the likes of Henry Johnstone need reminding of that, and Malina is so used to being independent that she forgets too.'

Mickey thanked him and went on his way feeling a little lighter. But where the devil were they? he wondered again. And why the hell hadn't Henry got in touch with him? Mickey had to admit that he was, like Cynthia, very much put out by this absence of contact. Very much put out indeed.

Mickey collected Sergeant Tibbs from the Criminal Records Office and they once again began their journey south.

'Fingerprint comparisons?' Mickey asked. The fingerprint bureau was proud of its ability to return most matches within a day of samples being submitted. Mickey supposed they were still well within that target, but he figured there was nothing wrong with being hopeful.

'Nothing turned up yet,' Tibbs told him. 'And the testing of the blood from the floorboards and the wall, if that's what it is, will be done later today I believe.'

Mickey nodded. 'Then at least we may have some idea if the blood is from one person or two. Unless the blood groups match, of course. Though Henry's is type B, so a little more unusual, and that makes it less likely. There are some files on the back seat,' he added. 'Make sure to read them later, but for now I'll fill you in on the broad details. Sidney Carpenter was a petty thief, rubbed a lot of people up the wrong way but was not important enough to come to the attention of anyone who might obviously want to kill him. He was the lookout on a couple of big burglary jobs over St John's Wood way – silver, paintings, jewellery, that sort of thing. One of the gang was picked up trying to fence some jewellery, fingered Carpenter but Carpenter remained shtum throughout. Sergeant Pincher was in charge of the interrogation and he was never, shall we say, too subtle about his methods, so there's a good chance that Carpenter didn't know anything useful, maybe didn't even know the real identity of the others. His job was just to keep watch. I doubt he made much out of it in the way of payment. My guess is he didn't know anything or had very good reason not to tell anything. It's hard to imagine many people more frightening than Sergeant Pincher when you are in a little room with him, so if Carpenter was scared to speak out it must have been because he was very much afraid.'

'I never met Sergeant Pincher,' Tibbs said.

'No, he was probably before your time. He retired and now runs a pub. Devon somewhere, I think, that's where he came from. Back in the day a lot of Metropolitan officers did their growing up in the countryside. The brass reckoned they were fitter and better fed and that was probably true. No one was particularly interested in brains when they were recruiting plod to manage the streets. How the hell Pincher made it through his sergeant's exam is anyone's guess but, well, ancient history. Things were different then.

'Anyway, Carpenter came to our attention now and again but never for anything major. Until he turns up dead. Single stab wound up under the ribs, hits the heart, no defensive wounds so—'

'He likely knew his killer.'

'Or he's approached by someone who looks harmless until it's too late. One single stab wound, Sergeant. The action of a moment. The killer could have just walked up to him, or asked him the time, or for directions. Carpenter pauses, killer steps in, stabs him, walks off.'

'Covered in blood. Surely someone would have noticed.'

'Blooded, yes, but covered? Probably not. The knife went in, came out, body fell, killer walks on. Bloodied knife goes into a pocket or a bag. The killer puts on gloves to hide the blood on his cuffs, wears a dark coat so it's not immediately apparent anywhere else that got spattered. Maybe even gets into a car or goes into a house. And would there have been anyone around to see on a miserable November afternoon when it's drizzling with rain and blowing a hoolie? He was found when the children were leaving school, a little after four. It's not clear how long he'd been lying there before that.'

Mickey frowned suddenly and Tibbs was quick to pick up on that.

'You've thought of something?'

'I may have done. It's a simple thing but I'm pretty sure it didn't get into the original report. Inspector Johnstone and I attended the scene, and we were there for the first hour or so before we got called away and handed it off to the local constabulary in S Division. We only picked it up again later when it became obvious that the Deans family had also gone missing and it was possible someone in the family was suspect. So far as Sidney Carpenter was concerned, everyone initially assumed it had been a falling out between thieves and if we followed up on every one of those that crosses our desk because it ends in a dead man on the pavement, we'd get nothing else done. But it occurs to me now and should have occurred to us then that it is odd no one saw the body when they were *on their way* to pick the children up from school.'

'The body was found by two young lads, running down the pavement ahead of their auntie and her friend. The two women were gossiping and the boys were running off ahead. So, I ask myself now, did the women walk that same path on the way? And if they did, why did they not see the body? If there was no body to see, then that gives us a window of opportunity – a very short window of perhaps a half hour between the women walking down that path and coming back the same way.'

'And presumably they were not the only parents or guardians collecting the young ones from school.' Tibbs paused. 'I was walking home on my own with the big kids from about five,' he said.

'As was I,' Mickey agreed. 'You and I didn't grow up in a posh house with servants and a fee-paying kindergarten and a prep school round the corner.'

Tibbs appeared to consider this but then he nodded. 'So

presumably there would have been other parents and guardians
around, walking down that street towards the school.'

'A few, yes. It might be worth having the constables knock
on a few doors, see what people remember from that time.
The incident was something of a *cause célèbre* in the area so
chances are that even five years on there will be people who
have good memories.'

Tibbs was recording these ideas in his notebook. 'When we
reach a telephone I'll call Central Office,' he said.

'Do that. But if, and it is only an if, Carpenter was murdered
at say between three thirty that afternoon and around four fifteen
when he was found, or perhaps we could even narrow it down
to a quarter before three and a quarter past, then it disconnects
his death somewhat from the other half of a mystery.'

He paused, waiting for Tibbs to catch up with the line of
thinking, and was satisfied when the young man said excitedly,
'The Deans had left their *lunch* unfinished. They would likely
not be eating lunch at three thirty in the afternoon.'

'It is *less* likely, certainly,' Mickey agreed. 'Perhaps afternoon tea would have been more appropriate, but it was certainly
lunch that was left on the table. Although there seemed to
have been no direct connection between the Deans and
Carpenter, we had considered the possibility that the death of
one led to the sudden desire for the other to flit. Perhaps this
was not the case after all.'

'You think that Inspector Johnstone suddenly realized that?'
Tibbs asked. 'But why would he be thinking about the
Carpenter murder? What would have brought it to mind?'

That, Mickey thought, was a very interesting question. So
far as he was aware, Henry had thought about the case from
time to time, as had just about everyone who had been obliquely
involved in it. No one liked unfinished business. But he did
not believe that it had weighed on Henry's mind in any particular way. No, it had been more of a mild irritation or an
interesting mystery to be mulled over the occasional pint or
as a fit subject for speculation at one of his sister's dinner
parties. So what might have escalated that into something
which not only led Henry to act precipitously, but which had
led him to disappear?

None of it seemed to make any sense, Mickey conceded and, unusually, he wasn't even sure what the next step in the investigation ought to be.

Tibbs said, 'Perhaps we should go back to the library and see if he left anything among the paperwork he was dealing with. All the records and notes we spotted in the drawers. See if perhaps there was anything there that might have called this to mind.'

Mickey nodded; it was as good a place to start as any. 'And then we proceed as normal, interviewing local business owners, neighbours' – not that there were close neighbours to the Barry house – anywhere Henry may have passed or people he may have interacted with when he went for his walks.' And Henry would have walked, Mickey knew that. It was something they had in common that they walked when problems gnawed at their brains. Only a good long walk could give them space to mull them over.

'I've asked Malina's brother to put the word out,' he said. 'It's possible she's made contact with family; it's more than possible Henry is with her.'

He observed the look of disgust that flitted across Tibbs' face but he said nothing. These kinds of prejudices, Mickey knew, took a lot of uprooting and it would take a while to shift the young man's perspective. Though shift it would, Mickey promised himself, and not only about Malina's people.

SEVEN

'How is the arm feeling?' She set down the bowl of water and began undoing the bandage.

Henry watched her, shifting his focus away from the view of the house opposite for a short time and on to his friend. 'It's sore,' he confessed. 'But he came off worse.'

He saw her grimace. 'So you told me. You got lucky, Henry. You can only ride your luck for so long.'

He winced as she slowly eased the bandage away from the dried blood and then winced again as she cleaned the wound with the saltwater. Henry turned his attention away from Malina and back to the window. No one had come anywhere near the house in the last day and a half and he was beginning to think that she was right, they had moved on.

'You know Cynthia is going to be worried half to death,' Malina said. 'She deserves better, Henry.'

'I'm keeping them safe. I've brought enough danger to their home. The last time they got caught up in something I was involved in, Melissa nearly died.'

And he had nearly been killed too, Henry thought. It was the injury he had received saving Melissa that had brought him to this point in his life. Forced him to leave the police force, forced him to try and find something else to do with his life. And that was working out really well so far . . .

'You think I don't know that? I was there, remember. A part of all that. But your absence will not keep those you love any safer,' Malina said. 'If one of the men you are seeking chooses to strike against you, any of those you love could still be the target and, thanks to the way you are handling this, they can't even prepare themselves. They have no idea there might even be a threat.'

'You should go back,' he told her. 'Go back and tell them. I brought you into danger and I had no right to do that.'

'I *chose* to be with you.' She touched his forehead and

frowned. 'You still have a fever. Henry, this is all ridiculous.'

'And I should not have told you any of it.'

'You leave clues to follow and people will follow them. People who care about you. You know that Mickey won't give up either. Now, please, call Cynthia or let me do so and tell them what's happening.'

She paused, waiting for his response. She had been patient with him so far, Henry knew, but he could feel that her patience was at an end. That anger was now taking its place. 'Henry, I swear, if you don't contact your sister then I will.'

Henry frowned. She was right of course. He'd thought . . . no, he'd felt that he was doing the right thing but he was now less certain that his judgement had been sound. He had missed Cynthia, and Mickey Hitchens too – his resilience and his common sense and his strength of character – but did he really want either of them engaged in this folly? And that was how Henry had come to think about this. How could he have got things so wrong? He had spent half his life investigating, righting wrongs, and now he couldn't even get his own thoughts to make sense.

He was aware Malina was watching him closely. Sometimes he suspected she could read his thoughts. He wondered if she made any better sense of his ramblings than he was doing.

Henry sighed deeply. 'Perhaps you're right,' he said. 'Perhaps I should just go back, speak to Mickey, tell him what I've learnt and hand the whole thing over to the proper authorities.'

'That's the most sensible thing you've said in days,' Malina told him tartly.

He glanced around at her again. She was putting some kind of salve on the wound in his arm. It smelt like lavender and wintergreen and it did soothe the pain. The wound was not life-threatening, though it had bled like the devil until he had managed to wrap a towel around it, and even then the blood had gone through the towel and stained his shirt. But he had managed to best his assailant and that was something.

She began to cover the deep cut with a fresh bandage and Henry watched her, feeling a deep pleasure at the sight of her dark hair, her slightly pursed lips, her concentrated focus. Was he in love with her? Henry wasn't sure he even knew what that felt like, but he enjoyed having her around. He worried that there should be more to it than that, and that he was failing this woman who had been such a good friend to him. Who, he knew, had gone beyond wanting simple friendship.

A movement in his peripheral vision called his attention back to the window. 'I knew they'd be back,' he said, a note of triumph in his voice as two men walked up the steps to the house, glancing around cautiously before they opened the door.

Malina sighed. 'So let me send a telegram to Mickey. Henry, you can't handle this alone. Next time it will be more than a cut arm. You said a moment ago that you thought you should go back and get help. That was a good thought; follow it through, for God's sake.'

He stood, and she steadied him when he swayed and almost fell.

'Sit down,' she told him sharply.

Reluctantly Henry obeyed her. The truth was he had over-exerted himself and had been doing so for months. He'd told everybody that his shoulder was healing and he was feeling better but there was nothing further from the truth. It still hurt damnably whenever he moved. It still felt as inflamed and sore and stiff. The trouble was the rest of him didn't feel much better. He'd let everybody think he'd been fit enough to go and live in the Barry house and work in the library, but the act of moving library steps, taking down books, cataloguing books, and re-shelving books had already stretched his stamina to the limit. Since leaving the Barry house he had pushed his body harder and even Malina's care could not compensate for that. Nor compensate for the fight he had won more by luck than judgement, back in the room with eight windows, then barely making it to the top of the stairs before faintness overcame him.

He'd known he'd have to leave that house; felt they were certain to come back and find him there and he would not be able to defend himself a second time, and so he had called for help and she had come. She'd found him stumbling in the lane, rain falling, blood dripping from his hand, the taxi driver having to be persuaded to take an injured man who might stain his seats. She had taken him to a hotel, and the next thing he remembered was waking up with Malina sitting at his bedside and his arm burning but cleaned and bandaged.

She had stayed with him ever since, been responsible for finding rooms in this cheap boarding house with its view of his quarry, but Henry knew she was, quite rightly, running out of patience. He was being foolish and bull-headed and she was right that they could not handle this alone.

Malina stood. 'Rest,' she said. 'Keep watch if you must, but nothing more. Promise me?'

He looked questioningly at her. 'You're going out?' She had left him briefly only on two occasions, both times to buy food. He had worried about her being seen and she had assured him, with good reason, that she could be as invisible as a mouse when she needed to be. But still he worried. He got to his feet, reached out for her.

'Where are you going?'

She took a deep breath. 'Enough of this nonsense, Henry. I am going to telegraph Mickey Hitchens and your sister. We've caused enough grief to those who care for us without adding to it.'

She unhooked her coat from behind the door and was gone before he could stop her.

Back on the outskirts of Rottingdean, Mickey and Tibbs had been busy with their door-to-door enquiries, working their way inward from Whiteway's Lane, parking up on the outskirts and then continuing on foot. This was largely guesswork on Mickey's part – he had made the assumption that if Henry had walked into Rottingdean he would have come in this direction, the lane leading to the Barry house forking off Whiteway's.

They took a circuitous route through the pretty little town with its mix of residential, shops, small commercial enterprises and religious communities. Its links to Kipling who had apparently lived there for a time, something Mickey had not known.

Personally he was not a fan. Tibbs seemed very impressed and Mickey had to remind him of the job in hand when he started quoting from *If*. They reached the High Street, chatted to people at the fruiterer's, and the medieval Black Horse pub. Mickey made a mental note that it looked like an appealing hostelry and should be investigated. The High Street narrowed considerably where it met the coastal road and they were forced to squeeze through the blockage caused by a face-off between a lorry exiting and an omnibus seeking to enter the cramped space between ancient shops.

A short loop later found them in Whipping Post Lane and Tibbs was speculating if there really had been a public whipping post there.

'I imagine there was, and I imagine it was as popular a spectacle as public hangings,' Mickey said darkly.

Tibbs glanced at him in surprise. 'Is public humiliation such a bad thing?' he asked. 'Would it not discourage perpetrators of crimes if they knew their fellow citizens could watch as punishment was carried out? Their faces would be recognized by everyone. There would be no further chance for them to commit crimes unnoticed or undetected. It might make the job of the constables a good deal easier.'

'And it would block all opportunity for reform,' Mickey said. 'Men are less likely to change their ways if society is always suspecting them, if every petty theft is then laid at their door regardless. It's my experience they then think they may as well commit the deed. That they may as well hang for a sheep as a lamb, as the saying goes.'

'The criminal mind does not change, sir,' Tibbs said stoutly. 'As often as not criminal acts begin in childhood and by the time adulthood is reached they are ingrained.'

'Which implies we should be looking at the causes of crime, of where it begins, of the poverty and desperation that drives so many. Yes, I agree that *some* are born to it, that some seem born with an evil streak in them, but most of those that commit petty thefts do so to survive. Most of those who enter into a life of crime do so because other avenues have been blocked. That is my experience at least.'

'And yet you told me yesterday that there are many

highborn, who have never known want or need in their lives, who commit heinous crimes.'

Mickey nodded. 'Indeed I did. And as I have also just said, I do not deny that some are born with an evil streak. For some all manner of mischief comes out of pure boredom and my solution would be to set those individuals to work, preferably somewhere they can do some good for those worse off than they are. Perhaps they might learn a lesson by that. I do believe that a few are irredeemable, but they are the minority. And for those types of people public humiliation would do nothing.'

He could see that he had given the younger man a lot to think about and he wondered how Tibbs had grown so rigid in his thinking. Then Mickey got to thinking that perhaps he was simply more flexible than most in their profession. He supposed he had Henry to thank for that, in part at least. Henry and Belle and Cynthia too, and opportunities for learning that had been denied to many of his class and background. On the whole Mickey Hitchens counted himself a lucky man.

They traversed ginnels and twittens that criss-crossed the centre of the town, the narrow alleyways speeding pedestrian access between the congested roads where horse-drawn carts still competed for space with motor lorries and cars and buses squeezed along streets too narrow to accommodate their bulk. The main building material seem to be flint. Mickey noted round, dark, polished nodules that no doubt would have sparkled and glowed richly in the summer sun but which on a day as dark and dreary as this looked sullen and drab, relieved only by decorative sections of deep red brickwork on some of the grander buildings, criss-crossing the flint and lime plaster. Mickey glanced at his watch.

'Time we took a break and found ourselves some grub,' he said. It had been a fruitless morning.

Late lunchtime found them close to the White Horse Hotel. A slipway led down on to the beach close by the hotel and Mickey noticed the building work that he guessed must be related to the grand project he had heard about – a walkway along the under cliff together with sea defences. At the bottom of the slipway he could see large blocks of dressed stone, and further along groups of men involved in hauling rock, digging holes and other activities he could not quite make out.

The board outside the White Horse declared that the restaurant was open to non-residents and the scent of food floating out through the door when it opened briefly was inviting. Mickey looked Tibbs up and down and decided that he probably looked respectable enough to go inside. Tibbs' jacket sleeves were worn, but his overcoat looked decent enough and his shirt was clean.

'It looks expensive,' Tibbs said doubtfully.

'Courtesy of Cynthia, we have expenses for lunch, petrol and taxis, should they be required,' Mickey said. 'And I'm famished. I find it hard to think on an empty stomach these days, so I suggest we take advantage of the lady's benevolence and treat ourselves to a decent meal.'

Turning on his heel, Mickey led the way through the wood and glass doors and into the panelled room set with linen-clad tables. They reminded Mickey of the dust sheets at the Barry house, though the cloths were spotless here, not grimed and grey from long neglect. On the wall were photographs of the White Horse and its environs, and Mickey was particularly drawn to one which depicted horse-drawn omnibuses and private carriages on the road in front of the hotel, while a single car visible just at the edge of the frame spoke of a time of transition between horse-drawn and motor powered, though from what he had seen today the mix was still eclectic.

The diners looked well-to-do but not top drawer, Mickey thought, and mostly female from that class of women who had the leisure and means to lunch while their menfolk were at work. The one or two men that he identified as being among the better sort of travelling salesmen – most likely representatives from pharmaceutical companies or office supplies, their occupation made clear to Mickey by their leather cases and pinstriped suits – reassured him that two detectives would not be so far out of their depth in this company.

'Relax, lad,' Mickey said when they had been shown to their table and settled with menus. Tibbs was looking distinctly uncomfortable, glancing around at the other clientele. Mickey worried that he'd made the wrong decision – the boy would obviously have been more at home in a local hostelry like the Black Horse up the road, hoovering up bread and cheese.

'Consider this part of your education,' Mickey told him. 'A detective should be able to cope with a meal in a halfway decent restaurant.'

Tibbs looked even more disturbed. 'The fact is, Inspector, my parents don't really approve of eating out. My mother says it's wasteful and frivolous.'

Mickey blinked, waiting for Tibbs to break into a smile, sure that must be a joke. He realized a moment later that Tibbs was deadly serious. 'And how are they going to feel about your staying with the Garrett-Smyths?' he asked. 'Will they consider that frivolous too?'

The arrival of the waitress saved the unfortunate Tibbs from having to answer. Mickey requested soup followed by the steak and kidney pudding and Tibbs nervously asked for the same. 'And if I could have a quick word with your manager?' Mickey asked quietly, showing the girl his identification. 'There's nothing wrong,' Mickey assured her gently, noting the sudden anxiety in the girl's face. 'We're just involved in a case and it's possible your manager might be able to advise us.'

'Advise us?' Tibbs questioned as the waitress left. 'Why should we wish for advice?'

'Information, then,' Mickey said. 'But it's all in the words, see. You ask for information and people baulk at the idea that they're gossiping. You ask them to advise you about a situation and they feel like they're in a position of authority and privilege and you're the one on the back foot.'

Tibbs looked unconvinced.

'I expect your father likes giving out advice, doesn't he? In his position as spiritual council to the congregation?'

'I suppose,' Tibbs said reluctantly.

A man in a black broadcloth coat approached their table and introduced himself as the manager. Mickey made his own introductions.

'From the Metropolitan Police?' The manager sounded impressed but also, Mickey thought, a little put out. This was not exactly their patch. 'And what may I do for you?'

Mickey had decided that something close to the truth would

be the best approach to take. He had spent the morning with a photograph of Henry, borrowed from Cynthia, asking shop-keepers, landlords, residents and passers-by if they had seen this man. He had been met with curiosity, suspicion, occasional misplaced eagerness to help (*I might have seen a man like him last Thursday*) and outright rudeness. He showed the photograph to the manager.

'His name is Henry Johnstone,' Mickey said. 'Until a while ago he was a close colleague of ours. Had to retire due to ill health and now he's gone missing. Frankly, as you can imagine, his family's frantic with worry. He'd been doing some work up at The Pines. The old Barry residence?'

'I know it, yes. I knew the older Mr Barry slightly. He used to come in here from time to time. He liked to walk and was very spry for his age. Often he would walk here and then take a taxi cab home. He was a very friendly gentleman. What, if I may ask, was your colleague doing at the Barry house? I heard the younger Mr Barry had got someone in to pack up the library?'

Mickey nodded. 'To catalogue it ready for sale, yes.' He grinned at the manager. 'Unlike some of us, ex-Detective Chief Inspector Johnstone was a learned type of man. It occurred to me that as he also liked to walk he might have turned up here? As I'm sure you'll understand, any sighting of him would make his family very happy.'

'I can ask the serving staff,' the manager said, 'if you would loan me the photograph. But surely he might have walked in any direction from The Pines.'

'True, but he's been here before in company of his sister,' Mickey said. 'So the place would have been familiar. It's just possible therefore that he might have walked in this direction. His sister, Mrs Garrett-Smyth, and her husband would be grateful for any information, I'm sure. Mrs Garrett-Smyth was a friend of Sir Eamon Barry. I believe she lunched here with him on occasion.'

The manager looked impressed. He took the photograph and left them to their meal, the first course of which had just arrived.

'You really think Inspector Johnstone might have been here?' Tibbs asked.

'Cynthia thought it possible; she did once bring him to dine here. And, as it happens, she also dined here with Sir Eamon, though that was several years ago when the old man was presumably in better shape.'

'You think the manager remembered her name?' Tibbs asked.

Mickey shrugged. 'I doubt he's heard it before, but if you say someone's name as though they are some kind of VIP then people tend to assume they must be.'

Tibbs nearly choked on his soup. 'I suppose that's also part of my education,' he said. 'Inspector, there's a smack of deceit to some of your methods, if you don't mind me saying so.'

'Of course there is, my boy,' Mickey said.

They had just finished their meal when the manager came over again, this time accompanied by a young man that Mickey had observed tending the bar when they had first come in. 'It seems your friend may have been here,' the manager said. 'Tell these gentlemen what you told me, Cribbins.'

'I saw your friend about two weeks ago, probably a Tuesday evening but I can't remember exactly. He was here with a young lady. Nicely turned out, with dark hair. Respectable.'

The manager was frowning as though the idea of a non-respectable young woman coming into his hotel was inconceivable.

'And you're certain it was him?' Mickey asked.

'I've got a good memory for faces,' Cribbins said. 'You have to in this business.'

The manager nodded sagely and Mickey decided that that particular piece of wisdom must have come from him.

'And how did they seem?' he asked.

'The gentleman didn't look well and I think there was something wrong with his left arm. He had it in a sling; his coat was pulled round it so the sleeve was loose. The lady seemed concerned about him. They had dinner and then they left. I didn't serve them dinner, you understand, but the young lady came out of the restaurant.'

Mickey nodded. The restaurant area and the bar were separated by a low rail.

'And she stood like she was going to come to the bar but

she didn't want to. Like I said, she looked respectable, so I got Rita, that's one of the waitresses, to go and ask if she needed anything and she said that her friend truly could do with a brandy. That he wasn't feeling too good. And would it be possible for us to call a taxi for her. So I had Rita take a brandy across to the table and I got Mr Jeffries at the front desk in the hotel to call a taxi.'

'Do you have any idea where they were going to?'

He shook his head. 'I did see the young lady helping the gentleman into the taxi when it arrived, and then she walked off down the Brighton Road. I thought she might be going to get the omnibus. It wasn't that late in the evening, probably about nine, so she could have caught the omnibus quite easily.'

Mickey nodded, told Cribbins that he had been very helpful, and asked the manager if it would be all right to tip the boy as a thank-you for his information. The manager demurred that he was sure it would be acceptable on this occasion and Mickey asked for the name of the taxi firm and where he might find them. And could they have coffee.

Mickey watched as Tibbs sipped the coffee, his expression uncertain as though he had expected it to taste different in such unaccustomed surroundings. It was actually very good coffee, Mickey thought. Perhaps this too was considered frivolous. 'So he was here and he met Malina,' Mickey said.

'The barkeeper said that she was a respectable lady,' Tibbs noted.

'And so she is,' Mickey growled. 'You've been warned, lad. A change of attitude if you please.'

He was aware that he sounded far more annoyed than he had perhaps intended, but Tibbs' mumbled apology at least seemed genuine enough.

'So Tuesday about two weeks ago. I'm sure the taxi company picks up a lot of people from here, but the cabbie might remember an occasion when a man got in the taxi and a woman walked away instead of the other way round,' Mickey said. 'That he was using his sling disturbs me – he had convinced everyone he no longer needed it. Not that any of us believed him,' he added. It was interesting that he had met Malina away from the house, Mickey thought, when at least on one other occasion she had gone to the Barry house to see him. Had she been unable to borrow a car that night? The house was set a good way back from the road and it was a good walk from this main road where the buses ran regularly. Malina would be naturally cautious both about walking all that way in the dark and of being able to catch a bus home. If she had not been able to borrow a vehicle on that occasion she would have asked Henry to meet her somewhere that was safer and better lit. That would make sense.

He frowned, something else occurring to him.

Tibbs noticed. 'Something else is concerning you?'

'I am wondering if she could have got home that evening or if she would have had to stay somewhere. If she caught the bus at around nine o'clock she would still have had a fair journey ahead of her to get back to Cynthia's house. The buses from here presumably run through Brighton and perhaps onto Shoreham and I know she has friends at Shoreham, so it's possible she broke her journey there and continued to Worthing the following morning. Cynthia would remember that, so we may be able to pinpoint the day more accurately.'

Tibbs nodded. 'So what now, sir?' he asked.

'So now we go and speak to the taxi company and hope the driver who did the pickup remembers something,' Mickey said. He paid the bill and left a substantial tip. Once outside he patted his stomach in satisfaction. 'Now the brain has been refuelled,' he said, 'I feel confident that we may make progress.'

He was aware of Tibbs looking at him as though he'd gone slightly mad. 'Something to learn, boy: if you get the opportunity to eat you take it. There are times when you're stuck in the middle of nowhere and there's not even a cup of tea for hours at a stretch. So, two pieces of advice. You eat when you can and if you're called away you take a flask, and if that flask has a little nip of something in it in addition to your tea, all the better.'

He walked off in the direction of the taxi office knowing that if he'd looked at Tibbs' face and seen the shock he was certain would be there, he would be unable to stop himself from laughing. He had met puritanical beat officers in his time and deeply religious constables too, but those who made it to the rank of detective sergeant had generally grown a little more flexible in their thinking. Being a detective called for a different set of skills, Mickey thought, though he found himself hoping that Tibbs would make the grade. He had decided that he quite liked the young man.

EIGHT

In the end Malina had decided that the telephone would be quicker than trying to send a telegram and she had called Cynthia's house hoping to find her in. She was desperately relieved when she came to the phone.

'I'm so sorry,' Malina began. 'I promised Henry . . . Mr Johnstone . . .'

'Henry will do,' Cynthia told her a little sternly. 'All I need to know is that the two of you are all right. And you need to know that I am furious and with both of you. Why didn't you come to me?'

'Because I promised I would not and I've been regretting it every minute since. But yes, we are . . . No, we're not. He is unwell, he's feverish and hurting. I've done all I can but he needs to be confined to bed for a few days – a comfortable bed with good food. He's got a bee in his bonnet about— Oh, Cyn, can you send somebody for us? Or better still come yourself. He needs forcing into a car and then forcing into bed and tying down if necessary. I've never met anyone so stubborn.'

Malina was shocked to hear Cynthia laughing. 'I'm just so relieved to hear from you. And I'm still furious, don't forget that. But let me know where you are and I'll come now. I'll have to borrow Albert's car. Mickey has mine.'

'Mickey? Is he looking for Henry?'

'Of course he is. Now give me the address.'

Relieved, Malina did so, then she hung up and walked quickly back to the lodging house.

Forty-five minutes later when Cynthia arrived she found Malina sitting on the bed, her face stained with tears and contorted with anger.

'I got here and he was gone,' she said. 'I only left him for perhaps ten minutes. I had to walk to the nearest telephone kiosk and then I spoke to you and then I hurried back. But it was a scant ten minutes. He is in no fit state to be wandering around on his own and certainly no fit state to be following anyone.'

'Following anyone?'

Malina indicated the house across the road that Henry had been watching. 'He is convinced that two men there are responsible for a death and came to The Pines up to no good. One of them attacked Henry.'

'Attacked Henry! Why didn't he report it to the police?'

'Stupid pride, I think, and because he thought he'd struck on something bigger than a mere assault. His words, not mine. He was shaken up enough when I went to the Barry house and found him halfway down the road, stumbling along like an inebriate, his arm bleeding like billy-oh. Please, Cynthia, don't worry about that part of it, he's healing well and I have to say he's in a happier frame of mind than he's been in a while. But he's got it into his head that something very big and very odd is being planned and that it has something to do with a man who was killed. A man called Sidney Carpenter around five years ago, I think. Cynthia, he thinks he's been keeping watch on a murderer but that he needs proper evidence before he reports it. I truly think he's losing his senses over this.'

Cautiously, Cynthia approached the window and looked at the house on the opposite side of the road. Like this one it had three stories and a basement and might once have been a smart residence here on the outskirts of Brighton, but now it was rundown and neglected and, at first glance, looked deserted. Instinctively Cynthia had moved to the side of the window, staying out of the line of sight of anyone looking from the house. She was uncertain why she felt this was important, but the back of her neck prickled and her instincts were shouting at her that they should leave. That there was still someone at the house and that they could prove dangerous.

Cynthia could handle most situations but this one she felt needed more brute force than two women, however determined, could be expected to bring to bear.

'Gather your things quickly,' she said to Malina. 'We should not stay here.'

Malina looked startled but then proceeded to do as Cynthia directed. Minutes later they were out of the house and heading back towards Albert's car. To Malina's surprise Cynthia had not driven herself – she had borrowed one of the young men who worked at the garages, that had once been livery stables, where Albert's Lagonda 16/80 resided.

Cynthia saw her questioning look and said, 'This is not the most salubrious part of town, and Albert's car is rather more expensive to replace than mine would be as well as being his pride and joy. I thought it best not to risk damage or theft and so had Billy here park around the corner. Some attention is inevitable – this is a rather beautiful vehicle – but we could do without the wrong sort.'

She smiled at the group of children who had gathered to examine the Lagonda and Cynthia handed a few coins out of the window. The children grabbed the coins and ran away.

'They are sure to remember you now,' Malina said a little dryly as the car pulled away.

'Of course they will. Two women in smart clothes and a very smart car. There is nothing to be done about that, but if someone is kind they are less likely to go out of their way to speak about them than if I had shouted and driven them off.'

She glanced at Malina, seeing that the other woman accepted the logic of the argument but was probably still not convinced as to the wisdom. She looked exhausted, Cynthia thought, and beyond anxious. 'What on earth is he doing?' Cynthia asked.

'Truthfully, I am no longer certain. He is convinced that he found evidence of a crime. He was equally convinced he could not confide in you and risk bringing danger to your door as he's certain he's done before because of Melissa.'

'Oh, for goodness' sake.'

'I know. Believe me, I do know. I now know how wrongheaded he is. We need Mickey Hitchens, we need the police, we need . . . I no longer know what we need. Can you forgive me?'

'For falling in love with my brother, for being loyal to him? For trying your best to look after him when he's in one of those moods where nobody can look after him? Yes, I think I can forgive that. But I am still furious with you.' Cynthia reached out and pulled Malina into her arms. 'We have been so worried, and when I realized that you had lied about the funeral, more worried still.'

'What frightened you back there?' Malina asked.

Cynthia shook her head. 'Hard to say exactly, just the sense that there was danger, that we should not stay. Has anyone seen you with Henry, was anything done or said that could link you to him?'

'No. If I went out then I went alone; he wouldn't leave the room. And I . . . I suppose I kept away from the window. Henry was not being as careful as he might have been and that made me more cautious. Whenever I left the house, I left by the back door and went down the little ginnel so I doubt anyone saw me.'

'But if he did go out and challenge them, or follow them, it's likely by now they would have worked out which room he was staying in and where he'd come from. It's also more likely that they took him than that he followed. You said he was in no shape to follow anyone.'

'He was still weaker than he wanted any of us to know. I realize that now and these past days have really taken a toll. He's barely slept and I've had to force him to eat. He's been surviving on tea and cigarettes.' Malina opened her bag and withdrew a small, much worn cigarette case. 'He left this behind,' she said. 'He must have been in such a hurry that he forgot to put it in his pocket.'

The two women stared at this precious possession and Cynthia felt her heart sink. With an effort she pulled herself together. 'At least you have it safe. You did well to stay out of sight and my instinct was to do the same. Hopefully I succeeded.'

Malina nodded. She sat back in the seat, closed her eyes and within moments she was asleep.

Cynthia sighed. She would have loved to begin her interrogation but now she wondered how much sleep Malina had had this past week. Instead of waking her she arranged the car rug over her legs and sat back with her own thoughts. *Henry*, Cynthia thought, *what in Hell's name are you up to and where the Devil are you?* The fear that he had not followed someone but that someone from the house had taken him was growing to certainty. She sensed that Malina had not fully appreciated the consequences of this conclusion yet, but that she would. And Malina was right, they really did need Mickey Hitchens now.

The taxi firm had its offices in a mews just off the High Street. An awkward spot to get in and out of, Mickey thought, but it had the virtue of being central and there was space for a small mechanics shop in one of the old stables. The sign over the door announced it as Tate's and Mickey had a vague memory of seeing a larger Tate's establishment occupying a large corner space on the outskirts of the town.

The controller consulted her worksheets, narrowing down which drivers might have picked up a fare from the White Horse, and Mickey and Tibbs settled down to wait until the driver returned from dropping off his fare.

Yes, he recalled picking up a rather sickly looking man, and by consulting the worksheets it was decided it would have been a Tuesday night, just over a fortnight ago.

'You say he looked sick?'

'Arm in a sling, looked about fit to drop. I took him to The Pines where old Mr Barry lived. I'd taken Mr Barry back there a time or two, but no one's lived up there since he died. I wondered what your man was doing up there.'

His curiosity was evident and Mickey saw no harm in telling him that Henry had been cataloguing the library ready for sale.

'I thought they'd already cleared the whole place out,' he said. 'Several times I've seen a van going up that way when I've been out and about. Other drivers too. Mick Baily commented not more than a week or so ago that it was strange they'd got removal men up there at night.' He laughed. 'We wondered what that was costing.'

'And always the same van?'

The driver thought for a moment. 'One of two, I'd say. A dark Morris, I think. No trader's name on it though and that's an oddity, isn't it?'

Mickey agreed that it was. 'And the second?'

'Smaller, a delivery van. Chevrolet Bedford, I'd have said, but it was dark, so I couldn't be certain.'

'And the young woman, when she saw your passenger into the cab, what did she do?'

'Walked off to get the Brighton bus. It's a funny thing, though. I saw her again ten days ago or thereabouts. She came to the office. You remember, San?'

The controller frowned. 'Young woman with dark hair and a pretty blue hat and coat. Bit of fur trim at the collar?'

'That's the one. Wanted to go to the Barry house but we didn't get there. The bloke she'd been with on the other night, he comes staggering down the road like he's definitely had one over the odds. Well, she had me stop and pick him up. I told you about it, San, he'd hurt his arm. The same arm, but there was blood this time. She took off his scarf and wrapped it up so he didn't get blood on the seats. Even so, I weren't that happy.'

'Can you recall the exact evening? Where did you take them?'

Another consultation of records and Mickey was satisfied that it was the same evening Malina had left Cynthia's house. Their destination had been the end of the street on the outskirts of Brighton.

'And did they say much to one another on the journey?'

'Look, I don't listen to conversations—'

'Hard not to overhear, though, isn't it?'

The man shrugged. 'She was mad as hell with him. Told him he wasn't being fair and that his sister would be worried sick. He said something about leaving his sister out of it. They both clammed up then, but she certainly wasn't pleased about something.'

'Anything else you can call to mind?'

He thought for a moment. 'Yes. The woman paid, but she had to ask the man for a bit extra. Said she'd spent her cash just getting here. I can't be sure, but I got the impression she'd taken a taxi into Brighton and then got the bus and then come to the office.'

Mickey thanked him, looked at Tibbs to see if he had anything further to ask and then they departed, Mickey in thoughtful mood.

'Well, that clears up some of the mysteries,' Mickey said. 'It must have proved an expensive evening for young Malina.'

NINE

Cynthia's speculation had been correct.

Henry had left the house just after Malina, knowing that whatever was going to happen must happen now. When Cynthia arrived it would be too late for him to take action. He knew himself to be feverish and weak and totally unsuited to any kind of exploit that involved moving more quickly than at a snail's pace, and while he was aware that he was not thinking straight and was behaving in the most stupid manner, he couldn't seem to stop himself.

He suspected that the men had been aware of him for a while. Truthfully he had not been as careful as he could have been. He'd behaved like a complete idiot and he was paying for it now. He had been grabbed by two men, thrust into the back of a van and his hands tied, an action which sent piercing flames of agony through his shoulder and down into his ribs. He was aware that he had yelled out in pain as those manhandling him had thrown him on to the floor of the van. One man aimed a kick which, when it made contact with his shoulder, nearly caused him to pass out. The whole incident had taken mere seconds and the street had been empty. Henry doubted anyone would have seen a thing.

He tried to focus on how long they had been travelling. It felt like hours but he guessed it had been perhaps ten or fifteen minutes and the last part of that over rough ground. He was dragged from the back of the van and taken into a house, half dragged, half carried into a small room and tied to a chair. Henry's whole body throbbed. Fierce, stabbing pain racked him and he came close to blacking out. They left him and Henry forced himself to breathe slowly to try to bring some control back to his body and his mind. When the blackness and then the redness cleared from his vision and he could see again, and the pain had receded slightly to mere agony rather than overwhelming torture, he opened his eyes and looked around.

He was in a space which he guessed had once been a pantry in quite a large house. There was a door through to what he guessed was the kitchen and through which he had vague memories of passing before they brought him in here. He could hear voices – three, perhaps four people, an accent that was not British. American? He could not make out the words at first until someone moved across the kitchen and opened the door. Henry let his head drop to his chest and closed his eyes. He was fighting hard enough to remain conscious that he did not have to feign very much at all.

'That bastard owes me a bloodied nose,' a voice said. It was a voice Henry vaguely recognized but took a moment to realize it belonged to the man who had attacked him at the Barry house.

'You mean you got beat up by a man with only one working arm,' another voice taunted, and laughter followed.

The door closed again and Henry could hear someone's voice raised in anger, someone else still laughing and the tone of yet someone else trying to placate. Trouble among thieves, Henry thought. These are perhaps people who did not necessarily get along. Was that to his advantage or not? Henry was under no illusions: he was in a lot of trouble.

Carefully and experimentally he pulled at his bonds to see if he could free himself, but they were tight and wrapped around the chair. The chair back and legs put additional tension on the cords that bound him and the difficulty in moving his shoulder further restricted his movements. Shifting his weight about on the seat, he managed to ease a little of the pressure on his arm. Whoever had brought him in had untied his hands and re-tied them to the back of the chair so that his shoulder was not quite so stretched out of place and for that at least he was grateful.

So what next? Malina would soon realize he was gone and would summon help – had summoned help already, he reminded himself. That's why she had left him. Had they known that she was with him? Was she in danger too? He thought about it and realized that she had probably never been seen in his presence. If anyone from the house had noticed her they would have assumed she was just another tenant of the boarding house – at least that's what he hoped.

So soon she would tell Mickey what had been going on, or at least the part of it that Henry had confided in her. How that would help, Henry was not entirely sure. He could have been taken anywhere, he had no idea where this house might be and there was likely no trail left behind, so how was Mickey supposed to find him?

For a moment or two he gave in to despair and then he got angry. It was his own stupidity that had got him into this mess and no one was about to come and get him out of it, so he would have to shift himself. He looked around to see if there was anything useful that could help him loosen the ropes or cut through them, but all he could see in the little room was shelves on both sides, a cold slab of marble on which dairy and meat would have been stored and, from the feel of the draft at the back of his neck, he was pretty sure there was a window behind him, high up in the wall. Pantries large and small tended to be built to the same pattern, Henry thought. Was the window big enough for anyone to get through? Many was the house that had been robbed by the agency of a child posted through such a window who had then gone on to unlock a back door for the rest of the gang. Reason told Henry that this opening would also only be child-sized, but he had to know.

Carefully, afraid of being overheard, he started to rock the chair. Had Henry had his feet on the ground this would have been an easier matter, but they had been hooked around the chair legs and tied in place, something which was making them go numb and which he knew would cause intense pain sooner rather than later as the muscles began to cramp. He made an effort to move his feet as much as he could, wriggling the toes and chafing his ankles against the cords and the turned wood, trying to keep the blood flowing. By dint of shuffling and rocking he managed to turn the chair slightly, enough that he could, in his peripheral vision, just make out the window. It was not large but neither was it barred as many downstairs storerooms were. Could he get through there? Henry wasn't sure but, given the opportunity, he would sure as hell try.

TEN

As soon as she had returned home, Cynthia had composed telegrams, one to be sent to Central Office in London, at Scotland Yard, and one to Belle hoping that she might have some idea of where Mickey and Sergeant Tibbs might be. She sent a third to the tiny police station on West Street in Rottingdean in the hope that Mickey might report in with his local colleagues. Beyond that there was little she could do.

She had sent Malina up to her room to get bathed and changed and requested soup and sandwiches for both of them. She wasn't particularly surprised when Cook delivered refreshments herself, assisted by Josie, and then stood with her arms folded in the doorway and asked her mistress bluntly if Mr Henry was all right.

Cynthia regarded her in surprise, wondering whether she ought to be annoyed and then gestured for her staff to sit down. 'The truth is we don't know,' she said. 'Malina went to telephone me and tell me where they were, but by the time she got back to where they had been staying Henry was gone. He seems to be investigating something but we don't know whether it has gone badly or not.'

Cook nodded. 'Is it another matter like that with Miss Melissa last year?' she asked. 'You know we all felt desperately for the way she was taken from our house. That man took her out through my kitchen.'

Not exactly true, Cynthia thought. The abduction had been from the London house and the abductor had gone out through the storerooms and the back door into the yard, adjacent to the kitchen, but this was clearly not the time to argue about such a fine detail. 'We don't know. We hope not.' She looked anxiously at the cook. The woman had stuck by them through thick and thin and uncertainty and rumour after the crash that had taken part of Albert's business and threatened the rest, and then through Melissa's kidnapping when the house had been in uproar and had had policemen everywhere. Cook had coped with all of this and more with unflappable equanimity, but was this one emergency too far.

It seemed that her staff knew what she might be thinking because the older woman nodded, stood, straightened her apron and said stoutly, 'You know you can rely on all of us, madam. Whatever needs doing we will do it. Now, when is Inspector Hitchens likely to arrive, and will the young man be with him? The one that needs feeding up?'

'Unless my telegram reaches him sooner, then I expect it will be this evening,' Cynthia said. 'And yes, I expect Sergeant Tibbs will be with him. Though, Cook, it might be wise to provide something that can be eaten on the run. I don't imagine they will have much leisure to eat a proper meal.'

'I'll make sure it's all sorted out,' Cynthia was told, and then she and Malina were alone.

Cynthia served soup and sandwiches – comfort food, she thought – that had been left sitting on the chafing dish. 'Now eat,' she told Malina, 'and then you tell me everything you know.'

Mickey finally telephoned Cynthia just before four o'clock in the afternoon, and Cynthia had never been more relieved in her life to hear his voice. It seemed that one of the constables in Rottingdean had tracked him down and given him the message she had sent. Cynthia had kept it plain. *News of Henry, call immediately.*

'Has he been found?'

'Found and lost again.' Cynthia could scarcely keep the exasperation from her voice. Quickly she explained what had happened and told Mickey that Henry had been watching the building across the road from the boarding house in which he had been staying with Malina.

'And do we know for what reason?' Mickey asked.

'From what Malina can gather, this has to do with some suspicion he had of activity involving the Barry house and also perhaps the death of Sidney Carpenter and the disappearance of the Deans, but he was being as close-mouthed as ever and she doesn't believe he had worked out the details. She thinks Henry found something or thought of something while he was working in the library. She says he thought the house was being watched, that he heard footsteps coming from an attic above his room, but he could find no entrance into the attic and he wondered if he might be hallucinating. But then twice a car pulled up at the house and drove off when they realized someone was there. Somehow from that he made the leap to the Deans and Carpenter. Malina thinks he recognized somebody who approached the house on foot. But frankly, Mickey, she can't be sure of anything; he was feverish and hallucinating and very ill and may well have been imagining the whole kit and caboodle. Which is why she said she was going to contact me. He had been adamant that I was not to be involved, that none of us were to be involved, and now she is thinking that he disappeared because she raised the alarm.'

'If he was in a state that is possible,' Mickey said. 'But you think otherwise.'

'I think he grew careless and they took him. He's not been in his right senses for months, you know that, and everything seems to have become exacerbated over the last weeks since he went to that bloody house. Mickey, I was very careful not to let anybody see me but I'm sure there were people in that building across the street and I'm equally sure that someone has taken Henry. Call it woman's intuition if you like, call it any damn thing that pleases you, but please—'

'You don't have to ask. We are on our way. Cynthia, you know that Henry left his journal behind for me to find. Well, he mentioned the car and he mentioned the footsteps coming from somewhere above his room, but he did not record anyone coming to the house on foot so perhaps we should assume this happened shortly before he left? Talk to Malina, see if she can put a timeline together and get her to write everything down. We'll be with you as soon as we can.'

No one had been anywhere near Henry for the last hour, or so he estimated. It was hard to know how much time had passed and he was judging purely by the light from the window and how this had faded and finally disappeared. He guessed it was therefore late afternoon but probably no later than five. He was cold; they had taken his coat from him in the van. He was exhausted but he was now burning with anger, most of it directed at his own stupidity. He had been working on the ropes as best he could, loosening them slightly about his wrists and a little more about his feet, but there was nothing he could do to free the knots that he could not reach.

He'd taken to listening very, very closely. The people in the kitchen came and went; sometimes there was silence and at other times two voices, sometimes three. One was definitely American, and this was the man that had laughed at Henry's assailant for having received a bloodied nose from a man with only working arm. He was, Henry judged, the sort of man who liked to treat people like wind-up toys, turning the key by making comments that were derisory or inflammatory and then setting the toy in motion and watching as events play out. It was a type of individual that Henry did not have time for under any circumstances and he was prepared to take an extreme dislike to this man.

The third man was something of a mystery. Henry had seen him standing in the background and he had an air of calm about him that the other two did not. Was he in charge? Henry felt he did not have enough information to judge, but the man certainly seemed cut from a different cloth.

He had been offered no water, no food, no opportunity to relieve himself, and that distressed him. He knew that this was deliberate; nothing would give them greater pleasure, he sensed, than to see him piss himself. No doubt the American would find that hilarious.

He must have dozed for a few moments because when he woke he could hear all three of them talking. The door was ajar so someone must have come to check on him and he soon got the sense that they wanted him to overhear, they wanted him rattled and scared and presumably as cooperative as possible. None of them had tried to interrogate him as yet, so he guessed that someone else would be coming to do that and the thought filled him with dread. Henry was no coward, but he knew he was not in the best state to withstand any kind of physical oppression, and although he had only just begun to

put things together in his own mind, he realized he might
know enough to put others in danger and had no wish to do
that.

He could hear a sound of crockery set on a table and they
sounded as though they were playing some kind of card game.
He guessed from the play, the request for cards, the calls
made that it was poker of some description.

'So what are we going to do with him?' the American voice
said.

'That isn't a decision for us to make.' The quiet man this
time, Henry thought.

'They should leave him to me,' said the man who had
attacked Henry and been bested by him. Luck had been on
his side that night, Henry thought; it would not be again.

'You might have better success now he's tied up.' The
American voice again. 'If you ask me, the best thing we could
do is make it look like an accident, or better still make it look
like he did away with himself. From what I've heard, no one
would be surprised.'

With something of a shock, it dawned on Henry that this
man knew about him, his history, his depression, having been
in a complete funk for the last . . . however long. Henry could
no longer remember. This man knew all about his despair. So
how did he know and *who* did he know that might've told
him?

Definitely this information would not have come from
anyone directly involved with Cynthia, but what about Sir
Eamon's son? Would someone, maybe even Cynthia, have
mentioned that Henry was not in great shape or, having met
him, would Mark Barry have been able to draw the conclusions for himself? Or Sadie, the little daily maid who had
come in and brought his supper and who had tried to be kind
to him. Would she have said something? Did she have some
contact with this man?

On top of everything else, Henry now felt humiliated by
the idea that he could have exposed himself in this way. He
had tried hard to keep his emotions in check, along with the
fact that he felt like his head was underwater and he was
drowning, but evidently he had not been nearly as effective at

hiding that as he thought. Henry closed his eyes and took a deep breath. This was not the time for self-recriminations or for sliding even further into the pits. If he was going to get out of this alive then he had to act, though exactly what shape that action should take still defeated him.

As quietly as he could, Henry set about rocking the chair again, moving it a fraction of an inch at a time until his back was against the shelves and he could get a better look at that window. It was, he thought, possibly just as well that he had lost so much weight these last weeks. With luck, it was possible he could get through. But first he had to get out of the bonds that held him to the chair and the desperate need to urinate was now becoming an all-consuming thought. It almost made him laugh; he was in an utterly desperate situation but the only thing he could think about was this commonplace need to relieve himself. It was hardly heroic thinking, was it?

Mickey halted the car a few hundred yards away from the address they had been given and sat for a moment surveying the scene. The boarding house was on the right, a tall building with lights in several of the windows. There was no light on the second floor at the front, and from Cynthia's description this was where Henry had been staying. The house opposite was equally tall and had the addition of a basement. He could see the steps leading down from the pavement. No lights seemed to be on.

'It looks as though there's no one there,' Tibbs said cautiously.

'That's what it looks like,' Mickey agreed. 'But we should make no assumptions.'

'Do you think . . .?' Tibbs paused as though not sure how to phrase the next part of his sentence.

Mickey put him out of his misery. 'Do I think Henry is off his head and is making all of this up? On balance no, not from what he wrote in his journal or what he told Malina. There is something going on, though it may not be what Henry thought it was. I think, young Tibbs, that we should maintain the possibility that the residents of this house are innocent parties that Henry has in some way tarred with the guilty brush, while maintaining also the possibility that Henry Johnstone's instincts were correct. I've worked with him for a long time, and though he can be erratic he is also an excellent detective.'

Tibbs nodded. 'So what do we do?'

'You knock on the front door and I will go round the back,' Mickey said. 'I doubt anyone will open the door to you, but you never know. If they do then make up the name of someone you are looking for, someone who gave you this address. Act the innocent.'

'And you?'

'While you are distracting them, I plan on finding a way inside,' Mickey told him. He could see that Tibbs was not particularly happy with this plan.

'We should have asked for constables to come with us,' Tibbs said.

'And had constables been available at such short notice then I would have done. But that outpost of Rottingdean is small and lightly manned. To have stripped the sergeant of his two constables would seem excessive, especially as we may well be chasing the shadows of a poorly man's mind. I would rather find out first.'

They got out of the car, closing the doors quietly and Tibbs, as instructed, waited in the shadows to give Mickey time to slip down between the houses and get to the back of their target. Mickey glanced back before he turned into the alleyway and was satisfied that he could not see his sergeant; hopefully no observers from the property would see him either. Mickey was satisfied the car was parked sufficiently far down the road to be out of direct line of sight and not attract attention.

He felt oddly nervous, and it took him a minute to put his finger on the cause of that nervousness. He realized that this was the first time he had gone into a potentially dangerous situation without Henry Johnstone as his backup – or vice versa. The task he had given to Tibbs was simple enough, but would the young man cope with it or would he fluff his lines?

Time to find out, Mickey thought.

The gate creaked as he opened it and Mickey stood very still, one hand on the latch, gate slightly open, peering through the gap between gate and post, up at the house. His eyes had grown used to the darkness now and so far as he could see nothing was moving. There was no twitch of curtain, no deepening shadows as someone came to the window. A little further down the road a dog barked and the door opened and then closed. With luck, whoever was in the house – if there was anybody in the house – would have assumed the noise was just one of the random street sounds inevitable in a residential area like this.

Mickey moved forward, keeping in the shadow of the fence until he was touching the house wall. He made his way along to the back door, peering up at the windows to see if any was open, glancing down at the fancy grating that covered the tiny window that must in daytime illuminate the basement. There would, he assumed, be larger windows at the front of the house. Mickey had no general liking for basements; his professional life had led him to too many secrets hidden in cellars including a handful of dead bodies, a kidnapped child and an injured officer.

As he reached the back door he heard a knocking on the front that told him Tibbs was in position. He paused, his ear pressed against the door, listening. Tibbs knocked again. Again, no response. *All right then*, Mickey thought, *let's get inside and see what we find.*

The door was old, rotting where it touched the bottom of the frame. Mickey turned the handle and pushed, then pushed harder when he met resistance, heard the lock give way and then . . . then all hell broke loose.

He saw the first shot, the muzzle flash, almost before he heard it. He threw himself to the ground and rolled, diving back into the shadows and then running for the gate. The second shot grazed his arm and then he heard shouting coming from the front of the house. His first instinct was to get to his sergeant. His feet pounded on the cobbles and then he turned back into the alley and ran full pelt back to the front of the house.

Tibbs was on the ground and there was the sound of a car engine revving hard and then screaming away. Mickey ran to his sergeant, cursing and swearing, and in his mind already trying to explain to the young man's parents how he had got their son killed.

Tibbs stirred and tried to sit up.

'Easy boy, easy, be still. Are you shot?'

Tibbs put a hand up to his head and in the light from the streetlamp Mickey could see that he was bleeding heavily. 'I'm sorry, sir, he opened the door and he hit me.' Tibbs sounded both distressed and outraged. 'They got away – I'm sorry they got away.'

People were coming out of their houses now, assured that the immediate danger seemed to have passed and curious to find out what was going on. There was anger too, at people making trouble in their quiet little street. Several of the menfolk had come out armed. Mickey noted one with a carving knife and another with a spade. He produced his identification, explained quickly that his colleague was hurt and then realized, when someone pointed it out to him, that he too was bleeding.

One of the men helped him get Tibbs to his feet, led them both into his parlour and then, when his wife fussed, into the kitchen.

'Quite right too.' Mickey attempted humour. 'My wife would not want me bleeding over her best rugs either.'

Tibbs was sitting in a Windsor chair, holding a handkerchief to his head. The white linen was already soaked with blood and it was oozing between his fingers.

'Do you have something I can use to wipe the blood away, and some hot water?' Mickey asked. 'And is there a local doctor who might take a look at this?'

'A local doctor would take time to get here, but I'm a nurse if that's any good,' a voice said, and Mickey turned. An older woman had come in carrying a Gladstone bag. She gave the woman whose kitchen they had invaded a quick hug and asked her to put the kettle on, and it seemed now that this lady had arrived all was right with the world.

The husband took himself off to 'clear the streets of any rabble' and summon the constable, and the wife busied herself with following instructions from the nurse who introduced herself as Edie Young.

'Let's take a look at you,' she said.

Mickey watched as she cleaned the wound. It was long but

shallow and Mickey recognized the shape of the bruising and the matted hair. 'Hit you with the blackjack, did he?' he asked.

'I have no idea,' Tibbs said. 'Only that one minute I was standing on the doorstep and the next I was on the floor. I think it caught on my hat brim first.'

'And lucky for you it did,' Mickey told him.

Edie Young interrogated him about headaches and double vision. Had he passed out? He might have done, Tibbs told her, but only for a moment or two. He was conscious by the time Inspector Hitchens had got to him.

A matter of moments, Mickey told her.

Gently she pressed the skull around the wound, examining the bone and announced herself satisfied. 'You need stitching,' she announced. 'I can do that for you.'

Tibbs did not look thrilled at the prospect but he didn't have much option on the matter, Mickey decided. Moments later she had her needle and thread sterilized in boiling water, the needle wiped with alcohol and she was repairing the damage to the sergeant's head.

'You should get him to a doctor just in case of complications from concussion,' she said when she had finished. 'And don't let him be alone for the next few hours, just in case.'

Mickey, who had wide experience of head wounds and being bashed by various species of weaponry, assured the nurse that he would take care of his young sergeant.

'And I'll take a look at you,' she said, and Mickey gave into the inevitable. The thickness of his overcoat and his jacket beneath saved him from the worst. The bullet had grazed his upper arm, made a hole in his coat and his jacket and ruined his shirt. The blood had run all the way down his arm and, Mickey admitted to himself, it hurt like beggary. But he had suffered worse. She cleaned and bandaged the wound, declared that he didn't need stitching, and then a constable had arrived and Mickey had to explain the events of the evening.

He realized that he'd been too concerned for Sergeant Tibbs to have taken steps to secure the house and he cursed himself for it. Leaving Tibbs in the kitchen drinking hot, sweet tea, he and the constable crossed the road to find Alf Peterson, whose kitchen he had been making use of, standing with a group of men outside the front door.

A couple of local kids had tried to get in, he explained, so had been given a clip round the ear and sent on their way. Alf would be reporting their activities to their mothers in the morning, a threat if he'd ever heard one, Mickey thought. Alf and some of the other men from the street had decided that they'd better hang around until the police arrived, to make sure no other youngsters got the wrong idea. There were two other men around the back apparently, tasked with the same duties.

Mickey thanked him fervently and he and the constable went inside. Mickey was cautious; the men were armed and clearly aware and must have seen him come in through the back gate after all. Perhaps they had been aware of Henry's observation and still been on alert. Whatever the reason, they were clearly dangerous. He wondered what they had left behind.

There was no electricity in the house. There were candles and lamps but Mickey was reluctant to touch any of these in case of fingerprint evidence, and so they made do with their torches. To Mickey's disappointment there was little present, the one obvious exception being a jacket left on the back of the kitchen chair. He rifled through the pockets and then put the jacket over his uninjured arm and told the constable that he was going to get his sergeant to a place where he could rest and see a doctor and that he would rouse reinforcements from the Brighton and Hove constabulary on his way. He gave the constable Cynthia's phone number and asked that he be contacted there later. If necessary, he would return once he'd seen to Sergeant Tibbs' welfare.

Peterson and the others agreed to stand guard until other police officers arrived. Already the women in the street were organizing tea and refreshments and boys were sent running to find other constables at the local constabulary. There was, to Mickey's surprise, an almost party atmosphere along the little terraced rows. It was, he supposed, probably the most exciting thing to have happened in long years.

Weary now, but satisfied there was nothing more that he

could usefully do that evening, Mickey was glad to collect his sergeant and drive away.

Henry heard a car, then he heard a door slam, and the sudden change of mood was palpable. Twice since they had brought him here he had heard a vehicle arrive and then leave quickly, no other people coming into the house, and he was certain that this was the same engine sound that he had heard before. Two more voices, one calmer, one furiously angry and raised sufficiently that Henry could catch the sense of what was going on. Someone had come to the house Henry had been observing, one man round the front, one at the back, and the angry man was guessing there would be more lying in wait.

His quieter companion seemed to be trying to reassure him that this was probably not the case. As they drew closer to the scullery door, Henry also heard the quieter voice reprimanding the noisy man for having fired his gun unnecessarily. 'I should have made you stay here,' he said. 'A lot of use you are when you could have just raised the alarm. I told you I would deal with it; in all likelihood it was one of the local kids or some nosy beggar from along the road just looking to satisfy their curiosity. I dealt with him quietly as we left. There was no reason to raise Cain.'

'And what about him?' The scullery door was kicked open and an angry man stood in the doorway, pointing at Henry. 'Mark my words, them as came tonight was something to do with him.'

Mickey, Henry thought. It would have been Mickey. Shots had been fired. Had anyone been hit? Had Mickey been hurt? He tried to stay calm, to stare the man down, but the man was in the room now, grabbed him by his shirt collar and, chair and all, lifted him off the floor.

'Put him down.' Henry recognized the one he had come to think of as the quiet man, one of the trio who had been there originally. For a moment Henry thought the man would ignore the order but then he was dropped, painfully and unceremoniously, back on to the quarry tiled floor. The chair tipped over and Henry was on his side. His bad side. A flash of pain stabbed through his shoulder and into his chest and he was gasping for breath. The world was fading to grey and he was vaguely conscious of somebody setting the chair upright.

'Have you questioned him yet?'

'Let me do it.' Angry man again.

'We want him capable of answering.' A calmer voice.

'We waited for you.' The American this time. He sounded as though he resented the fact.

'Did you get everything out?'

'There wasn't a lot left, nothing much for them to find. Except muggins here left his jacket behind.'

'There was nothing in it but a pocket handkerchief,' the angry man objected.

'That had better be the case.' The quieter of the two men who had just arrived went to the kitchen and fetched a second chair and then sat in front of Henry, studying him thoughtfully.

'Ex-Detective Chief Inspector Henry Johnstone,' he said.

Henry stared right back at him. 'I've been offered neither food nor drink nor a chance to go to the lavatory since I've been here. If you plan to kill me then do so but at least have some decency about it.' He was aware that his voice sounded parched and dry, but he managed to keep it steady.

'Well, there's a pity,' the man said. He was dark-haired and thin-faced and wiry but probably stronger than he looked, Henry considered. There was coiled tension about him that worried Henry far more than the bluffness of the American, the out and out resentment of the man whose nose Henry had bloodied or the short fuse of the angry man.

The phrasing of his words and the slight inflection made Henry think Anglo-Irish in terms of origin, but he could not be sure.

The man seemed to be considering Henry's words. 'Fetch a bucket,' he said, and a bucket was duly fetched. The angry man untied him. He stank of cheap whiskey and onions, and his face was florid and jowly with broken veins across his nose and scars on his forehead and neck and a cauliflower ear. Henry would have bet on him as being a fighter, and from the look of his fists: bare-knuckled, the joints laced with scars and swollen in a fashion he had noticed such men seem to acquire over time.

Henry stood; almost collapsed. The man grabbed him by the back of his jacket and pulled him upright.

'A pot to piss in,' the quiet man said. 'So piss.'

What choice did he have? He was aware of the others around him, comments deriding him, laughter, the enjoyment of humiliation. Of the man still holding on to his jacket so that he did not fall. Henry reached out and held on to one of the shelves, using his injured arm to undo the buttons on his trouser fly. He closed his mind to the others in the room and he relieved himself, pissing in the pot, feeling the blood go back into his feet and his hands, feeling the strength and the anger grow within him. Relieved, he refastened his buttons and turned back to face his persecutors.

'You've got work to do, so go do it,' the quiet man said, and the three who had originally been there – the American, the man with a bloodied nose and the quiet man – turned obediently and left. The blow came out of nowhere, knocking Henry to the ground, knocking the air out of him. He was hauled upwards and sat back on the chair.

The quiet man pulled his own chair opposite, sitting astride with his arms across the back. 'Now what the fuck are you about?' he said.

ELEVEN

Mickey and Sergeant Tibbs arrived back at Cynthia's just after ten in the evening. Mickey had, as he had promised Alf and the constable, spoken to the constabulary at Brighton and Hove and arranged for back-up for the constables. He left the house and the detective to examine the scene, warning them that they would need to take portable lights with them. He volunteered to return when he had seen Tibbs settled into a comfortable bed and with proper medical attention, but was assured that they could deal with this and frankly Mickey was only too glad to agree. Brighton and Hove was a well-established constabulary, with its own team of detectives and a reputation for efficiency, and Mickey left with the promise that he would speak to the detective in charge in the morning. In truth, he didn't expect them to find anything; he had the jacket and had shown that to the officer he had spoken to, who had agreed that it didn't really help matters. Mickey had been prepared to leave this small piece of evidence behind and in preparation for that had already examined it closely and recorded the name on the tailor's label inside. Having the jacket itself was a bonus.

He had also taken the opportunity to telephone Cynthia, knowing that she would be worried. She was still worried when he ended his call, but at least, he thought, she knew what was going on even if they were no closer to finding Henry.

The doctor had arrived and was drinking sherry with Cynthia and Malina, Albert in attendance, when Mickey helped Sergeant Tibbs up the steps and into the drawing room. Albert poured Mickey a large measure of single malt and the doctor and Josie helped the injured man upstairs.

'You look all in,' Albert said.

'Nothing that a bath, a good feed and night's sleep won't fix,' Mickey said practically. 'And a needle and thread,' he added, examining the hole in his jacket revealed now he had removed his overcoat.

Cynthia came over and examined the garment. 'I think the shirt is beyond help, but Nanny should be able to fix the jacket and the overcoat. She's better with a needle than any of us and you can borrow something of Albert's for tomorrow. I suppose there is no news of Henry?'

'Had I anything useful to tell, I would have told you on the telephone,' Mickey said gently. 'We will find him and at least tonight's business proves that he was on to something. This wasn't all in his mind.'

'His investigating days are supposed to be over,' Cynthia said. She sounded angry, Mickey thought, but angry because she was afraid.

'And we will find him,' Mickey said. 'He's been using his brain, Cyn – the first time in weeks that's happened. It may have got him into trouble, but at least he's thinking again. Trouble caused by thinking, we can deal with. Trouble caused by a man in the depths of despair is much harder to fix.'

Cynthia nodded, wanting to be convinced, he could see that. He told them what had happened at the house in more detail, and then went out into the hall to fetch the jacket he had brought from there. 'The quality looks good,' he said. 'Not top drawer but from a decent enough tailor and it does not look second hand – there is not much wear on it, or perhaps it was given away when still quite new and the fashion changed. Do you recognize the tailor's label?'

Cynthia shook her head. She handed it to Albert, who examined the cloth and the cut and said, 'There was a lot of this kind of check about in autumn of last year. Personally it's a little loud for my taste. The cloth is not the finest, but not cheap either.'

Mickey himself was a big user of the thriving market in second-hand clothes. His overcoat had been one of Belle's most excellent finds, not much worn and made of wool a great deal heavier and better quality than Mickey could have afforded new. Once brushed and the buttons tightened – and Belle had ministered to the armpits and odd stains with a dabbing of

diluted alcohol – it had been in fine fettle. He suspected Tibbs
was at least as familiar as he with the second-hand trade.

'Leave it to us,' Cynthia said. 'Malina and I will track the
tailor down and find out who ordered this.'

Mickey nodded, satisfied. He had no doubt that Cynthia
would do exactly that.

'And now,' she said, 'top up your whisky, go and have your
bath and then you will eat and so will Sergeant Tibbs, and
then nothing more till morning, Mickey dear. If you are to get
to the bottom of this, you need your rest.'

Mickey could see how much this was costing her. She and
Henry were very close. She had effectively raised her younger
brother and loved him dearly, and he did not want to imagine
the pain she must be going through.

The doctor came back and said that Tibbs had been very
lucky: though he had a mild concussion he would take no
long-term harm. He was complimentary about the stitches
and said he could not have done a better job. He suggested
that Tibbs had something light to eat and then suggested that
before he left he should examine Mickey's arm. Reluctantly,
a little fed up of being pulled about, Mickey agreed.

In the bright electric lights of Cynthia's drawing room the
wound looked red and raw and deeper than he remembered.
Gaslight had a way of softening things, Mickey thought,
making them look less severe. He accepted the painkillers the
doctor gave him, swilling them down with another swallow
of whisky, and then, Albert having topped up his glass, he
went gratefully to his room and wallowed in a deep, hot bath.

TWELVE

Morning light filtered in through the window. Henry lay on the cold floor. Consciousness slowly returned and he was aware of how chilled and stiff and pained he felt. He moved. It hurt. Starting with his feet, he experimentally tested out each part of his body, flexing his toes, his ankles, his knees, at length sitting up and examining himself for breaks. He decided he was mostly just very badly bruised – apart from his ribs. Henry had endured broken ribs before and was familiar with that particular agony. He had a loose tooth in his upper jaw and had lost one from his lower. His face, when he probed with careful fingertips, felt puffy and swollen. He must look a sight, Henry thought.

There was no sound coming from the kitchen. They had not re-tied him and Henry decided that was because they didn't think he'd be going anywhere. Beaten unconscious, they probably thought he would remain that way for some time to come and he had to admit that oblivion would have been welcome. It would have been far less painful.

The bucket still stood in the corner of the room and he struggled over to it, fumbled with the buttons on his trousers and urinated, the sound uncomfortably loud, and in the light coming through the high window he could see that there was blood in his urine. Considering the kicking he'd received, he wasn't entirely surprised.

He could not quite understand the questions they had been asking him, but in a way that had been a relief because he could not give them answers that could incriminate anyone or even contribute the suggestion of involvement by another party.

What did you see, what did you find, why were you at the house, why were you watching us? He had seen nothing, he had found nothing that made sense, he was at the house to catalogue the library, he had been watching the house because the address had been in the pocket of the man who had attacked him at the Barry residence. Henry had taken pleasure in telling them that. He would have told them that for nothing, even without the beating. In the scuffle several things had fallen from the bloody nose man's pocket. A matchbook, a penknife, a few coins . . . but on the matchbook was a scribbled address. Henry was still too much of a detective to pass up that gift of information.

As he lowered himself painfully back into the chair, Henry dimly recalled the altercation that had happened after this revelation. The quiet man had left the room and had no longer been quiet, shouting and threatening recriminations. Shortly after that a car had started up and someone must have left.

Henry realized that it was dawn, light coming in through the window. He stared down at the floor, at the bloodstains that he realized must be his, at the bloodied hands from where he had felt the wounds on his face, and it occurred to him that the gang might have thought that they had killed him.

He closed his eyes, remembering the beating, the fists, the boots, the pauses for the questions posed by the quiet man who struck no blows but sat and watched, his face impassive. He remembered the moment when he had realized that his mouth was so bloodied and his lips so swollen he could barely speak. When his aching head told him that he was concussed, the difficulty in focussing reinforced that information.

He had to get out of here before they came back – that is if they had actually gone and not simply moved into another part of the house.

Henry struggled to his feet once more, grasped the scullery door and pulled it open. There were cups on the table, one still half filled with tea, and he lifted it with difficulty. His bruised lips unable to make a seal around the cup, he spilt as much on to himself as he did into his mouth, but even so, cold and scummy though it might be, it was the most wonderful thing he had ever tasted. It did not fully quench his thirst but it was better than nothing. He listened but could hear nothing except the wind outside, rain against the window, and the creaks and groans of an old house settling.

Henry stumbled out of the kitchen and into the hallway. He could see what looked like a front door but the hallway seemed as though it went on forever, his vision was swimming and his whole body crying out for rest. It came to him suddenly how they might have known who he was. Unless they had known already. Who might have told them? Had he previously arrested any of the gang or their confederates? He could not call such an event to mind.

They had taken his overcoat. In his overcoat pocket was his wallet and in that wallet was a old copy of his police identification, something he had kept as a souvenir when he'd had to surrender his current one on leaving the Metropolitan Police. That and other papers in his wallet would have filled in any gaps they might have had as to his identity, and his only worry now was whether there was anything in his possession that might link him to Cynthia.

He didn't think there was. He had no need to carry Cynthia's address on him, or her telephone number, but it still worried him.

He was certain now that the house was empty but had no way of knowing whether or not they'd left for good. He knew he had to take the chance. He must leave now, even though he barely knew how to put one foot in front of the other.

Struggling, one hand placed against the wall, he came to the foot of the stairs and the front door was almost in reach. Thrown into a corner, he saw something familiar. His coat. His talisman. Blessing the gods that he had long since ceased to believe in, he managed to pick it up, get an arm into one sleeve and pull the other around him, then he opened the door and stumbled outside. The sound of a car engine, distant but still terrifying, panicked him. The house was surrounded by an overgrown garden and somehow he managed to make it into the trees before falling on his face and lying still. The sound of the engine receded and Henry realized that it was not coming here, that it was simply passing by, and then he realized something else: that must mean there was a road, and if there was a road there would be people, and if there were people there might be somebody from whom he could get help. He just needed to lie still for a little longer, just rest for a moment and gather his strength. The world went dark and Henry passed out again.

THIRTEEN

At Cynthia's house, breakfast brought a morning conference. Mickey had been up for hours already, checking up on what had been found at the house Henry had been observing – very little, just a half bottle of good brandy – and being briefed on what the neighbours had to say about the men who had been staying there.

One of them had called at the local shop and bought basic provisions. He had been polite but tight-lipped, deflecting even friendly, casual questions. There had been at least two others who had come and gone at the house at various hours of the day and night.

The one small, intriguing piece of information was that the owner had arranged for building work to be done. He had agreed a price, arranged for materials to be bought, checked references and was now seriously alarmed that those he had employed were certainly not builders.

His money was gone, the referees now identified as bogus, but Mickey was struck by the elaborateness of this. The house had been unoccupied for months and, according to neighbours, squatters and local itinerants had taken advantage of that fact on more than one occasion. So long as they behaved, the community tended to ignore these intruders; usually homeless men who only hung around for a day or so before moving on. One had been caught thieving and been persuaded, none to gently, to 'sling his hook', as the sergeant Mickey was speaking to reported. But for some reason, probably instinctive caution, Mickey guessed, the locals had given the latest incomers a wide berth.

Most people living on the edge, for whom ruin was the result of a lost job or a bout of ill health, recognized predators, Mickey thought. They knew when and how to turn a blind eye and stay out of the way.

Tibbs had come down to breakfast and he was looking much

better, if still a little daunted by the company and, from the look of his face, the range of available breakfast comestibles. Mickey watched as he stood by the sideboard, spoon raised, clearly uncertain as to how much of anything he was allowed to help himself to. The previous morning there had just been Tibbs, Mickey and Albert present and, as usually happened when there were fewer people at the dining table, Cook sent up a classic English breakfast for each person, plus toast and marmalade, much as she would have done had they elected for breakfast in bed.

To have everything set out on the sideboard was much more daunting. Mickey was about to intervene but Cynthia came to the rescue with a usual tact. 'Sergeant Tibbs, please do sit down and help yourself to some coffee. Melissa, darling, see how Mr Tibbs likes his coffee, please. And now I'm sure you'll do what everybody does on their first visit here and sample a little bit of everything.'

Moments later Tibbs had a loaded plate in front of him and Cynthia had turned the conversation away from the young man and was asking Mickey what his plans were for the day.

Mickey dipped his sausage in his egg yolk and stared at it thoughtfully before answering. 'I must return to London, make my reports, and I wish to re-interview the neighbours, if there are any left from that time, on the street where Sidney Carpenter was found. I'd also like to speak to Carpenter's wife if I can track her down. And I have promised that I will try to be at Belle's last performance if I can possibly manage it. I don't mean to seem insensitive, my dear. I'll not slacken my efforts to find Henry, but I doubt I'll get back here – today, anyway. I can travel down with Belle first thing in the morning.'

'Mickey, you're being pragmatic, not insensitive, and it's about time you went to see the performance. She is rather splendid,' Cynthia added with an attempt at enthusiasm, though Mickey could see the strain in her eyes as she tried to remain cheerful. 'We went to see her last month.'

'I'll come with you,' Tibbs told Mickey.

'No, you remain here. I want to be sure that your head injury isn't more serious and the doctor will be coming to check on you this morning.'

Tibbs looked uncomfortable. He'd been anxious the night before about covering the cost of such an eminent physician and even more uncomfortable when Mickey told him that Cynthia would be footing the bill. That discomfort resurrected itself now and he seemed about to voice it. Mickey interrupted him, knowing that as far as Cynthia was concerned the matter was settled and the young man would only embarrass himself further. 'But I also have a task for you. There is no sense in duplicating our efforts and I will need you to liaise with the local constabulary. Cynthia, I'll be travelling to London by train, so if Tibbs can make use of your car, I'd be very grateful.'

'Of course, though Malina was going to use it to drive over to the boarding house. She needs to reassure the landlady that she wasn't dealing with villains and collect any other belongings that were left there. I'm afraid I bundled her out rather quickly.'

'Then we can go together,' Malina said, 'if that's all right with Sergeant Tibbs?'

Tibbs blushed bright red and Mickey looked suspiciously at the young woman, wondering if she'd caught a whiff of Tibbs' prejudices, but her expression gave nothing away. It would not be the first time she had met with such an attitude, Mickey knew, or that she'd dealt with it in her own inimitable fashion . . . which was generally head on.

'That's settled then,' Cynthia agreed. 'More coffee, Sergeant Tibbs? Or,' she added, noting he'd not drunk the first cup, 'would you prefer tea?'

'How's the head feeling?' Mickey asked as Cynthia poured tea.

Tibbs touched his stitches carefully as though to check. 'It feels sore,' he confessed, 'but I'm quite well, Inspector. I can still carry out my duties.'

Mickey nodded thoughtfully. 'You were lucky, young Tibbs. I've seen men killed with a blow such as that.'

'I know,' Tibbs said soberly. 'I'd decided there was no one home, I'd turned away and was coming to find you when the door opened and the man leapt out. He hit out at me as he passed and my hat brim took the worst of the blow as it came off. Had I not moved a moment earlier . . .' He broke off and his face paled as though he'd just realized what a close shave he'd actually had. 'I think I lost my hat,' he added suddenly. 'Inspector, did anyone pick it up?'

His look was so tragic that Mickey almost laughed.

'I'm sure we can provide you with a hat,' Albert said. He'd been hiding behind his morning paper. He folded it carefully and set it aside. 'Mickey, could you spare me a minute when you've finished breakfast?' He bid everyone a good morning and left the dining room.

Mickey raised a curious eyebrow at Cynthia, who shrugged. He finished his final cup of strong tea and then set off in pursuit of Albert, guessing that he would be in his study.

When he got there, he found Albert sitting at his desk and polishing a very fine handgun. Mickey took a seat opposite and Albert pushed the weapon over to him. It was a Mauser 1914, a weapon Mickey knew well, having liberated several from their owners during the war. It was small enough to be pocketed and had a peculiar, two-action safety catch that Mickey had come to like. A lever pushed down with the thumb made the weapon safe. A push button released the lever.

'What's this then?' Mickey asked.

'You were shot at. You're going up against dangerous people, Mickey, old man. I want to make sure you can defend yourself.'

Something in Albert's expression told him he should not argue. Instead, he thanked Albert and pocketed the gun along with a spare magazine. The weight of it in his jacket felt oddly reassuring.

'So, this new sergeant of yours, is he up to the job?'

'He's still wet behind the ears, but he's got potential,' Mickey said.

Albert nodded. 'You know that Cyn is on the brink,' he said. 'God knows what happens if . . . Mickey, do you think he's still alive?'

Would he know? Mickey asked himself. Would he feel it in his bones if Henry was gone? Perhaps he would. 'I'm aware what she's going through,' he said quietly. 'Albert, I'm trying to keep my dealings with Cynthia as optimistic as possible. But I will admit to you that I'm very afraid. My question is why didn't they take him before? They must have been aware of him watching them. Malina tells me he was not always cautious.'

'And have you reached any conclusions on that score?'

'I can only think that perhaps they previously took him for just a nosy parker – and Lord knows there would be enough of those in that little neighbourhood. Working folk are rightly suspicious of strangers who refuse to be neighbourly. I believe that when Malina left him he must have decided to go and poke his nose more obviously and was caught in the act.'

'You know it was Henry who chose where they must stay? Malina scouted around and discovered the boarding house and its apt location. He demanded they stay there, and fortunately she managed to secure two rooms. I must say, old chap, that his recent behaviour has been strange, even for Henry. There was a time or two I almost felt I should step in and say something. He was downright rude on occasions. You know how fond we both are of the old curmudgeon, but I have to admit it was something of a relief for the entire household when Cynthia found that little job for him.'

Hardly a little job, Mickey thought, but then Albert had probably not set eyes on the library.

'I'm familiar with the way Henry behaves when the black dog is nipping at his heels,' Mickey said. 'He either retreats into himself or he behaves as though the whole world is his enemy. He doesn't seem to have confided much in anyone,' Mickey added ruefully. 'Albert, I'll be frank with you. It's hard knowing where to start. He could be anywhere. He could be dead. We have to start preparing for that eventuality.'

Albert was silent for a moment and then he nodded. 'I'll do what I can to cushion the blow, but after all that happened with Melissa last year and . . . everything else that's troubled this family—'

He means the financial crash, Mickey thought.

'This would be a terrible blow. God knows he was a . . . an awkward cuss, but he was an honest man and a good friend.'

'And may be still,' Mickey said firmly. 'God's sake, man, don't let Cynthia hear you using the past tense.'

Albert laughed harshly. 'No, indeed not,' he agreed. 'Have

my guts for garters, she would. No, chin up, Mickey. You'll find him alive. Nothing more certain.'

They're all hurting so much, Mickey thought as he left Albert's study. *And they are all depending on me to get it right.*

For a brief moment solid, dependable, stolid Mickey knew himself to be at sea, the ground beneath his feet shifting like wet sand. Then he shook himself. They had come through worse than this in wartime. Henry had survived that. He could survive whatever vicissitudes he was facing now. No question of that. No question at all.

FOURTEEN

Had anybody at that moment asked Henry Johnstone if he felt like a survivor, he would have answered in the negative. He regained consciousness slowly and painfully and was aware that he was very cold and there wasn't a part of him that didn't hurt. He began to move and then stopped, listening cautiously for any sound that might suggest the men had returned. Finally he got to his knees and then struggled to his feet. Walking was difficult. He suspected he had several cracked ribs and hoped they were only cracked and not broken, knowing how easily he could pierce a lung. Breathing was hard but not impossible. His abdomen was black with bruises, as observed when he tucked his torn shirt and undershirt as best he could into the top of his trousers. He pulled his overcoat tight, but his hands gripping the thick black wool were incapable of fastening the buttons. They were bloodied and bruised and swollen and useless, and he inventoried his injuries while allowing that his theory that he had probably been left for dead was most likely true. The truth was he barely felt alive.

Alert to every sound, he staggered down the path and on to the road. Once there he looked back towards the house, trying to commit it to memory. He thought it had once been a farmhouse, solidly built but not large. Slates were missing from the roof and several of the windows were broken. It was clear that the place must have been abandoned for some time, and as he turned back to the road and looked left and right his heart sank as he realized that he might be miles from anywhere.

With an effort, he rallied himself. At least there was a road. It had to lead to somewhere, but should he go left or right?

He chose left because the road to his right climbed upwards and he realized he was not capable of anything that took more effort than the massive struggle to put one foot in front of the other and not fall over. Even that proved beyond him. The road at first began to slope downwards and Henry's feet, though just about capable of the process of taking baby steps on a level surface, took exception to the idea of walking downhill. Suddenly Henry was falling and tumbling and rolling and it hurt like hell. Rolling into the hedge halted his progress and for a moment or two he lay there, winded and unable to move. He struggled into a sitting position and looked around, trying to get his thoughts into order. The hedges were low, the road narrow, but the rolling landscape told him that he was still on the Downs and therefore had not been taken too far from the coast. This hinterland he remembered was an area dotted with small villages and settlements, farms and sheep and, hopefully, with the occasional car going by.

What if the men came back? What if the car he tried to wave down was them?

He struggled back to his feet, deciding that whatever he was going to do he would have to do it under his own steam, that he couldn't risk exposing himself to more danger in the shape of a stranger's vehicle. His brain, overwhelmed by all that he had gone through, suggested to him that perhaps he couldn't risk talking to anyone. Anyone might be in league with these men. How would he know? Was there anybody he could trust?

Mickey and Cynthia and Malina, he thought. They would be looking for him, and with that thought he returned to the process of putting one foot in front of the other and trying to keep his balance on a road that was descending steeply now. He managed a few more steps, and then his balance went completely and he fell once more, rolling and tumbling again until the world around him went black.

At some point later he was dimly aware of voices. Of being lifted and someone saying, 'Put him in the back.' And of fighting because the last time someone had said that he'd ended up in the back of a van and then in the pantry in that house, and then there had been nothing but pain.

Hands pushing him down, voices he did not recognize as the American, the quiet man or the bloodied nose man, and then there was nothing beyond a vague sensation of cold moving air and the sound of an engine and hard boards beneath him.

*   *   *

Cynthia had discovered that the tailor who had made the jacket Mickey had recovered from the house had two branches. One was in London and one along the coast in Brighton. She had Albert drive her there; he had no objection, being always ready to examine the possibility of a new tailor, and arriving in the Lagonda, Cynthia knew, always impressed.

Hughes and Pickering was a good-sized establishment. Cythia had noted them on occasion but had never had reason to venture in.

Albert was soon in discussion with the under manager, examining swatches and bolts of winter-weight suiting, and Cynthia had the full attention of the manager.

'The trouble is,' she told him, 'we had a bit of a party. Guests brought impromptu guests, you know how it is, and someone left this jacket behind. I have called all and sundry but no one seems to know who owns this poor abandoned jacket. So, I wondered if you could perhaps look at your records and help me to return it?'

She smiled, head tilted just a little to one side, eyes wide, her manner just a little helpless. The manager was smitten.

He examined the cloth and was able to estimate from the style when it might have been made. Vaguely recalled . . . yes, let him look.

Half an hour after entering the tailors, Albert had booked an appointment to be measured for a new suit and Cynthia had a name.

'Goodness, I did not expect that,' she told Albert as they returned to the car.

'Surprises abound, old girl,' Albert agreed.

After a little thought, a check of his records and a consultation with someone wielding scissors in the back room, the manager had the answer. The purchaser of the jacket had been Mr Mark Barry, and Cynthia got the distinct impression that the young man had not yet paid his account.

Malina had driven Cynthia's car back to the boarding house on the edge of Brighton. She had gone into the house to collect the remainder of their possessions and speak to the landlady. Henry had paid in advance for two rooms for the sake of propriety. She had in fact spent barely any time in her own room, being far too busy keeping an eye on Henry. The land-lady was not best pleased at having trouble brought to her door, but was mollified by the small cash gift, courtesy of Cynthia.

Malina stood in the front doorway – a doorway she had never actually used while in residence – and studied Sergeant Tibbs who was speaking to the constable left on watch. She had promised to take him to the police station after she dealt with the boarding house, and had tried hard to make conversation with him on the way. He had been polite though somewhat stiff, and was obviously uncomfortable in her company. He was, she thought, probably a nice enough young man, but so stiff-necked and clearly not sure what to make of Malina. Mickey had warned her of his prejudices but Malina was undaunted. There were things he had to learn, this young constable, and between them they would make sure he did.

He came back across the road and they walked to the car. 'I'll drive the car to the police station and then Cynthia thought you might like to drive back,' Malina said.

Tibbs looked startled and then nodded enthusiastically. 'You are quite sure that Mr Garrett-Smyth won't mind?' he said and then corrected himself. 'I mean Mrs Garrett-Smyth.'

'It was her suggestion. It's a nice little car and very easy to drive. Even I can do it.'

She laughed as he opened his mouth to reply and then thought better of whatever he was going to say. 'Did they find anything useful at the house?' she asked as she started the engine.

'Whatever was there seems to have been cleared out,' he said. 'And they've made a thorough job of it. I shan't be long at the police station,' he added. 'You would perhaps like to wait in the car? I mean, a police station can be an uncomfort-able place—'

'For a Gypsy, you mean?' Malina laughed. 'For goodness' sake, Sergeant, I spend a lot of time around police officers these days and it might surprise you to know that I have never actually been in trouble with the police. I moved to London when I was fifteen, stayed in a nice hostel for respectable young women, took typing classes – paid for by my mother and my aunt, I might add – and found a boring but secure job in the typing pool. Then I worked as a temporary secretary for various managers and executives, and then, in rather unusual circumstances, I met Cynthia and eventually became her personal secretary, a very happy member of her household and her friend. My brother Kem is a boatman. Some of my family still travel and some are more settled. Most come back to winter quarters in Gillingham at the camp on Ash Tree Lane and I go and visit them. Often Cynthia goes with me, as does Melissa. Cynthia is capable of friendships across barriers of class and wealth, I'm sure you recognize that. As am I. Even friendships with police officers.'

'I meant no offence,' he began.

She knew that was not entirely true. 'And none was taken. I recognize that your upbringing has probably taught you to view my people as thieves and vagabonds and no doubt your professional employment as a police officer has brought you into contact with the worst kind. It's easy to assume that everyone who is not *you* must be *non you* – at best unreliable and at worst potential miscreants. I'm used to having to change people's minds, Sergeant Tibbs.'

'Miss Beaney, I am aware that you are an unusual woman,' Tibbs tried again.

'For a Gypsy?'

'No, I meant—'

'I think we should change the subject,' Malina said gently. 'Minds are changed when you get to know the person and I am prepared to change my mind about you. I hope you will be prepared to the same. Now, do you have a name other than Tibbs?'

'Um, yes, it's Bexley,' he said.

'Bexley Tibbs – an unusual name. So, here we are and there is a little cafe across the road. You go and deal with your business at the police station and I will go and buy myself a cup of tea.' She pulled up at the side of the road and cut the engine, smiling at him. 'And then you can drive me home.'

FIFTEEN

Vagrancy Act, 1824, Section 4

Persons committing certain offences to be deemed rogues and vagabonds.

Every person committing any of the offences herein-before mentioned, after having been convicted as an idle and disorderly person; every person pretending or professing to tell fortunes, or using any subtle craft, means, or device, by palmistry or otherwise, to deceive and impose on any of His Majesty's subjects; every person wandering abroad and lodging in any barn or outhouse, or in any deserted or unoccupied building, or in the open air, or under a tent, or in any cart or wagon, not having any visible means of subsistence and not giving a good account of himself or herself; every person wilfully exposing to view, in any street, road, highway or public place, any obscene print, picture, or other indecent exhibition; every person wilfully openly, lewdly and obscenely exposing his person in any street, road or public highway, or in the view thereof, or in any place of public resort, with intent to insult any female; every person wandering abroad and endeavouring by the exposure of wounds or deformities to obtain or gather alms; every person going about as a gatherer or collector of alms, or endeavouring to procure charitable contributions of any nature or kind, under any false or fraudulent pretence; every person being found in or upon any dwelling house, warehouse, coach-house, stable, or outhouse, or in any enclosed yard, garden or area, for any unlawful purpose; every suspected person or reputed thief frequenting any river, canal or navigable stream, dock or basin, or any quay, wharf or warehouse near or adjoining thereto, or any street, highway or avenue leading thereto, or any place of public resort, or any avenue leading thereto, or any street, or any highway or any place adjacent to a street or highway with intent to commit an arrestable offence, indictable offence; and every person apprehended as an idle and disorderly person and violently resisting any constable, or other peace officer so apprehending him or her, and being subsequently convicted of the offence for which he or she shall have been so apprehended shall be deemed a rogue and vagabond, within the true intent and meaning of this Act; and it shall be lawful for any justice of the peace to commit such offender (being thereof convicted before him by the confession of such offender, or by the evidence on oath of one or more credible witness or witnesses) to the house of correction, for any time not exceeding three calendar months.

'So what's your name then?'

It was hard to get his mouth to frame the words. 'Henry Johnstone, Dectective Chief Inspector.' No, that wasn't right, he wasn't a detective chief inspector any more, he was just a mister.

He heard laughter. 'Delusions of grandeur, is it. Here's one for the nuthouse then. Thinks he's a policeman; thinks he outranks us. What do we say to that, boys?'

Henry was pushed and shoved. His coat was pulled from his shoulders and the pockets turned out.

'No identity. Not even a pocket handkerchief. No money to pay your board. Looks like the Vagrancy Act applies, don't you think, lads?'

Again, there was laughter. Henry could see that he was surrounded by constables and the sergeant at the desk. He was trying to make sense of the situation but couldn't even bring them into focus. 'Section four,' he said almost automatically, '"*Not having any visible means of subsistence and not giving a good account of himself or herself.*"'

'Oh, been here before have you, mister, and been fighting too from the look of your face and the rest of you. Boy, do you stink. And where did you get this coat? Stole it, did you?'

'My sister,' Henry managed. 'She gave me the coat. Call my sister, she will vouch for me. She gave me the coat.'

To Henry's relief the coat was thrown after him when he was shoved into a cell, and with further relief he realized that he was the only one occupying it. He lay down on the hard wooden bench, pulled his coat around himself and closed his eyes. He understood what must have happened now: someone must have picked him up on after the road and chucked him in the back of the wagon. He remembered the sound of the engine and the pain of being jolted around in a flatbed truck. He must have been dropped off at the local police station, though he had no idea which one, only that it was big enough to have a desk sergeant in it and at least three constables. He needed to get a message to Cynthia, Mickey or to his superintendent at Central Office who would, he felt, at least vouch for him. But how to do any of that?

Henry groaned, the pain in his back and ribs and everywhere else unbearable. If the sergeant in charge was to do his job properly he would call for the police surgeon to examine him. He doubted anyone would be in any hurry to do this, but it would happen sooner or later. He could tell he was in a state and the surgeon would not particularly want to risk him dying in a police cell and having to fill out the paperwork for that, vagrant or not. The Vagrancy Act tended to scoop up anyone who wasn't obviously employed, capable of paying for lodging, travelling . . . It crossed his mind that Malina's people were well-versed in the application of the act, which had been brought into law in 1824 as a way of dealing with soldiers returning from the Napoleonic wars and, having no provision for their welfare, been forced to beg on the streets. *Every person wandering abroad, and endeavouring by the exposure of wounds or deformities to obtain or gather alms; every person going about as a gatherer or collector of alms or endeavouring to procure charitable contributions of any nature or kind*, Henry reminded himself. For a few brief seconds he allowed himself to marvel that he had been caught up in a law that he himself had applied on occasion. It was a good catchall for a thief-taker if you couldn't find immediate evidence of a particular misdeed. Just about anybody, acting in any particular fashion, could be said to be a *suspected person* within the law, whether or not they might in fact be one of the persons mentioned in the act.

He supposed he might well look like an idle and disorderly person given the state he was in. At least, he supposed, he was relatively safe for the moment. They would have to give him food and water at some point and call for medical assistance to get him patched up. In the meantime, he was too exhausted to think of anything else and decided the best thing to do was to try and sleep. Despite the pain.

He recalled how the man who had been interrogating him – the one asking the questions rather than the one using his fists and boots – had wanted to know how Henry had tracked them, and Henry took great pleasure in revealing that the man with a bloodied nose had been careless enough to lose some of his possessions during his fight in the room with eight windows: some coins, a penknife and a matchbook on which the address of the house Henry had been observing was written.

'You should employ a brighter class of people,' Henry had said. 'You should tell your men to memorize the address and then burn the paper.' He had even managed a crow's laugh. He recalled the silence that had followed his revelation and guessed that the future would not be as bright for the bloody nosed man as he might have hoped.

A twitch of a smile curved Henry's mouth as he thought about this, and then he thought what he'd like to do to his persecutors and that there were some advantages to no longer being a policeman. He was no longer restricted by the rules of his profession when it came to taking his revenge.

SIXTEEN

Mickey had made his report to the superintendent at Central Office and had then gone to question any neighbours that might remember the Deans family. He had also requested any additional records kept by the local constabulary in S Division at the time, but which had not automatically been passed back to Scotland Yard. Henry and Mickey's involvement had actually been quite brief, so all he had easily to hand was the part of the enquiry they had been involved in. Mickey didn't know what follow-up there might have been on a local level. Some of it might indeed have been quite informal, constables seeking to settle the local community after the trauma it had endured. He knew from experience that it was often the case that constables gathered snippets of intelligence due to their intimate relationship with people living on their ground, that their beat would bring them into contact and casual conversation with shopkeepers and newsboys and nannies and household staff as well as house owners and lodgers. Though his hope of accessing these valuable snippets after all this time was not great.

The Deans' house was now occupied by another family, the Appletons, who knew nothing apart from rumours and what had become local legend. 'Was anything left behind?' Mickey asked, remembering how the house had been after their disappearance, full of food, clothing and books.

Mrs Appleton shook her head. 'Everything was gone by the time we arrived, apart from some furnishings that the landlord said we could make use of if we so wished.'

'Who cleared the house before you arrived, do you know?'

'No, but Mrs Hamblin might be able to tell you something. She's been here forever and she knew the Deans.'

Hamblin, Mickey thought. That was the woman who, with the next-door gardener, had kept guard on the dead body until the police had arrived. A formidable woman from what he remembered. He checked that he had the address correct, just three doors down from the Appletons, and went and knocked on her door.

Mrs Hamblin was tall and austere-looking until she smiled, and in that smile he caught a glimpse of the handsome woman she must have been when she was younger. She had no soft prettiness about her, but her eyes were dark and intelligent, and she had what Cynthia would have called good bones, Mickey thought.

She sipped her tea, studying Mickey carefully. 'You were here that day with another man – a taller man, a bossy man.'

Mickey grinned. 'Inspector Johnstone, he would have been then, Detective Chief Inspector . . . Before he left the force.'

'No longer a policeman?'

'Ill health,' Mickey said shortly. 'Injuries received unfortunately in the line of duty.'

'I'm sorry to hear that. He struck me as an intense kind of man, a terrier. Albeit a little large to be a terrier.'

'More of a mastiff,' Mickey agreed. 'So when the Deans had gone, who cleared the house after them?'

'Well, there is something of a story there. A police constable remained on duty for a day or two, in case of other evidence to do with the murder coming to light, I suppose. When he had gone – well, you can imagine that the rumours had spread and the house was left completely unattended with all of the family possessions remaining. The local children tried to break in of course – they were convinced that there were ghosts and some magic trick involved in the family's disappearance. And twice – twice, mark you – there were disturbances when housebreakers tried to gain access. Because the neighbourhood was aware this might happen and the servants had been charged to keep special watch, the constable was soon summoned. It was decided that the family's personal possessions should be removed, but I believe some of the furniture was still there when the Appletons arrived six months later. It took the landlord quite some time to re-let the house. Once a house has gained a bad reputation, people are naturally cautious.'

'Had the wider family not been contacted and not come to fetch the possessions?'

'But that was a curious thing,' Mrs Hamblin said. 'It seems there was no family.'

Mickey frowned. He had memories of interviewing people who had known the Deans in that first day or two after their disappearance, and also recollections that others had been spoken to. But then, how often is recollection incorrect?

'We spoke to local tradespeople,' he said, 'and to other members of the golf club and the local Rotary Association, I believe.'

Mrs Hamblin nodded. 'Yes, that would be right, but think, Inspector, did you actually speak to family? To friends, perhaps. They were a popular family and there was a woman who Mrs Deans referred to as her cousin, but it turns out she was not related, merely that they by coincidence shared a similar name. The so-called cousin was called Samantha Dean and she met Mrs Deans – Mrs Angela Deans – when they were both helping with some local fundraising effort or other. A May fair, I believe. This caused them to strike up a friendship and so it remained. I suppose whoever interviewed Samantha Dean assumed there was a relationship.'

Mickey nodded; he remembered the name from the reports but could not recall having spoken to the woman personally. It would probably have fallen to one of the constables.

'And so, what did happen to their possessions?'

'Well, as I say, the landlord eventually leased the property partly furnished, and much of what the Deans had brought with them was still there when the Appletons moved in. It was obvious they weren't coming back, not after such a passage of time. There was a certain superstition about the place, I suppose, because of the strangeness of the circumstances. However, the Appletons, so far as I know, have had no problems.'

'And the more personal possessions? The clothing, the books, the items most precious to the family?'

'Well.' Mrs Hamblin took another sip of her tea and then refreshed both their cups, and Mickey got the distinct impression that she was enjoying the process of spinning out this yarn. 'Because they had left so precipitously in the middle of their luncheon, it was assumed they had taken nothing with them. As you know, the clothing was still in the wardrobes, the hairbrushes on the dressing tables and so on, but when I went in there with the intention of packing what remained of their possessions – I ended up volunteered for this task, Inspector, because no one else wanted to take it on – it became very obvious to me that certain things had been taken and that there was an element of what I believe you might call deception at work. While it's true that there were still clothes in the wardrobe, I knew the family well enough to recognize that certain favourite items were missing. A blue dress that Mrs Deans was particularly fond of and her good coat. Two pairs of shoes remained, but her boots and another pair were gone, and the same with the others. Someone had been clever. They may have packed in a hurry and left a great deal behind, but they did pack. A mirror had been left on one of the dressing tables but not the hairbrush. The lipsticks had gone. Mrs Deans was fond of hers. She didn't wear overmuch, just a touch before she ever went out, but I know she felt underdressed without it. It occurred to me that they had some warning before they left and that their departure was perhaps not as sudden as was first thought.'

'That is very interesting,' Mickey said. 'And did you think to mention this to the police officers who were still investigating?'

'What police officers? Once the constable had gone we never saw hide nor hair of any others. I would not have become involved at all, but the landlord wished to rent and the Appletons wished to move in and we could not watch over the house forever. So I agreed to pack things up and store them in my loft. I have enough space. There are three suitcases and two boxes, and if you wish to take them away, you can either fetch them down yourself or you can wait until I can borrow a van from one of the neighbours.'

He would need a taxi, Mickey thought. 'You suggest the police seemed uninvolved and uninterested.'

'The consensus seemed to be that the man found on the pavement was a ne'er-do-well who had simply met his end in an unusual place. The consensus on the Deans seemed to be that they had skipped out on their rent. That happens less in a street like this, I suppose, but it's not a particularly unusual occurrence, I imagine. The police constable I spoke to seemed to think that they had deliberately added an air of mystery in order to cover for the fact that they left debts behind. That was partly true apparently. The rent was paid, but they owed the corner shop and their electricity bill and Mr Deans was overdrawn at the bank, or so the gossip goes. I doubt very much whether Mr Deans was allowed an overdraft. He might have been a chief clerk at some establishment in town, but it was still a fairly humble occupation. Not the kind of occupation for which a bank manager allows an overdraft. In fact, the mystery was always how they could afford a house like that. Mrs Deans did not work. The brother seemed to have an occupation of some kind; he went off in a suit every morning and at least *looked* respectable enough.'

'But you have doubts about this.'

'Well, it's unusual for respectable families to have visitors at eleven in an evening. Or at two in the morning. Visitors who go to the rear entrance not the front door and who seem very disquieted if they are noticed.'

'I'm guessing you don't sleep well,' Mickey said.

'I do not, and my room overlooks the street behind. Rear gates from the gardens and yards open on to that street. I can see, if I lean out of the window, all along the street.'

Mickey laughed out loud. 'And of course a noise in the night would make you curious, so you're bound to lean out of your window,' he said.

'Insomnia is very boring, Inspector. Any kind of relief from that boredom is welcome.'

Mickey nodded. 'And when you were packing the Deans' things into their suitcases and boxes, what did you notice?'

'How little there was in terms of personal possessions and how little there was that was older than perhaps a year or two. Which is how long they lived at the house – just over eighteen months. It is almost as though they decked themselves out to play the role of a happy family in a respectable neighbourhood.'

'It is an intriguing notion,' Mickey said. 'Did they give any indication of where they had lived before coming here?'

'Daventry, in Northamptonshire. Beyond that I know nothing about it. And I know nothing about them. I liked them, they were pleasant enough neighbours, sociable. I went to supper there on occasion and found them intelligent and well-read and willing to talk about the affairs of the day, the theatre, books, but not themselves. Though I have to admit this is not something I considered until afterwards. The truth is I do not like to talk about *myself* and so I found it very convenient.'

Mickey raised an eyebrow. 'You were widowed,' he said. 'That seems to be the one thing people remember about you.'

'Indeed,' she said. 'Inspector Hitchens, I may well be widowed by now, but I left my husband long before he might have died, was glad to do so and very glad to have been helped to do so. That was close on twenty years ago and for all I know he had me declared dead and married again. It's unlikely the Great War took him; he would have been too old for service. What I do know is that the man was a brute and I discovered that within two months of my marriage. I'm only thankful that I had no children with him. My parents saw what was happening and distant family agreed to help me.'

'You were fortunate,' Mickey said. 'I know of many a young woman who was told that she had made her bed and must lie in it. And what excuse did they give for your sudden disappearance?'

'My family were inventive,' she said. 'I trust you will go no further with this, but what it did teach me is that there are many people who move elsewhere to begin again and who have reason to do so. The Deans may well have been escaping debt and this may not have been the first time they did so, but I have the feeling they had been keeping one step ahead of something for quite some time before this.' She paused thoughtfully and then said, 'Someone observed Mrs Deans and her brother getting into a taxi on the afternoon they disappeared. I did not hear about this until sometime later. I do not know how reliable this information is, as it is second or third hand, but the greengrocer's boy claimed to have seen them getting into a taxi.'

'And does the greengrocer's boy still work for the greengrocer?'

'The greengrocer's boy is now a young man who has now grown up, married and moved away,' she told him with amusement.

Mickey laughed. 'I suppose he would have done,' he said. Time had passed, the trail was cold and it was quite likely that the gossip was correct, that the family had merely been fleeing the debts they owed. He was satisfied in his own mind that they had nothing to do with the murder of Sidney Carpenter as he now believed that it happened later in the day. Unless the abandoned lunch had been another misdirection of course. But was this getting him any further? Were the Deans even now just a distraction?

'I will call the taxi, and if I can trouble you for the suitcases and the boxes I'll take them away and relieve you of your duty of care.'

'And I'm glad to be relieved of it. Inspector, I don't believe they have done anything seriously wrong. Will you have to pursue them intently or can you let the matter slide into past history? Surely that would be the kindest thing.'

'And what about the dead man on the pavement?' he asked.

'Sidney Carpenter, I believe he was called. If the Deans left at lunchtime then what is the likelihood that the body of a man would not be found until four o'clock? This is a quiet street but not a deserted one, people come and go, residents and tradespeople and delivery people and . . .' She shrugged. 'I do not believe the body could have laid there unnoticed for all of that time. I said as much to the constable, but he told me that I should just let the police do their duty. The implication being that being just a poor little woman, and a widow at that, what could I possibly know?'

'Some constables are ignoramuses,' Mickey told her.

He had less luck searching for Carpenter's wife. Gone away, he was told. She had taken up with a sailor and Mickey gained the impression that this had been before her husband's unfortunate demise. So how sound was her alibi? Mickey wondered.

SEVENTEEN

'Wake up, sunshine, shake a leg.' Henry was woken by the sound of the opening door and the sergeant's loud instruction. He opened his eyes and tried to bring into focus the rotund sergeant and the man beside him, dressed in a suit and raincoat and carrying a tan leather Gladstone bag.

'You must be the police surgeon.' Henry's voice was slurred.

'So, you're familiar with the process,' the man said. 'Been drinking and brawling, have we?' He clicked his tongue. 'Look at the state of you, man. And it was the middle of the day as well when you were picked up.'

What time was it? Henry thought suddenly. His hand moved to his wrist, suddenly noting the absence of a watch. 'My watch,' he said. 'I don't have my watch. Or my cigarette case, or my lighter.' He felt in the pocket of his coat. The pocket was empty. 'Do you have them safe?'

'Your pockets were empty when you were brought in.'

Henry was distraught. These things could not be gone. He was aware of the doctor scrutinizing him closely and the sergeant's impatient muttering. 'Watch indeed. What would the likes of you be doing with a wristwatch? Now, up on your feet and let the doctor take a look at you, sign your papers as fit to stand. You'll be up before the judge in the morning.'

Then, as Henry made no move, he said more loudly, 'Up with you now. You're wasting the gentleman's time when he's better things to do.'

'For his five shillings,' Henry said.

'Why you insolent—' The sergeant's hand was raised and Henry instinctively flinched.

'That's enough, Sergeant. I can deal with this man. You've your own duties to attend to.'

The sergeant scowled but left as requested and Henry breathed a sigh of relief. He had goaded the man, he realized, though he wasn't certain exactly what he'd done. He looked like a vagrant, he supposed. That was probably sufficient.

'Where am I?' he asked. 'And what time is it?'

The doctor glanced at his watch. 'It's five minutes past four,' he said. 'You'll be fed at five, so it's to both our benefits to get this over with. Been in a fight, have you?'

'No,' Henry told him. 'Someone wanted some information that I didn't have. He still believed he could extract what wasn't there with feet and fists.'

'Well, this is what happens if you fall in with the wrong crowd.' He came over to where Henry sat and began to feel his skull with hard fingers that sent spikes of pain through Henry's face and head. When the doctor felt his cheekbone he could not supress a yelp.

'A small fracture by the look of it,' he said. 'Severe bruising to the jaw. There's a lot of swelling there, so there might possibly be a fracture too, though I think not. Now stand up and turn around.'

With difficulty Henry did as he was told. The same strong fingers tugged what was left of Henry's shirt out of the way and examined his spine, back and ribs. Henry let out a groan of distress.

'Keep still while I listen to your lungs. Breathe in. Good. Breathe out. Good. Your lungs are still functioning normally, despite someone kicking seven shades out of you. Lucky for you. Though frankly, if you'd had a punctured lung you'd not have made it this far, would you?' The police surgeon laughed as though this was a big joke that Henry could not understand.

'Your ribs will hurt like the devil for a while, especially when you try and exert yourself.'

Damn that, Henry thought. *They hurt enough just trying to breathe.*

'I could strap them for you but it wouldn't do much good. I'll tell the sergeant you're fit enough to appear before the magistrate. At least you've earned yourself a few days inside and three square meals.'

'Doctor, please. I need to get a message to my sister. She'll be worried sick.'

'Seems to me you should have thought of that before you fell in with thieves,' he said. 'You sound like an educated man; what the devil were you doing to land this far into the pits?'

'Doctor, I was a police officer—'

'Then you should be doubly ashamed.'

'No, it's not what you think. Please, Doctor, just telephone my sister. Do it for her peace of mind if not for me.'

'I'll give the matter some thought,' he said. He took the number down and Henry breathed a sigh of relief.

When the police surgeon had left he sat down once more and put his head in his hands, as close to despair as he'd been in a long time. What if the man disregarded the request? What then? Perhaps he could persuade the magistrate?

Henry sighed, knowing that was unlikely to happen. He'd seen the morning cattle market brought before the circuit judges – men and women marched in, their name and offence recorded, sentence handed down. Five days' incarceration, seven days, ten days' hard labour. Short sentences that, in theory, dissuaded acts of public nuisance but which Henry knew did nothing of the sort.

Please let the doctor call Cynthia. Henry found that he was praying, though not to any God he could have named. He had come to hate religion in the first days of the war and never recovered one iota of belief in the years since. What God could have sanctioned such indiscriminate carnage as he had seen?

And now there was the further hurt of losing his watch and lighter – both gifts from Cynthia and Albert – and, worse than that, the worn and battered cigarette case he had carried with him since it had been given to him in August 1917. By September the giver of that gift, his initials painstakingly inscribed on the underside with a sharpened nail, was already dead and gone.

EIGHTEEN

Mickey had managed to catch the last performance of *Lady Windermere's Fan*. His wife was playing Mrs Erlynne and Mickey admired the performance even while his mind was elsewhere. They had found him a seat at the back of the stalls, and Mickey was pleased that this was because the performance was sold out. Pantomime season in the small theatre was about to impose itself until the middle of January, when a brief vaudeville season would take over while the main troupe was in rehearsal for the next production. He vaguely remembered that Belle had said rehearsals would begin at the start of January and the next play – he was ashamed to say he couldn't remember what that might be – would be staged at the end. She would likely be working pretty much non-stop after that until the summer, he thought, but at least she wasn't travelling around the country any more. He saw her every night when he was in London. They usually ate a late supper together and talked about their day, and Mickey was shocked by how much that meant to him.

He had never interfered with Belle's career even though her itinerant lifestyle had impacted on his own, the powers that be on the promotion panel taking a dim view of a man who could not even control his wife but allowed her to go waltzing off around the country getting up to who knows what kind of mischief as all actresses did. Or at least according to the gentlemen of the panel. But now that she was London based and had the legitimacy of appearing in 'proper' plays that got reviewed in proper newspapers, attitudes had shifted a little.

Mickey's thoughts wandered. Where the hell was Henry? What shape was he in? Where could he look next? Truthfully he was at a loss, though his instinct was that the answers lay at the Barry house and that he must look there again more closely – dig more deeply.

* * *

The telephone call arrived just before the family were about
to sit down to dinner. Albert took the call and then came to
find Cynthia. 'It's some doctor or other,' he said. 'Reckons he
knows where Henry is. That Henry gave him our telephone
number.'

'Where?' Cynthia demanded.

'In a police cell, down in Shoreham. Says somebody found
him in the middle of the road, picked him up and dropped him
off at the police station and he's being charged with vagrancy.
He'll be put before the magistrate in the morning.'

'Like hell he will. Get me my coat.'

Tibbs and Malina had been drawn out into the hallway by
the exchange and Tibbs intervened at once. 'Mrs Garrett-
Smyth, please let me handle this. Let me telephone to Shoreham
and then to Central Office; if my superintendent speaks to the
police officers there, it will smooth your path and then if I
may come with you? A detective sergeant with the Metropolitan
Police—'

'May have a little more authority than the brother of a man
locked in a police cell,' Malina finished for him. 'Listen to
him, Cynthia – he's right about this.'

Cynthia looked from one to the other but knew that they
were correct. She threw up her hands, relinquishing control,
and Albert led Tibbs into the study where he could make his
phone calls in peace. Cynthia paced for the half-hour this took
him, impatient to be off without any delay. Finally Tibbs
emerged from the study and said that he had spoken to the
sergeant in charge at the Shoreham station, and also to his
bosses at Central Office, who would be contacting Shoreham
directly to verify his story. He had told them that Henry had
been the victim of a kidnapping and that he must have somehow
escaped. The police surgeon had examined him and he was
badly hurt.

'Hurt. How badly?'

'I don't know, some broken ribs and a lot of bruising,' Tibbs
said. 'It might be an idea to summon your doctor.'

'I'm coming with you,' Albert said. 'You're in no fit state
to drive the Lagonda and that will be by far the most comfortable option if Henry is hurt. You and he can ride in the back;

the sergeant can sit with me in the front. Best bring some blankets too.'

Cynthia nodded, knowing he was right. She was shaking, anger and anxiety fighting for supremacy. 'Malina, will you send a telegram and notify Mickey. Sergeant Tibbs, when we return can you motor up to London in my car and collect Mickey and his wife? They had planned to come down by train tomorrow but Mickey will not want to delay. Malina, will you add that information to the telegram, please.'

Moments later they had collected their coats and were walking round to the repurposed livery stables where Albert kept his car.

Henry had been unable to eat. Food had been brought, and water which he drank gratefully, though even that was hard to swallow. He wondered if the doctor's conclusion that his jaw was not broken was in fact correct or if he was just avoiding the idea of sending Henry to be X-rayed – someone, of course, would have to foot the bill for that. He asked for more water and after a time this was brought, but the food seemed to be beyond him. It was some kind of slurry masquerading as stew with grey, granular mashed potato. The sight and the smell of it nauseated him. He tried to eat, knowing that he ought to, mixing a little bit of the potato with the thin gravy, but when he put it in his mouth he wanted to vomit. With difficulty, he swallowed and then drank more water, spilling half of it on to his front as he tried to gulp too quickly. He set the tray back in the hatch and tried to sleep, wishing the doctor had offered him some pain relief. Wondering if he had in fact telephoned Cynthia or simply left the police station having collected his pay and forgotten all about him. Police surgeons were often peremptory in their duties – payment was inadequate for being on call at all hours of the day and night and the job was often inherited with their practice, generations of GPs having held the same post and often no one else in the area being willing to take it on.

He must have dozed and did not know how much time had passed, but the sound of familiar voices roused him to a sitting position. Cynthia sounded angry and Albert placating, and there was a third voice that he did not know. This one sounded officious, and a few minutes later the cell door opened and Cynthia hurtled in and grabbed him around the shoulders.

Henry yelled in pain and Cynthia backed off, startled. 'Oh my God, look at the state of you,' she said. 'Let's get you out to the car.'

'There's paperwork to deal with,' said a sergeant that Henry had not seen before. He presumed the other had gone off duty.

'All of which will be taken care of by Central Office at Scotland Yard,' a young man Henry didn't recognize told him. 'You've spoken to my superintendent; you know all of this has been cleared with them. Mr Johnstone is to be released into my custody. He is pertinent to my enquiries and those of an ongoing murder investigation.'

Henry blinked. What on earth was this man rabbiting on about? Though he was reassured that Cynthia looked uncon-cerned and was helping him to his feet, and with Albert's help then leading him past the recalcitrant sergeant who was still arguing with the young man. Moments later they were out by of the car. Henry was installed in the oxblood leather seat and Cynthia was wrapping blankets around him as though he was a newborn that needed swaddling.

'Here, have a nip of this, old man,' Albert said, handing over his hip flask. Cynthia held it to his lips and Henry managed to take a swallow and then another. The liquid was fiery and then smooth and then warm, spreading through his body.

'More,' Cynthia said. 'You're going to find the journey uncomfortable. This will help.'

Obediently Henry swallowed more of the rather fine whisky and then closed his eyes. He was dimly aware of the young man arriving and getting into the front seat beside Albert, the engine starting, Cynthia checking that everything was in order and the young man reassuring her that it was all going to be fine.

'Thank you,' Cynthia said, and then added, 'I can't keep calling you Sergeant Tibbs – surely you have another name.'

'It's Bexley,' the young man said. 'But if you don't mind, I prefer Tibbs.'

And then there was nothing else. The warmth of the whisky

spread through his body and the warmth of the blankets eased his hurts from without, and Henry relinquished himself to the simple gratitude of being safe.

The telegram arrived at the theatre just before the performance ended and the manager brought it to Mickey just as the cast were taking the second curtain call. Mickey was outside the dressing room when Belle came offstage. He gave her the news.

'While you change I'm going to ask the manager if I can use his telephone,' Mickey told her. 'I'd like to know what's happening.'

A few minutes later he was back with good news. Malina reported that they had just brought Henry back and that the doctor was with him. He was injured but he was at least alive. She sounded profoundly relieved, Mickey thought, but then so was he.

'So what do we plan to do?' Belle asked. 'We could catch the milk train, be there by morning.'

'There's no need, Tibbs is coming up to collect us. He set off about forty minutes ago so perhaps another two hours and he should be with us. I will drive us back; the lad will be exhausted. In the meantime I suggest we get ourselves something to eat. I've no doubt you're already packed, but I need to put some things together. We'll get a taxi home.'

Usually they walked. It took about half an hour and they enjoyed the quiet wind down after the performance. If Belle was alone then she caught the late omnibus which dropped her at the end of their street. But tonight a taxi from the rank around the corner seemed like the best plan.

'What sort of shape is he in?' Belle asked as they settled in the cab.

'Malina isn't sure yet. She says he's been badly beaten and the doctor was with him but that's all I know.' Mickey closed his eyes and breathed a sigh of relief. His worst fears had not been realized and anything else he could deal with. Belle took his hand and squeezed his fingers tightly.

'So with luck and a following wind, your sergeant will be here just after one. He will need some tea and a sandwich.

Now don't object; Henry's in safe hands and a poor young man will be half starved. We will be with Cynthia by about four in the morning. Tme to grab a few hours' sleep before breakfast and then I have no doubt you'll be off investigating again.'

Mickey was amused by her matter-of-fact tone. 'I plan to go back to the house – Tibbs and I need to tear the place apart. The answers are there, I'm certain of it.'

NINETEEN

Three men returned to the house where Henry had been held but only one would leave. The quiet man who had interrogated him, the big man who had beaten him senseless and the man Henry had awarded a bloodied nose were parked in the drive in the shadow of the trees and made their way inside.

Their torches revealed blood on the step and in the hallway, but Henry was gone.

Briggs, the one Henry thought of as the quiet man, turned to the one Henry called bloody nose man. 'Did it occur to you to wonder how he found us?' he asked. 'When you got your backside handed to you in a sling, you failed to realize something had fallen from your pocket.'

Bloody nose man looked startled, his hands instinctively going into his coat pockets. 'Lost something? I don't understand.'

'You wrote down the address of our safe house.' Briggs' voice was now dangerously quiet. 'You wrote it on a matchbook and then you lost it and guess who picked it up?'

'I—' He seemed to be searching desperately for an excuse or an explanation, but he didn't get further than that first word. Briggs had taken a gun from his pocket and shot him in the head. He fell to the floor where Henry had lain.

'And you swore you'd finished him off,' Briggs said to the other man.

'I told you. The man was dead, couldn't of been anything else, not by the time I'd done with him.'

'But clearly you were wrong.'

'Someone must've come for him.'

'"Someone must've come for him",' Briggs mimicked. A second shot and the big man had fallen to the floor beside his comrade. Briggs turned on his heel and walked away.

TWENTY

A constable arrived at Cynthia's house on the Saturday morning carrying a folder with information for Mickey on a local thug by the name of Sean Matthews. He had a record for GBH and general violence, and his finger-print had been identified as one of those found in Henry's room at the Barry house. He was known to both the Metropolitan Police and Brighton and Hove, and if they were so inclined then Inspector Hitchens and Sergeant Tibbs could accompany the locals in making the arrest.

Mickey agreed with alacrity and the pair of them left with the constable and drove back along the coast road, through Rottingdean and to the nearby settlement of Saltdean.

The address that had been given was a small brick and flint cottage on the outskirts of town. It was part of a terraced row and Mickey accompanied one of the constables to the rear, leaving Tibbs with those preparing to hammer upon the door. A low wall separated the houses from a ginnel that ran between this row and the one behind. A small gate led to a tiny, paved yard, at the end of which was a shed housing the privy. Mickey could hear the front door being opened and the officers as they made entry and the shouts of a woman, indignant but, to Mickey's ear, resigned. According to the records this was not the first raid on her house by police looking for her husband. A few minutes later the back door opened and Tibbs came through.

'No sign of him, I'm guessing,' Mickey said.

'His wife reckons he's been gone about a week; she says he's often gone for a period of time. She doesn't seem too bothered about him.'

Mickey followed Tibbs back into the house. The woman, presumably Mrs Matthews, was standing by the kitchen table. She had been rolling pastry and had the pin gripped in her hand. She looked quite ready to use it on anyone who got out of line, constable or not. He wondered if she ever came to blows with her husband.

'I'm telling you, I've not seen him, not this past week. Friday last was when I last set eyes on him. He got in the car with two men.'

'Did you see the two men?' Mickey asked.

'One was a big bruiser in a loud jacket that looked too small on him and one was a toff,' she said. 'More than that I do not know.'

'Had you seen either of them before?'

She shrugged and, somewhat to Mickey's relief, set the rolling pin down on the table. 'Big chap sometimes drinks in the Ship. I seen him in there. Fists like a prizefighter, knuckles all bruised and calloused and spread. I don't know 'is name.'

'And the toff?' Mickey asked.

'Never seen him before.'

'And why do you think he's a toff?' Tibbs asked.

'Dressed like one. All fancied up. Hat and big overcoat like the gentry wear. Nothing like the likes of us could afford, not in a month of Sundays.'

When pressed she thought he had a moustache, neatly trimmed, and got the impression that he was the one in charge. She had no idea of the make of car beyond the fact that it was blue – deep blue. 'Glassy blue,' she said. 'Like you could dive into the paint. And big. A posh bloke's car.'

'So what do we do now?' Tibbs asked as they were leaving. He seemed somewhat deflated, Mickey thought.

'There was always a good chance he wouldn't be here,' Mickey said. 'For today I think we try and get what we can out of Henry. See what he recalls, see what leads we can scare up. Then we go back up to the Barry house and we'll take the place apart.'

Tibbs nodded. 'Tomorrow is Sunday,' he said. 'I told my family I would try to be home for the Sabbath. As it is I think it is too far to go back to Bermondsey and then come back here. I suppose I could attend church locally. I'm sure there are churches in Worthing.'

'I'm sure there are,' Mickey agreed. 'On the occasions when Cynthia goes I think she trots along to the C of E down the road. I have a vague idea that Cook is Baptist, or Methodist, or something of the sort.'

He could see that Tibbs was about to object and tell him that while both churches might be nonconformist they were very different in nature. Mickey grinned at him. 'I'm sure Cynthia will be able to advise,' he said. 'And we may as well have Sunday as a day of rest – we need to pull together what we know and look at what we don't and come back to it fresh. I do not think that questioning Henry is going to be a quick enterprise.'

'How is he?'

'Better now he's had a bath. I was able to help him with that this morning, though it'll be a while before he can shave. The doctor doesn't think his jaw is broken, but it's certainly dislocated. He hopes that as the swelling recedes it will reset on its own. His cheekbone is fractured and his ribs will take their own time to heal, as ribs do. He was severely dehydrated and is black and blue with bruises. But he'll live. He is also mad as hell, at himself and at those who hurt him, and that's a good thing. Henry in a funk is not a good thing. Henry on the war path, on the other hand, now that is a useful resource.'

He could see Tibbs considering his words and not quite understanding something.

'Spit it out, boy,' Mickey said.

'I understand you are good friends, and that you have known Mr Johnstone for a very long time, but sometimes your relationship seems strange. He was your superior officer and yet—'

'And yet our friendship was stronger than that,' Mickey agreed. 'When you work with somebody for a length of time you get to know them perhaps better than you know your own spouse. Their strengths and weaknesses, their difficulties, your difficulties. You come to depend on them to have your back and you must always have theirs. Surely you've known that kind of comradeship.'

Tibbs considered and then shook his head. 'I think I have always been a little strange,' he said.

'Nothing wrong with strange,' Mickey said. 'Not so long as your heart's in the right place and you do a good job. Now come along, young Tibbs. We missed breakfast, so we must make it up with an extra-large lunch.'

And then a long talk with Henry, Mickey thought. See what the blazes had got into him and, if he was up to it, deliver a long lecture on the stupidity of acting alone.

Henry was looking a little better, Mickey thought. Nanny, Malina and Cynthia had been sharing his care between them so he had been thoroughly pampered. His bruises were less black today, more purple with green around the edges, and his face a little less swollen though Mickey knew it would take several weeks for him to get back to normal and the ribs probably even longer to heal.

He had just finished soup that Cook had prepared especially for him. He was going to be killed with kindness at this rate, Mickey thought, amused by the idea.

'So,' he said, drawing up a chair beside the bed. 'You've played silly beggars before, but this time takes the biscuit. What the hell were you thinking, Henry?'

Henry managed a smile. It was a mere twitch of one corner of his mouth. His lips were pulped and swollen and Mickey realized that talking was going to be a major effort. 'Not thinking,' Henry managed. 'I think I gave it up for Lent.'

'And we're now approaching Advent.' Mickey paused, taking a long look at his friend. 'You're a fool, Henry Johnstone,' he said. 'But let's just acknowledge that and put it aside. Can you tell me what happened to you? Malina found you on the doorstep of the Barry house. You told her someone had attacked you, and Tibbs and I found blood and more on the poker. Now I'm assuming the blood on the floor and pyjamas was yours from that gash on your arm, and that on the poker was his?'

Henry nodded. 'Heard him on the stairs. I'd been hearing footsteps before but this was different.' His voice croaked and he closed his eyes against another wave of pain. Mickey put three drops of laudanum in the glass of water set beside the bed and helped him drink it down.

'Now don't you try to talk, you just listen and nod if I've got it right. The man who attacked you left his dabs behind for young Tibbs to find. So we have a name for him. He's a brawler by all accounts; you did well to best him. I'm guessing you got your hit in first and struck lucky. His name is Sean Matthews. Does that mean anything to you?'

Henry shook his head and then frowned. He began to speak but Mickey halted him and instead handed over a notebook and pencil. *Press cuttings in the library drawer about him,* Henry wrote. *Sir Eamon seems to have collected them but I had no time to make a proper inventory.*

'Then Tibbs and I will take a look,' Mickey told him. 'Is that why you wrote Carpenter's name on the blotter? Were his clippings in the drawer?'

Henry shook his head and wrote again. *Sir Eamon seemed interested in him. I saw a man watching the house one day.*

'You spoke to him?'

No. Watching the house like he was casing it. That put me on guard. Then he was in the car.

'The car you mentioned in your journal?'

Henry spoke again. 'Yes. With a big man. And another.'

'You didn't recognize the make of car or you'd have written it down,' Mickey said. 'Matthews was seen getting into a posh blue car with two other men. One described as a bruiser and the other as a toff.'

Henry nodded. 'That sounds like them. The toff was calling the shots. Asking questions. The other did this to make me talk.' He indicated his face and Mickey winced.

'He really worked you over,' Mickey said. 'Would you know them if you saw them again?'

'Oh yes.' The laudanum was working. Mickey watched as Henry's face relaxed and he drifted into sleep. There are so many more questions he wanted to ask but they would wait.

A quiet knock on the door made Mickey realize that he too had fallen asleep. The room was warm and the chair comfortable and he'd had no more than a quick nap when they had come down from London. Cynthia came in.

'How's he doing?'

'He's going to be fine,' Mickey said. 'There's more light in his eyes than I've seen in months and I think his brain is working more clearly. The rest of him will catch up.'

'Come and have afternoon tea,' Cynthia said.

'Is that the time? I seem to have lost most of the day.' *And it has been a frustrating day for the most part*, Mickey thought. No arrest in the morning and not enough answers in the afternoon.

'Malina and Tibbs have been working through the afternoon on your behalf,' Cynthia told him playfully. 'They've gone through everything that Henry told her, everything she observed, and she's given good descriptions of the men she saw at the house. And Tibbs can draw, did you know that?'

'Beyond the fact that he can't play the piano very well and his mother thinks eating out is frivolous, I know very little about the young man,' Mickey admitted. 'What's he been drawing?'

'Well, hopefully portraits of the men Malina saw,' Cynthia told him. 'She seems to think they're pretty close.'

'Has he indeed,' Mickey said. 'Well, perhaps the lad will earn his keep after all.'

He stood in the doorway and observed for a moment. Albert had brought his microscope through from the study and set it by the window, and was instructing Sergeant Tibbs as to its use. Melissa he could see was trying hard not to correct her father when he got things wrong.

Malina was sitting by the fire looking very amused. Spread out on a folding table were pencils and paper and a stack of portraits. Belle was pouring tea and handed Mickey a cup and a plate of delicate little sandwiches. Mickey would never have admitted it to anyone but he liked these tiny dainties. Even though he could dispose of them in one bite and they made his fingers look positively enormous. He set his plate down and picked up the sketches. 'So you reckon they're good like-nesses?' he asked Malina.

She nodded. 'Take them to show Henry to see what he thinks, but I saw three men go in and out and one I saw at the corner shop, so I got quite a good opportunity to study him. As you know I've got a good memory for faces, Mickey. I was always very careful to keep out of the way so they couldn't see me through the window. I'm afraid Henry wasn't always as cautious,' she added. 'He didn't seem to care if they saw him. I was always very careful that they didn't see us together; in fact, I was very careful that they didn't see me at all apart from that one day at the shop, and he didn't pay me any attention.'

She took the papers from Mickey and sorted through, showing him the picture of one particular man. He looked to be about thirty, Mickey thought, and Tibbs had made notes as to eye and hair colour. Dark brown hair and blue-grey eyes.

'He was polite enough, quite well spoken, but I wouldn't have said particularly educated. No particular accents that I could discern, in fact that was quite interesting, it's almost as though he was avoiding anything that might make his speech distinctive. It was all "please" and "thank you" and "can I have" and "yes, it is bad weather, isn't it", that sort of thing.'

'Well, we can send these to Central Office and see if they match anyone in the portraits we have there,' Mickey said. 'And it is possible we can have copies made and distributed. Though I don't want to tip our hand just yet – not that it's my investigation of course. Now Brighton and Hove are involved, everything will have to go through them. They've not formally asked for help and they have a good detective squad down here so—'

'But that doesn't mean we can't continue investigating.' Tibbs seemed quite disturbed at the idea. 'I mean, I know Inspector . . . Mr Johnstone's been found, but—'

'Don't you worry about that, lad, we've been given a few more days' grace to see what we can turn up and we've got eyes on the Barry house, The Pines, for the next day or so. Two constables settled in the kitchen and patrolling the house. Making themselves as obvious as possible. Monday morning fresh and early we'll be up there again and tomorrow, while you're having your chat with God, I plan to drive out to where Henry was found and see if I can pick up his trail. Hopefully he can give me a description of the house before then and estimate how far he travelled. From the state he was in it would not have been far.'

Albert was on his feet and looking excited. 'You'll be

needing maps,' he said. 'Now come with me, I've got just the thing.'

'Before you disappear,' Cynthia said, 'Mickey, we have a guest for dinner tonight. They might be useful to you and Tibbs. I've invited an old friend of Sir Eamon's. Though he's old as the hills he's sharp as pins and may be able to give you some details about that son of his. Mickey, I'm still really angry with myself for getting Henry into this situation in the first place. Hopefully this will go some way towards making amends.'

'You've got no amends to make, old girl,' Albert told her. 'This will be sorted in no time and Henry will be back on his feet and all the better for it.'

Mickey shepherded Albert out of the room before Cynthia could say more. He could see in her face that she was not particularly impressed at the idea of her brother being better for being beaten to within an inch of his life. Sometimes, he thought, Albert could really open his mouth and put his foot in it.

TWENTY-ONE

B riggs was aware of all the grousing that had gone on quietly in the background since he had come back alone. He had made no secret of what he'd done and then sat down and cleaned his gun, knowing that his nonchalance would add both to their anger and their fear. He had since sent Josephs out on an errand and Cookson had settled in the parlour with his nose in a book.

Briggs, too, was annoyed – he was now two men down and while they weren't the brightest of the bunch they had been useful. Well, perhaps Sean Matthews hadn't been particularly useful, though he would miss Pedersen if only for his fists.

So that left him with Josephs, the American fixer, and Cookson, the quiet man and one of the best safebreakers in the business, who knew every fence in the south of England, capable of dealing with the kind of cargo they had stashed. Not that there had been much call for his skills so far, but there would be, Briggs decreed, there certainly would be. Or there had better be or someone would be in deep trouble, and Briggs had already showed that he had no patience with failure.

The sound of a car engine spoke of Josephs returning. Josephs had found them lodgings now that the safe house they had been using was compromised. The woman whose home they were inhabiting was now in her own cellar and this time Briggs had ensured the kill – he wanted no more mistakes. The house was set well back from the road, there was food and drink and Cookson, who looked the most inoffensive of the bunch, would pose as a nephew looking after the place in the unlikely eventuality anyone should question.

He heard Josephs park around the back of the house. He came in through the kitchen door. 'Two constables on watch,' he said without preamble. 'Look set for the duration.'

'Why would they be on watch at The Pines?' Briggs asked, the question rhetorical. 'Because we were seen by a man who should be dead and yet who is miraculously living. Because a man who should have been disposed of when he got in our way, on two occasions mind, two occasions, is still walking around free as a bird. And that bird will have tweeted and sung his heart out by now. That's why there are two constables at The Pines, because they know the place was watched but they don't know why. They know the man was attacked and then beaten but they don't know why. They know someone wants something there but they don't know what. So that's why they would be on watch at The Pines.'

'We should cut our losses and clear out,' Josephs said. He had always been the only one who would stand up to Briggs.

'No, we just wait them out. When nothing happens, and no one shows up, their superiors will find something better for them to do. I take it no one actually saw you today,' he added dryly.

'I took the car nowhere near, I walked across the back fields and circled in through the trees. No one saw me.'

Briggs sat back in his chair and surveyed the three remaining members of his diminished gang. 'Look at it this way: bigger shares for all. A three-way split.'

'Aren't you forgetting the son?' Josephs asked, but Briggs could hear from his tone that he wasn't expecting an affirmative answer.

'Why should he get anything? What has he done? Besides, he owes us. What's he done to deserve anything?'

'We could do with an extra body for the heavy work,' Josephs said. 'Now we're . . . a little short-handed.'

He was careful not to meet his gaze, Briggs noted.

'Fine,' he said shortly. 'And then we're done with him.'

TWENTY-TWO

Cyril Cartwright was a frail looking and frankly ancient man, Mickey thought, with an admirable mop of white hair framing a face that looked like a contour map. Frail looking he might be, but Mickey estimated he had managed to eat his own weight in beef Wellington.

There was a slightly festive air to the evening, Mickey thought. Henry was home and safe and the relief was palpable. As a special treat Melissa had been allowed to join the party, and it was clear that she knew Cyril Cartwright very well and that they shared common interests. She was sitting on one side of him while Tibbs, solicitous of the old man's welfare but clearly also interested in the conversation, sat on the other.

Cyril Cartwright was promising to lend Melissa a book he had recently purchased, *Astronomy* by John Charles Duncan. It was a complex text, he said, but was sure Melissa could manage it and the star charts were rather wonderful. It was clearly a subject that Tibbs knew nothing about and Cyril and Melissa were doing their best to instruct him.

Henry was not well enough to come down yet. Mickey thought he would have enjoyed the evening in his own quiet way. With Cynthia and Albert and Melissa, Mickey and Belle and of course Malina. He would even have got on well with Sergeant Tibbs, Mickey thought, because the young man caught on fast and showed a keen interest in all manner of subjects.

After dessert Melissa was sent off to bed and the rest of the party retired to the drawing room for coffee and brandy. There was none of this nonsense about women withdrawing and leaving the men to their port in Cynthia's house, Mickey thought, though he knew that was different if Albert was having business colleagues to dinner. It was then Cynthia's job to entertain the wives while the men argued about this commodity or that investment or the purchase of new machinery. Mickey knew this because on odd occasions he had been present with

Henry. Truth to tell, Albert got slightly bored of these business dinners and was often glad of the dilution provided by the presence of two police officers. It could be guaranteed that the other dinner guests would be curious about the murders they had investigated. Mickey had collated a fund of stories that could be told in an entertaining but still respectful manner. Henry could be counted upon to correct the fine detail and Albert could then take the opportunity to enjoy the company, do his bit for public relations, or commerce, or whatever it happened to be that evening, and drink his port without over-taxing his tolerance for what was often quite priggish and boring company.

Tonight though, there was no need for pretence. The conversation had flowed, lubricated by the best Albert's still considerable cellar could offer, and everyone present actually liked one another. Mickey could see that Tibbs was even growing used to thinking of Malina as a respectable member of their company – although he had acknowledged that he'd been a little shocked at the idea of the young woman and Henry both being booked into the same boarding house, even if they did have separate rooms.

He was a little old fashioned and stiff for a police officer, Mickey thought, and wondered vaguely how he had managed to keep so many of his idiosyncrasies intact in the five years he'd been in the force.

Cyril Cartwright settled into an easy chair, coffee in hand, a plate of tiny pastries and other delicacies on his chair arm. Mickey quite frankly wondered how he could stuff any more in. He sat back in his own easy chair, hands clasped comfortably over his very full belly, and came to the point of the evening.

'Cynthia tells me that you were good friends with Sir Eamon Barry,' Mickey said.

'Oh yes, indeed, we were at school together, went up to Oxford together. He did rather better than me of course – came out with a first. I was always rather more interested in the sporting side, but I did well enough. He lectured for a time, did you know that?'

Mickey shook his head. 'No, I didn't.'

'And then after he married, of course that allowed him to take to research full-time. He published regularly and made quite a name for himself. It's a pity Melissa didn't meet him. They would have got on famously – he was interested in microbes, don't you know.' Cyril Cartwright waggled his fingers as though to demonstrate. 'Tiny little wiggly things that cause no end of damage but apparently we can't live without them.'

Mickey regarded the man solemnly and decided that Cyril Cartwright, judging by the conversation he'd had with Tibbs and Melissa, knew a lot more and was a lot more erudite in that knowledge than he liked to make out. 'And did the son follow in his father's footsteps?'

Cyril Cartwright's expression changed and he shook his head. 'Indeed not. Mark Barry is not only a complete idiot, he is unkind with it. He was a nasty little boy and grew into an even nastier young man. It just goes to show you can never tell. Caroline, his mother, wasn't very bright, but she was the sweetest woman you'd ever like to meet. She had the money of course, which allowed Eamon to do his research in peace, equipped his library and a little laboratory he had in the basement at one time. I believe he married for the money, and for the fact that she was a sweet woman, but he did fall in love with her, there is no mistake about that. When she died he was devastated.'

'Mark Barry must have been about seven or eight,' Cynthia said.

'I think perhaps a little older, I believe he was ten, but still far too young to lose his mother. Not that he took much notice of her even then. You see, Eamon knew she didn't have a brain, Caroline knew she didn't have a brain, but they found things in common. She went and peered in his microscope whenever he requested and he took her to the theatre with great regularity. He encouraged her to host parties and dances and could even be prevailed upon to dance on occasion. They found a way of communicating with one another which disparaged neither of them, and I believe they were very happy.

'Mark, on the other hand, though he had no great brain himself, decided that his mother was not worth his notice. As

I say, he was a nasty piece of work from being very young. His father tried to interest him in science, and when that didn't work he looked for other things. He thought that Mark might have been sporty. You have to understand that Eamon married quite late, but Caroline was a good deal younger. They had twelve years together, twelve very, very convivial years, and when she died I think a part of Eamon died with her. He perhaps did not take as much notice of Mark as he should have done. The boy was away at school by then of course, and Eamon gave him the choice of coming back home and schooling locally, but Mark would have none of it. But then a time later he was expelled, sent down for misbehaviour. Serious misbehaviour. A boy was badly hurt. Of course everybody tried to make excuses for him, that his mother had recently died and that he was grieving and that his misbehaviour had emerged from that source.'

'But you don't think so.'

'I had known the boy since he was born. I had watched his parents expend every effort they could to interest him in something, anything, but the only thing that seemed to interest him was tormenting—' He broke off as though this was very uncomfortable. 'Eamon and Caroline were dear friends,' he said. 'It pains me to speak of this. I don't want to diminish their memory or diminish them in your eyes. You never knew them.'

'I never knew Caroline, but I got to know Sir Eamon fairly well,' Cynthia said. 'He was a lovely man, amazingly intelligent and very kind. I knew there was trouble with his son, but he never spoke about it and I know it made him uncomfortable. So I never pushed him but, Cyril, this is important. Can you tell us what was happening with Mark in the last few years?'

'Did you visit Sir Eamon in the last year or so?' Mickey asked. 'I don't know if you realized it, but he seemed to have fallen on very hard times. The house is in a terrible state and he had taken to sleeping in the butler's pantry. He employed a young girl who came and brought him shopping and looked after his food and did so for my friend Henry Johnstone, Cynthia's brother, when he was staying at The Pines recently.'

'I had hoped to meet him tonight,' Cyril Cartwright said, clearly seizing on what he saw as a more neutral subject.

'Unfortunately my brother was seriously beaten and injured,' Cynthia said. 'It seems he uncovered something untoward going on at The Pines and tried to investigate – the habit still hasn't left him – and as a result he was almost killed. Truthfully, had I known what state the house was in I would not agree to him going there, but I thought . . .' She shrugged. 'Sir Eamon was such an erudite man, I wanted to ensure that his library and his work were catalogued correctly and I knew that Henry was capable of it. Mark Barry agreed and said he would accommodate him. Which he did, badly.'

Cyril Cartwright was taking this in. 'And you believe that Mark was involved in what happened to your brother?'

'Not directly. He is apparently in Scotland with his wife, on her family estate, and Mickey has been told to approach him only through his solicitor. This is all too much trouble for him.' Mickey had rarely heard her sound so bitter about anyone.

Cyril looked thoughtful and then shook his head. 'Oh, he's definitely not in Scotland, or if he is he's not with Martha and her family. She left six months ago. Her solicitors are looking . . . Well, not to put too fine a point on it, they're looking at a way of extracting her from this marriage. Mark's funding has been cut off. Most of it was her money – what his father had, Mark had run through within the couple of years. He had persuaded his father to give him power of attorney. Martha's family and mine have been friends for a very long time, and she confided in me that if he continued with his expenditure there would be nothing left. And, of course, he had control of her allowance, though fortunately not the bulk of the money she would eventually inherit. Her father still has control of that and if you ask me just as well. She was already contemplating leaving her husband. In their five years of marriage she had encountered cruelty and abuse, the like of which no woman should have to put up with.

'Mark can be charming. He charmed Martha; I believe he even charmed Martha's father though not her mother. She is a wise old bird and can see through men like other people see through windows. Martha will not inherit the estate of course, that will go to her brother, but provision has been made for her, substantial provision, and now that line of credit has been withdrawn from Mark Barry—'

'You find it believable that he's fallen in with bad company?' Tibbs asked. 'What happened to the house, why has nobody lived there? You mentioned that there was a laboratory in the cellar?'

Mickey looked at the young man in surprise, but they were all good questions, even if he had asked them in a heap when he should have separated them out. Mickey felt he would have to have refresh the young man's interrogation technique.

'Mark found bad company since he was a schoolboy. He gravitated towards it. He was easily bored, not particularly intelligent and not particularly talented. He likes tormenting people which, although it does not surprise me, does sadden me a great deal.

'As to the house, Caroline died, Eamon tried to continue as she had done for a time, but I think it was all too much for him. One by one the staff left for better employment. However nice your employer, however pleasant, if there is only one man in a house that is fit for a large family then the work can become tedious and dispiriting, I suppose. For days at a time he would shut himself in the basement, continue with his experiments, come up to the library to write them up. Meals would be cooked for him and not eaten, letters would arrive and not be answered; the staff felt unappreciated. And I think Eamon realized he had no use for them and so he let them go until those that had remained were finally given notice. For the last eight or nine years or perhaps more I think he has lived only in that part of the house with the library in the kitchen and the rest has been neglected.'

'And Mark Barry has no love for the place,' Mickey said.

'I hate to go against my old friend and say anything that calls his essential goodness into question, but when Caroline died he became neglectful of the house and of his son. The boy was dismissed from school, came back, was enrolled in another school, sent down again. This happened three or four times and Eamon finally sent him to a military academy in

Scotland. The only good thing that came out of that, or perhaps on reflection not so good, is that he met Martha as a result of living up there. When he had finished school he seemed uninterested in coming back and his father uninterested in inviting him. He had his allowance and his so-called friends, and a respectable enough veneer. Martha's family estate is near Stirling and that's where he settled. His name was good enough that he was invited to participate in hunting and shooting and all of the activities of the local gentry.'

'Why was he sent from school?' Malina wondered. 'You say a boy was badly hurt.'

'There were rumours that I do not wish to go into. Distasteful rumours that followed him from establishment to establishment. But in this instance he tormented a boy younger than himself so greatly that the child threw himself into the river and would have drowned had he not been seen from the bank and two local men were able to pull him out, at great risk to themselves I might add. The river was in spate. It came out that his despair was very much down to his treatment at Mark's hands. I will leave it at that.'

There was a moment of silence while everybody considered this and Mickey speculated about the things that Cyril Cartwright was unwilling to say.

'Where in the basement was the laboratory? Is it still there?' Tibbs asked. 'We noticed no door to a basement when we were at the house.'

Cyril Cartwright laughed and seemed to be grateful that he could talk about something other than Mark Barry's sins. 'No, no, dear boy. You go out through the kitchen door, and across that bit of yard, and then there is an outbuilding that was part of the carriage house and later used for parking cars. The chauffeur used it for storing tools and petrol cans and that sort of thing. Well to the right-hand side of the door you will see what looks like a cupboard. You open the cupboard and it leads down into the basement. There are stairs from the basement that go up into the house but I'm not sure where it leads to; there were servants' passageways in the walls at one time, though I don't think Eamon ever used them. He wasn't one of these employers that thought servants should be invisible and only appear, as if by magic, when somebody summoned them.'

Tibbs and Mickey exchanged a glance. This probably explained a great deal – the footsteps Henry had heard among other things. *Nice question, young Tibbs*, Mickey thought.

He did not push Cyril Cartwright for more information; they had built up a useful picture of Mark Barry's current circumstances. Mickey asked only two more questions. 'Mr Cartwright, do you have a telephone number for Mrs Barry in Scotland, and would you mind giving it to me if so? Or perhaps to Cynthia, if you feel a woman should make the first approach.'

Cyril Cartwright considered this for a moment or two but then he nodded gravely.

'And could you perhaps tell me what Mr Barry was spending his money on? To get through so much in so short a time suggests he was a gambler perhaps.'

'It would seem so, and not in respectable establishments.'

'And was the power of attorney rescinded before his father died?' Sergeant Tibbs asked.

'With difficulty, it was. He tried to claim that his father was not of sound mind but we managed to debunk that piece of absurdity. He was very angry with Martha for interfering and I think that was the straw that finally broke their marriage. He became violent. He had been violent before but this was, well, beyond the pale.'

'Would you like more coffee?' Cynthia asked. 'And perhaps more of the little pastries. Apparently they are Polish, little spiced biscuits, and I have to admit they are rather delicious.'

Cyril Cartwright beamed and accepted both. The conversation drifted to other things and the rest of the evening was a pleasant one.

'That was an interesting conversation,' Tibbs said when they had waved Cyril Cartwright away home, just after eleven o'clock.

Mickey watched the car as it drove away, a Morris Isis and a very pretty one. It was not particularly grand in the scheme of things, but it suited Cyril Cartwright. The driver, he noticed, looked almost as old as his master.

'You opened a good line of questioning, lad, well done. So we know some very interesting things. That Mark Barry, as we had come to suspect, was not a paragon of virtue. That Henry was not hallucinating when he heard footsteps in the house, and we must investigate the property more thoroughly. But, more troubling, we have no idea where Mark Barry might be and if whoever entered the house found what they were looking for. If an opportunity arose since Henry left, why did they not take it? Or have they done so? That house has been left unprotected for over a week.'

'If they'd found what they were looking for, surely they would be long gone by now. Did they ask Mr Johnstone about the house? Or perhaps there is some kind of timetable to their scheme. That they cannot act before someone else does their part?'

'A valid idea,' Mickey agreed. 'From what Henry has told me they seemed most concerned as to why and how he came to find them and be poking his nose in their business, which in itself is interesting. I suspect if he'd been seen anywhere near the basement stairs their attitude might have been different. As it is, their only concern was how and why he had followed.'

'It seems likely one or other of the men had visited the house several times; he reported footsteps twice, reported the car appearing and disappearing. What is the reason for their hesitation? Forgive me, Inspector, but Mr Johnstone would not have even looked like a threat. If they had been intent on getting into the house and searching properly, then they could have hit him over the head with a poker and that would have been that.'

'It seems one of them tried that and came off worst,' Mickey reminded Tibbs. 'So perhaps they are not looking for something in the house; perhaps they are looking for something to arrive at the house. Perhaps something that Mark Barry has promised them? It seems clear from the fact that the jacket we found at the house was once owned by Mark Barry that there was a strong connection between the son and the gang.'

'Unless they killed him and took the coat.' Tibbs shrugged. 'No, that seems unlikely. But why employ Mr Johnstone? Why have someone there?'

'Possibly because having someone there would dissuade casual thieves from entering. Possibly because Mark Barry is still looking to gain all he can from the old man's estate, and the books are valuable, as presumably are his papers if he has two universities eager to look at them. He got both his library inventoried and a caretaker for that damned house in one package and likely on the cheap.'

'We should go tomorrow and look at the house again, find the basement, find the hidden staircase, explore further.'

'And so we shall, when you have finished having your chat with God and I have found the house where Henry was held. When we have both completed that business, then we return to The Pines and find ourselves a hidden staircase. I must admit, young Tibbs, the thought of that does excite the child in me.'

TWENTY-THREE

Armed with Albert's maps, Mickey had driven through Shoreham-by-Sea and then inland to the location where Henry had been found. He had stumbled out in front of a builder and his mate driving a flatbed truck and fallen into the road. At first they thought he was drunk but then had realized that he was hurt and, not knowing what else to do with him, they had taken him to the nearest police station. Mickey, now he had seen the state of Henry, knew he could not have travelled far. Henry vaguely remembered leaving the house and stumbling down the drive, and that there had been trees and overgrown hedges and some kind of thick shrubbery shielding it from the road. A large front door with steps in front of it, and he recalled that the house itself was in a bad shape with broken windows and missing roof tiles.

The driver of the truck had provided the police with an approximate location but Mickey appreciated that it must be hard to know exactly which bit of this winding road across the downs, with almost identical-looking hedges and ditches either side, was the actual place where they picked up the man they assumed was a vagrant.

With the help of Albert's maps he had picked out four possible houses that were close enough to this road to be where Henry had fetched up. Slowly and systematically, Mickey checked each of them and the road between. Heavy rain the night before would have washed away blood traces, so he had little hope of picking up such transient evidence. However, Mickey was nothing if not persistent.

The first two houses he dismissed very rapidly. The first was a farmhouse with tractors in the yard and cattle in the field. Henry might have noticed the odd cow and certainly would have noticed the large red Massey Ferguson, Mickey thought.

The second house, set back between trees and shrubs,

initially looked promising but even from the road Mickey could see that it was in a good state of repair and clearly inhabited. He drove on.

The third house was further along the road than he had anticipated from the builder's description and just proved his point that it was hard to differentiate one bendy bit of road from another. But there it was. He could see the chimneys poking up behind the line of trees and as the car nosed cautiously into the drive that there were roof tiles missing, windows broken and a large front door.

Mickey sat for a moment just inside the driveway and waited for a reaction. It was just possible that the men had come back to the house, but Mickey anticipated that if they had and found Henry gone then they would know it was only a matter of time before someone else came looking. He wished Tibbs was with him, a thought that surprised him greatly, though Tibbs was proving himself to be an efficient sort and Mickey was inclined to like him.

He eased the car slowly up the drive and then turned it around so that should he have to get away in a hurry he could do so. He engaged the handbrake and left the engine running knowing that he was doing exactly what he had rebuked Henry for doing and walking alone into what might be a dangerous situation. He was glad of Albert's Mauser in his pocket.

Mickey pushed the door and was not terribly surprised to find it open. The house had the feel of one that had been deserted, and he was almost certain that there was nobody present, but still he entered with the gun drawn and the safety off, and here there were signs of Henry. Blood on the tiles, dry, dark and brown and impossible to see against the darker tiles though clear enough against the white, the hall laid with a geometric combination of blue and red and brown and white. Mickey followed the blood trail into the kitchen and then into the pantry beyond and then he backed out. Two bodies lay on the floor, and he didn't have to go any closer to recognize that both were dead, the single bullet wounds to the centre of the forehead telling him that much.

Mickey turned, walked quickly out of the house, got into the car and drove away, apologizing to Cynthia as he over-revved the engine. He was pretty sure that one of the dead men was Sean Matthews and that the other was the big man that had beaten Henry to a pulp and who Malina had described and Tibbs had drawn. Now he was in a position to judge, Mickey realized Tibbs had in fact depicted him with considerable accuracy.

Shoreham police station was the closest. Mickey lost no time in reporting there and they lost no time in summoning assistance. This was now very definitely a murder enquiry – a double murder – and even if it had been a falling out among thieves it ratcheted the seriousness of the offence up a great many notches. Within the hour Mickey, already being at the middle of all of this, had received the formal application from the Brighton and Hove constabulary. His support had been approved by Central Office in Scotland Yard. Inspector Hitchens was taking charge of his first double murder.

TWENTY-FOUR

I t was strange for Mickey to watch others working on the crime scene, developing fingerprints and taking photographs and examining the bodies.

The police surgeon had arrived – by coincidence the same as had examined Henry in the police cell. He raised the matter as an amusing anecdote to be shared with Sergeant Fox, from the local constabulary, and Mickey was able to tell him that the man in question had indeed been a detective chief inspector with the Metropolitan Police and that this house was the location where he had received his injuries.

He got the impression that the police surgeon was not particularly interested, beyond the possibility of dining out on his involvement in the story when it finally broke in the press.

At least he had telephoned Cynthia, Mickey thought.

The two men having been certified as dead, Mickey knelt to examine them more closely. He had Tibbs' drawings in his overcoat pocket and he took them out and compared them to the two bodies.

'Whoever drew these has some talent,' Sergeant Fox commented. He was, Mickey thought, a man who suited his name. Sharp-featured and sharper-eyed.

'My present sergeant, and yes, he does. He's not a bad detective either.' He showed the other pictures to Sergeant Fox, explaining who they depicted and asking if he recognized the men.

'Not that I call to mind, but it would be helpful to get these copied and distributed. The *Brighton Argus* would take them on, and I can have constables take them to hotels and post offices and public places along the coast.'

'And I'll be asking you to do that, but hold off for the moment. I'll be sending Sergeant Tibbs back to London to look through our mugshots. If he can identify the others that would be to our advantage, and if Central Office can liaise with the London press, get these images out in the city as well and coordinate our efforts, that would also be to our advantage.'

Mickey signalled that the bodies could be taken away, then he and Fox went to stand outside while the mortuary ambulance attendants did their work.

Fox lit a cigarette. 'So how did your ex-boss come to be mixed up in all this?'

Good question. 'Put simply, he poked his nose into someone else's business. He's good at that, but then it's been his duty to do so, since coming back.'

Fox was of that generation that Mickey did not have to explain he meant back from the Great War.

'Where were you?'

'Too many places. Ended up in one of those damned mechanized death traps. Nearly finished me.'

'You were a Tanky?' Fox shook his head. 'My God, I'd rather go out looking the enemy in the eye than stuck in one of those infernal contraptions. And your boss?'

'Was the one who pulled me out,' Mickey said shortly.

Fox nodded. 'So fill me in on what he was doing to get his nose trapped,' he said and Mickey, accepting one of Fox's smokes, did just that, realizing as he told the story just how full of holes it was.

'So he was attacked at the house, his assailant dropped a matchbook with the address of the house the gang were using. No wonder he ended up with a perforated brain. Your boss follows up, observes the house, fails to let you in on what he suspects, and ends up beaten half to death for his pains.'

'That's about the size of it,' Mickey agreed. 'I was up in the north of England on a case and likely he couldn't have reached me. It was only when I realized it was Henry who had gone missing that I stepped in, and it soon became obvious there was more to it than Henry taking it into his head to wander off somewhere.'

'Given to doing that, is he?'

'Wounded in the line of duty. Had to take retirement. He's like a lot of us would be – no idea of what to do with himself after. Hence his sister organizing the job at the house.'

'But you figure this Barry bloke, he's involved in—'

'Whatever this is. Believe me, the state Henry was in he'd not seem like a threat to anyone but himself.'

'Ah. Like that, was it.' Fox nodded.

'It's to my mind a strange thing to do if he'd got something nefarious going on. To invite a man into his house that's spent his life as a detective and thief-taker.'

'Perhaps you should turn that thought around,' Fox said. 'Barry is a man already up to his neck in rumours regarding the company he keeps and the debts he owes. What could put a more respectable veneer on such a man than having a very respected ex-detective chief inspector of the Metropolitan Police as effective caretaker of his estate? Your boss's reputation is well known, even down here. Yours too. There was that nasty business at Shoreham a couple of years ago for starters. To have such a man of good repute administering your father's last wishes, what could look better?'

Fox took a last drag on his cigarette and dropped it to the floor. Ground it into the dirt. Mickey regarded the man with not a little respect.

'I'd not thought about it that way round,' he admitted. 'But it does make sense when you see it from that angle. The big question is what was Barry doing at the house that needed attention deflecting from?'

'Or what was he allowing to be done. From what you've said, the bloke's now on the lam. The man wants clear. What's the betting he owes too much to these people ever to be able to pay? He's likely been promised his debts will be cleared and there'll be a share of whatever profits in return for doing a good turn. In the meantime, he's decided not being around is the safest option.'

'That's the way I'm seeing it,' Mickey agreed. He stubbed out his own cigarette and offered another to Fox, who declined.

'Want to take a turn about the house?' Fox asked. 'See if they left anything but bodies behind?'

Mickey nodded but he doubted there would be anything useful. Identification and personal possessions had been stripped from the bodies, not even a pocket handkerchief left behind. The man in charge, Mickey felt, was skilled and organized and experienced. So why work with such amateurs?

He put this bit of speculation to Fox, who nodded. 'Watch your footing on that step. It's rotten as a pear. So you reckon he's run with a more professional operation until now and now he's making do?'

'Wouldn't surprise me,' Mickey agreed. 'So if that's the case, why did he leave and are his old partners in crime sanguine about that? I'd guess they're not.'

They had gone up to the attic floor of the house. Holes in the roof had let the rain come through and the bedrooms had been uninhabitable for quite some time, Mickey guessed. The floorboards were rotting and Mickey soon decided that no one in their right mind would have come up here. There were signs of the rooms having been used for storage at some time: large tea chests and other smaller boxes were strewn about. The smell of rodents and damp filled his nostrils. A brief inspection of the empty packing cases revealed droppings and nest material.

Down on the first floor the ceilings had taken damage, but beyond an ancient bed fame and a long disused washstand there was nothing of note.

The ground floor had been mostly protected from incursions of rain and there was less evidence of rodents. It was still damp, chilly and comfortless. Evidence of occupation had been cleared and Mickey recalled that Henry had told him of the tin mugs left on the table and the paraffin stove he had spotted with the kettle still in place and which they presumably used for making tea and providing a small modicum of heat.

The other house had been warmer, Mickey recalled. When he and Tibbs had gone through the place and found the man's jacket, there had also been a fire in the grate and food on the table.

'So,' he said, peering into the now-empty pantry, 'what might our felons be involved in down in this neck of the woods?'

'Same as they are in any place else,' Fox suggested. 'Though I take your point that this has the feel of something bigger and more elaborate, even if those involved don't seem particularly up to the task.'

'Or have been judged not to be,' Mickey said. 'Which suggests their boss is a man with expectations. And what criminality might be specific to this area?'

'Specific to this area you get the usual thefts from the larger houses, many of which are occupied only at certain times of the year. Agricultural crime is an issue – you wouldn't think anyone would try and steal a tractor, but it happens, though for the most part it's sheep and sometimes cattle. You get men out lamping and rabbiting and sometimes they'll take a sheep in preference, but for the most part that isn't organized crime, it's crime of opportunity. And of course, it being coastal, you get smuggling.'

'There's a long history of it in these parts from what I've heard,' Mickey said.

'Indeed there is. The Black Horse in Rottingdean was a watering hole for smugglers and Captain Dunk across the way in Whipping Post Lane was an infamous bootlegger. We're only a short hop, skip and a jump from the continent. Only the goods change and even those not a great deal. This past year or two we've had heroin come in for the first time, but it's more commonly booze and cigarettes and luxury items that have duty on them, much as it ever was. And with the shortage of excise officials, it's no surprise.'

Mickey nodded. Back in 1923 there had been three thousand coastguard patrolling the English coastline, a number now reduced to 850 thanks to the so-called Geddes axe, a drive to cut government spending in the wake of the Wall Street crash and the ongoing depression. Mickey thought again of the headlines he had read; America seemed intent on spending its way out of trouble. Britain was on a policy of slash and burn.

'And people,' Fox went on. 'From time to time you get people coming in. Most of the time they end up working for no pay somewhere, and from time to time we stumble across them. And a lot of the time there is nothing we can do. Proving coercion is the challenge. That and getting someone to work out what the hell they're saying or even what language they're speaking.'

'Let's hope the Forced Labour Act does some good,' Mickey said, aware that there was no conviction in his tone. In June of 1930 the general Conference of the International labour Organisation had convened in Geneva with the aim of protecting those who had been coerced or tricked into what amounted to enslavement. He was aware of Fox's sharp look and then even sharper laugh.

'The higher-ups can legislate all they like,' he said. 'People who are looking for a better life will still get caught up with the criminal gangs. First of all, you have to prove these people were coerced and lied to and to do that you have to catch up with them and the people what brought them here. Then you have to argue the toss with people who are their so-called employers, giving them bed and board and a bit of money, and who keep them in conditions that are often not much worse than those the so-called respectably employed find them-selves enduring.'

Mickey thought of the mean little rooms at the top of the Barry house. It was quite possible, of course, that they had once been in better condition and been comfortable and welcoming for those employed. It was equally possible they had not.

'And has there been much evidence lately that people are being brought here? And to what purpose? I would not have thought with the country in its present state that cheap labour would be a problem. If it's like London, the rich hang on whatever happens, and if they have to cut costs then it's those at the bottom that they are cut from. Wages are slashed, staff dismissed and the unions crushed.'

Fox laughed again. 'Bit of a bolshie, are we?'

'It has been said,' Mickey admitted with a smile.

'As to what purpose? Why take cheap labour if cheaper labour is available or if a man can be worked to death for a pittance and not missed, or a woman sold into the worst of situations and no one come looking for her? Some women choose to sell their bodies and choose what price they charge and set themselves up in a nice little flat somewhere where only the men they choose come through their front door. But for most, and not just women, let's be truthful about this, men and children too, the trade is more than rough and the only ones that profit are the men who control them.'

'Have you seen much evidence of this lately?'

'Specifically, no. There was a man brought into Shoreham about six months ago, bullet wound to the back, found lying on the beach like he had been washed up, though it wasn't the sea that killed him. He was taken to hospital but he didn't live above an hour, and we never did figure out where he'd come from, poor sod.'

Mickey had decided that they had probably seen enough of the house. He departed for Cynthia's and left Fox and his constable to drive back to the police station and await reports. There seemed little point in leaving a guard on the house; it was unlikely the men would come back. Whatever the residence had been used for before, it was now simply a body dump and they would have found somewhere else to hole up.

But they would go back to the Barry house, Mickey was certain of that. There was likely unfinished business there and the next thing to do was search the cellar that Mickey and Tibbs had been unaware of on their first visit. Fox had dispatched men to look for the hidden staircase and report back. He had also arranged for two constables to take up residence for a day or so and to be as visible as possible. Mickey wanted to be the one controlling the next move.

TWENTY-FIVE

Tibbs had returned from church and was waiting for Mickey when he arrived at Cynthia's. Mickey quickly brought him up to speed on developments and it was decided that straight after lunch, Cook having delayed it for them, the sergeant should catch the train to London armed with the photographs and the identification of Sean Matthews and see if he could put names to the others.

The Criminal Records Bureau would quite likely have a list of known associates; Mickey knew that Sean Matthews had spent some time in London, and he thought it likely that the other man would also have a broader criminal record. Fox would be doing the same with the local constabularies, being now armed with photographs of the dead men.

'If you find a name for the big man, and his known associates, ask for information from the new register on *modus operandi*. To be frank, I think this will be less useful to us than for Matthews and the thug he was with. Their MO seems to have been to use your fists first and ask questions after. But you don't know what the KAs will turn up and their signatures may be of more interest.'

Tibbs was also to organize copies of the drawings and photographs if they had them on record and for these to be sent to the local press and added to the *Police Gazette* for wider circulation. The *Gazette* went out to every constabulary and Mickey planned on all police in the area, from the humble beat bobby to the south coast CID, being informed.

They ate a hurried lunch, not really doing justice to the fine meal. Mickey took a moment to go down to the kitchen and thank Cook and apologize for their haste. He also took the opportunity to ask for sandwiches and a flask for his sergeant, knowing that, travelling on a Sunday, other rations would be hard to come by. Tibbs went on his way well supplied for his journey.

'And where are you off to now?' Henry asked when Mickey went up to see him. He was much improved and had managed to eat some lunch, he told Mickey. It had chiefly been soup followed by proper mashed potato and gravy, the rest of it taking too much chewing.

'You look less black and blue, more green and orange,' Mickey told him. 'As a colour scheme it leaves a lot to be desired, but you look better, Henry, a lot less close to death. I'm off now to track down Matthews' wife and tell her that she no longer has a husband. Fox would have done it, or sent a constable, but I'd rather speak to the woman myself.'

'It's likely she already knows,' Henry said. 'News travels fast and these smaller communities are close-knit.'

'You're probably right, but I will go anyway. She is a formidable woman, Henry; I wouldn't want to get in the way if she decided to wield that rolling pin on anything but pastry. Then on to the Barry house, and I'll be bringing you back something to work on. I think you need the distraction.'

Mrs Matthews was at home and did indeed know that her husband was dead. She had other women with her, bustling around and making tea and taking care of the bereaved as, in Mickey's experience, women did. Especially those from the working classes, where it seemed to him that widows were made more often.

He took the proffered chair and the proffered tea and regarded the woman with interest. She had clearly been crying and he wondered what kind of relationship she and Sean Matthews had. Was she really grieving for him, or was she angry at the man who had killed him, or a little of both?

'I'm told he was shot.'

'He was, once in the head. From the look of him he didn't even have time to react – it would have been quick.' He took a sip of his tea. It was strong and sweet. How many cups of tea had he drunk in the homes of the bereaved over the course of years? Mickey wondered. The women were hanging back now, listening, ready to intervene if he should upset this new widow further. But he could see they were also deeply curious, and who could blame them?

'He was found with another man, likely the one you describe as the bruiser. I wondered if you'd managed to think of a name since last we spoke?'

She glanced up at one of the women who said, 'Most likely it's Gilbert Baker. It sounds like him.'

'And where am I likely to find family of Mr Baker? Where did he live?'

The woman shrugged. 'Here and there, no family that I know of. Sometimes he works the boats, sometimes he goes inland and sometimes he's gone for weeks. Sometimes he fights.'

Mickey nodded. 'An itinerant sort then.'

'Men go where the work is.'

'I asked you last time we spoke if your husband ever had dealings with Mark Barry. His father owned the big house, The Pines, not a half-mile from here.'

'I know who you mean, and I know the house. What would he have to do with someone like that?'

'From what I hear, Mark Barry liked slumming it. He was always in trouble of one sort or another, and he liked to gamble.'

'Sean never gambled, I'd of brained him if he had. We don't have money to throw away.'

'How will you manage now he's gone?'

She glared at Mickey as though he'd asked a totally inappropriate question, and he heard the other women murmuring, the voices shocked, and realized that he had in fact insulted her. 'I'm sorry,' he said. 'I'm sure you're capable of looking out for yourself and it is none of my business what you do next.'

She held his gaze for a moment and then nodded. 'I have good friends,' she said, 'and I can turn my hand to most things. You don't survive here if you can't.'

'Unless you're very rich, you don't survive anywhere unless you can,' Mickey told her. 'And you have no idea what your husband was involved with. You don't know the identity of the toff he got into the car with?'

'I told you, I never seen him before. I keep out of his affairs. I *did* keep out of his affairs. He brought money home and I was fond of him and he was fond of me. I know what folk said about him, that he was rough and violent and hadn't got the sense he was born with, but we did all right together. The only sadness is we never had kiddies.'

Mickey nodded and took his leave shortly after.

Mickey returned to Cynthia's that evening with occupation for Henry. He had spoken at length with the two constables who had searched the cellar and they had taken him down into the house and shown him the staircase that led up to a corridor behind the library which then seemed to be blocked off. Mickey speculated there must be other such entrances and exits to the house and the constable said they would try and find them. He got the impression that they were enjoying the task. There was nothing left in the cellar beyond some broken glassware to indicate that there had once been a laboratory there.

The constables who would be camping out in the house for the next day or so, until Mickey decided it was time to pull them back, were well enough provisioned. They had noticed a man walking through the woods and gone out to challenge him, but it turned out to be a local taking a shortcut through the estate. They had taken his name and address. He'd been curious about the police presence and, as Mickey had instructed, the constables told him that the man who had been looking after the house had been assaulted and that there had subsequently been reports of individuals possibly casing the house with a view to breaking in. There been also been kids playing in the woods that afternoon but nothing of significance had happened.

Mickey had gone up to the library and started to empty the drawers with their ephemera and their half-drafted scientific papers, their newspaper clippings and letters, and then decided that it was easier simply to take the drawers back. So the constables had helped him load four of them into the car. He had used the plaid car rug that Cynthia habitually left there to protect the seats and hope that nothing slid around too much on the drive back, but hope proved futile on the first stretch of downhill two minutes after leaving the house.

He arrived at Cynthia's to find paperwork all over the place, fallen into the footwell, and anything that hadn't been disarranged before certainly was now.

'What on earth have you got there?' Cynthia demanded as he began to bring everything inside.

'Something to keep Henry occupied, and probably Malina and Melissa too, and you I hope.'

'These are Sir Eamon's papers?'

'And in a right jumble they are. I'm not surprised Henry gave them a wide berth. But it occurs to me that the old man might not have been the one to have left them in disarray. He seems to have loved his library and been careful with his books, but this,' Mickey indicated the mess of notes and theatre programmes and newspapers, 'reminds me of the mess made when someone tips out a drawer and then picks up the contents with no concern for order or organization. It makes me wonder if the son deliberately upset the apple cart, so to speak. And then realized that there may actually be some value in these papers, which is why he was looking for someone to sort them out.'

'After the two universities approached him,' Cynthia said.

'That's my thinking. He knew there was value in the books so he left those alone. He is not the sort to cut off his nose to spite his face; if there is money to be had he's going to be wanting it. But as you can see, it's hard to see the wood for the trees. It will give Henry something to do, and if he has help it will give him something to talk about and I think it might be useful. I want to know what was going on in the old man's mind in the months before he died, and I think the answer's written here. He realized what his son was doing, and how misguided he had been in giving over power of attorney. From what Cyril Cartwright said last night, he was trying to correct that mistake.'

'Then we'll do what we can,' Cynthia said. 'Mickey, there are mouse droppings in this drawer. I certainly hope you've not brought the mouse with you as well.'

TWENTY-SIX

B y Sunday evening, much of what Mickey had brought
back from the Barry house had been sorted and collated.
Sir Eamon's papers had been separated from the rest,
even though they were in themselves sadly disordered. These
had been put aside for later attention. The ephemera he had
gathered over years, the playbills and programmes and tickets
and photographs that were largely memories of his marriage,
had also been separated from the rest. Interesting as they might
be, they were not relevant to the enquiry.

They were left with the bundle of press clippings, some
handwritten notes and what looked like a ledger, albeit
composed in a cheap copy book of the sort a child might use
at school. Tucked into this book were also bank statements
and letters from a solicitor and bank manager, clearly Sir
Eamon Barry trying to sort out the tangle of affairs his son
had left when the power of attorney had finally been rescinded.

Albert and Cynthia examined these between them and came
to the conclusion that there had been very little left by the
time Mark Barry had finished. It was clear that Sir Eamon
had been trying to work out where the money had gone,
and had come to the conclusion that much of it had been
gambling debts. Mark Barry might have been a keen gambler,
but he was certainly not a successful one.

'He is also desperately extravagant,' Cynthia observed.
'Tailoring and hotel bills and travel expenses and a florist's
bill that would probably stock Kew Gardens for a season, and
I don't suppose these flowers were for his wife.'

'I've been trying to get hold of Barry's solicitor,' Mickey
said.

'On a Sunday? That is unwarranted optimism,' Cynthia told
him. 'Unless you have a number for his home and he deigns
to answer it, then you will have to wait until Monday morning.'

Henry had been examining the newspaper clippings. 'I came

across some of these when I first looked into the drawers, and to be frank was daunted. I did not know where to start. We have made more progress this afternoon than I would have made in weeks, I think.'

His words were still slurred, his lips being bruised and swollen, and he was still finding it very painful to move his jaw. But he looked brighter, Mickey thought. At least he was getting some nourishment inside him. Cynthia had brought folding tables into the bedroom so they could sit beside Henry's bed and work together. Melissa had proved very apt in sorting and was now concentrating on putting Sir Eamon's notes in some kind of order. It was, Mickey thought, a safe task, Cynthia having no great wish for her daughter to be mixed up in discussing criminal activity. Frankly, he thought, horse, stable door, bolted, but after last year when Melissa had been taken and they all thought they had lost her, Cynthia had felt more need to shelter her daughter.

She had gradually loosened her grip, which for a time had been strangling, and Melissa apparently only rarely had nightmares, but they were so close to the anniversary of those events that Mickey could understand why everyone felt a little oversensitive. Besides, Melissa seemed genuinely interested in the scientific papers Sir Eamon had produced.

'You mentioned that you thought Sir Eamon was keeping tabs on his son's activities,' Mickey said, 'and the ledger would certainly bear that out, so can we link what's in the ledger to the press clippings?'

'I suppose we have to make the assumption that Mark Barry mentioned these people,' Cynthia said. 'Perhaps even brought them to the house.' She paused. 'Though perhaps not that. I don't remember the last time Sir Eamon invited anybody to the house. He always made the excuse that he didn't have the staff for entertaining and either visited elsewhere or met his friends in a restaurant.'

'Seeing the state of the house, I'm not surprised at that,' Mickey said. 'I've seen more comfortable slums.'

Cynthia flinched and he was immediately sorry for the sharpness of his words.

She said, 'It's more likely he took them to his own house

and introduced them to his wife, and perhaps his wife told Sir Eamon. From what Cyril was telling us, it seems that Martha Barry and Sir Eamon got along well. She certainly helped him when her husband was taking advantage.'

'Well, I'm hoping to speak to her tomorrow. She and her parents were visiting elsewhere this weekend, but according to the head butler or whoever it was I spoke to, they'll be back late tonight and I can telephone tomorrow. We might get a clearer picture from Mrs Barry. She seems to have turned against her husband and grown very tired of his games and financial mess.'

Henry, he noticed, had lain back against the pillows and closed his eyes, so Mickey decided to call it a day. Hopefully Tibbs would be back on the Monday with some names and they could start pulling the strands of this investigation together.

Sergeant Tibbs had caught an early train and arrived at Cynthia's just as they were finishing breakfast. He was soon ensconced at the table with his own repast and more tea and coffee for everybody else. The young man looked excited, Mickey thought, and guessed he would have good news for them.

Mickey let Tibbs satisfy his appetite first and then, over toast and marmalade, Tibbs explained what he'd found. With the help of the experts in the Criminal Records Bureau he had discovered that the man who had beaten Henry so badly was almost certainly Gilbert Baker, the name that Mickey had been given when he'd gone on his death knock visit to Sean Matthews' wife. He handed Mickey the folder containing Baker's records.

'He's local to this area, but also spent some time in London and is a known associate of this man. Emory Josephs.' Another folder was produced. 'Came over from Chicago about two years ago. From what the Chicago Police Department could tell us he was lucky to escape with his skin. He'd been running a speakeasy for Capone, was skimming and Capone found out. Over here he teamed up with a housebreaker by the name of Terence Olds, but they soon had a falling out and Olds hasn't been seen since. Whatever he's been doing in the last year, he's kept a low profile but is a known associate of this man, Wilfred Briggs.'

Tibbs munched on his toast while Mickey skimmed the records. 'And Briggs was in Birmingham, affiliated with one of the bigger gangs there from the looks of things. He's dropped out of sight though.'

'Had a major falling out with Jimmy Lee.' Tibbs reached with the folder and flicked through several pages until he found what he was looking for. 'Culminating in him taking off with Lee's wife.'

Mickey raised an eyebrow. 'Very sure of himself or very stupid,' he said. 'And do we know where they fetched up?'

Tibbs shook his head. 'She surfaced again a couple of years ago, suspected of running a gang of shoplifters and muscling in on Diamond Annie's territory. Annie and her Forty Elephants didn't take kindly and Corah Lee took off again.'

'She was lucky to be in a position to run,' Mickey said. 'Annie doesn't take prisoners.'

'And this Briggs.' Mickey looked at the man's sheet. Armed robbery, attempted murder, suspicion of the same. He was a violent man in his own right, Mickey thought, though he seemed to prefer keeping his hands clean. 'Likes his firearms,' he commented.

Tibbs nodded. 'And Josephs is known to be a knife man. Not an ounce of conscience between them.'

'Indeed not. Right, lad, you finish your breakfast while I take these up for Henry to look at.'

Tibbs looked startled. 'I mean no disrespect, Inspector Hitchens, but Mr Johnstone is no longer—'

'Henry is a witness. And he's also looking over documents I brought over from Sir Eamon's house. Among them are certain ledgers and bank statements and newspaper reports we've been trying to make sense of – I seem to remember Briggs' name coming up. So we'll allow our ex-detective chief inspector to be useful, shall we? And what's being done about liaising with our brethren in the press?'

'Both my drawings and the photographs we have are authorized for use and will be in the evening papers, both here and in Brighton and Rottingdean and in London. Names and descriptions and known associates will also be in the *Police Gazette*, possibly not today but certainly by tomorrow. And the superintendent's put out a statement that makes a big play of the fact these men attacked an ex-Metropolitan Police officer, one of very high standing.'

Mickey nodded, satisfied. 'Let's give the buggers nowhere to hide,' he said.

Mickey was thoughtful as they drove up to the Barry house. He had finally managed to contact Mark Barry's solicitor and had initially received short shrift from the man. He owed money and Mr Terry was not inclined to speak about what he now regarded as an ex-client.

'If it's an ex-client then you're no longer bound by confidentiality,' Mickey had pointed out cheerfully. 'Frankly, you're well shot of him. The man is up to his neck and drowning.'

There was a moment of silence on the other end of the telephone, and then the solicitor said, 'I don't think I want to know.'

'So you can tell me this. When his father's lawyer eventually broke the power of attorney, what happened to Mark Barry's affairs? Was an allowance reinstated, or was he totally reliant on his wife's money?'

'His father told him he would have to fend for himself. That he was a married, adult male who had shown himself to be unreliable, unworthy and unfilial. There may have been more, but that's all I remember. As far as his wife's money is concerned, her father made a settlement on her at the time of her marriage and Mr Barry tore through that within the first three years. She knew nothing about it, and it was only when debt collectors arrived at the house that she was apprised of the situation. As you can imagine, she was less than impressed.'

'Was that when they separated?'

'No, that was when Mark Barry persuaded his father that he should sign a power of attorney, just in case anything should happen to him. That's not an unusual provision, as I'm sure you know. I was aware that old Mr Barry was in ill health and I was informed that he was also losing his acuity, shall we say. It is not an uncommon situation and I drew up the papers in good faith. Then some six months after that, Mrs Barry got wind of the situation and intervened and I have to say that she and her father brought certain pressures to bear. It was not easy to rescind the power of attorney, but I did so to keep my reputation intact.'

'Because it shouldn't have been signed in the first place, because Mr Barry was not losing his marbles,' Mickey said bluntly.

'I would not have phrased it in quite that way, but yes.'

'And it was then that Mrs Barry departed.'

'I'm not privy to the exact details, but she was certainly absent from the marital home by the time the paperwork was sorted out. I suspect she may have left well before and just been maintaining appearances.'

'I'll be speaking to Mrs Barry later, see if she can add anything of interest to this sad tale,' Mickey said. 'However, it is interesting that Mark Barry is still giving out cards with your name, that you are still the recommended point of contact for anyone trying to get in touch with the man.'

Mr Terry sighed. 'A situation of which I am now well aware,' he said. 'Not a day passes when I don't hear from some creditor or other or their agents. I tell them all what I've told you: that I am no longer acting for a client that does not pay my bills either. But that does not stop the letters coming, or the personal visitations, or the telephone calls.'

Mickey commiserated, perhaps a little too cheerfully. 'So where might he run to?' he asked.

'I have no idea. I am not, as they say, my brother's keeper, and I'm certainly not Mark Barry's.'

Mickey had then telephoned Martha Barry at her family home in the Highlands. 'I'd be happiest if he threw himself of the nearest cliff,' Martha told him.

'Well, he would have plenty to choose from where I am right now,' Mickey told her. Somewhat to his surprise, Martha Barry laughed. 'Feel free to give him a little shove from me,' she said. 'All I do know is he'll get no more money from this direction, and I doubt he has much to come from what little remains of his father's estate.'

'I imagine the house and land will make something,' Mickey suggested.

'Perhaps, if whoever buys it plans to pull it down and start again. And he still has death duties to pay, don't forget. I can't think the Exchequer will be more forgiving than everyone else he owes money to.'

Good point, Mickey thought. 'Mrs Barry, did you visit The Pines often?'

'Twice. I met Sir Eamon on quite a few occasions, but not at The Pines.'

'Then you never visited his laboratory? You knew nothing about the hidden passageways in the house?'

She laughed. 'Of course I did. Sir Eamon loved all that kind of thing. He took great pleasure in showing me every dusty, cobwebby space. Apparently the previous owners liked their servants to be invisible, not so uncommon in a house of that age. There were also smugglers' tales, of course, but I took those with a large pinch of salt. The house is not old enough to have been used by smugglers, is it, and it's far too far from the sea for there to be tunnels they could have used.'

Mickey didn't bother to inform her that illegal trafficking of goods was a profession that was alive and well and did not always involve men with eye patches and peg legs or eight-eenth-century frock coats. 'And would you remember how to get into any of the spaces? We found the one from the shed next to the stables, down into the basement where we think he had his lab, and from there between the walls towards the library. But it's blocked off after that. You're telling me there are others?'

There were certainly others, and though she did not know how to get into all of them, she had given Mickey an idea of where the other cellars might be accessed and the other passageways might lead.

And of course, Mickey was thinking as they drove up to the house, Mark Barry would know all of these and he and his confederates would have made good use of them.

'There are children playing in the woods,' Tibbs commented as they entered the drive.

'Indeed there are.' And there had been children playing in

the woods the previous day – Mickey remembered the constable commenting on them. 'No one takes much notice of children,' Mickey said. 'They can be everywhere and go anywhere and no one pays them any mind. They are observant little souls, and will do anything for a few coins.'

Tibbs was staring at him. 'You think they are being used to spy?' he asked. 'Then we should round them up and question them.'

'Then we should use them to our advantage,' Mickey corrected. 'Besides, I might be wrong and then we'd have their mothers to deal with. No, leave them be; if they are spying for Briggs then we can make use of that and if they are innocent parties then no harm done.'

The constables declared that everything had been very quiet, but Mickey sensed they were uneasy. It was not a comfortable house, he acknowledged; it was nothing you could put your finger on exactly, and the discomfort had nothing to do with it being run down and chill and neglected. It did not feel like a friendly house; it had become curmudgeonly in its old age, or was he simply being fanciful.

He took the constables up to the library and told them what Martha had said about other passageways. 'She can't remember how to get in from the outside, only that she went out through a door that was somewhere at the rear of the house, in one of the outbuildings. Chances are that's how Sean Matthews and the others gained entry to this place for whatever purpose they were using it. But she and Sir Eamon entered the passageways from this room. The only snag is the door was open when she came in, so we are going to have to play like kids looking for a secret hidey hole – move some books and press some mouldings and see if we can find a way in.'

'There are only so many outbuildings, Inspector. Would it not be quicker to look from the outside?' Constable Knox asked. He was a large, imposing man with a fierce moustache.

'No doubt it would, but it would also allow us to be observed and I'd like to avoid that if I can. So far as Briggs and his gang are concerned, we know nothing about secret ways into this house and out again, or into the cellars beneath, and we should keep it that way for now.'

For the next hour they poked and prodded and moved the books around and Mickey was beginning to think that Martha Barry had been pulling his leg when one of the constables shouted in surprise and a panel swung back.

Mickey examined the moulding that the constable had moved. 'A fine piece of work,' he said admiringly. 'The carpenter that made this certainly knew what he was about. Well done, Constable. Now wedge the door, drag that table across it so it can't close on us, then fetch the torches and we'll see what's at the bottom of this.'

TWENTY-SEVEN

Henry had read through the files that Tibbs had brought back from London. He looked again through the press clippings and ledgers and found a direct link in the form of payments made to a man called Briggs. These were regular and occurring over about six months. They stopped four months before Sir Eamon had died, presumably when Mark Barry's finances had been cut off.

There was certainly nothing wrong with the old man's mind, Henry thought. He'd had a very good sense of what was going on and what was more had apparently made several visits to newspaper archives in London to follow up his own enquiries. He also seemed to have employed a private detective. There were letters from a detective agency in London talking about Briggs and his origins and also mentioning known associates that Tibbs had also mentioned. One by the name of Terence Olds was a name which rang a bell with Henry.

Telephone calls to ex-colleagues and another to the detective agency confirmed Henry's memory; Terence Olds was a housebreaker. He was also a cousin of Sidney Carpenter, the man whose body had been found outside the Deans' house. It must have been for this reason, this connection, that Sir Eamon had news clippings about the Carpenter murder. He was, Henry guessed, slowly building up a picture of his son's network of associates and the depths to which he had sunk.

Henry had the sense of things beginning to fall into place. Briggs and Corah Lee had fled from Birmingham to London and presumably lost themselves in the underworld there. Later, Corah had attempted to cut territory from Diamond Annie and Briggs had teamed up with this Emory Josephs at some point. Whatever was the full story, the capital did not seem to be supporting them in the manner to which they were accustomed.

This must have been a blow to someone like Briggs who

had once been Lee's right-hand man, employed in race fixing, drug dealing, prostitution and intimidation. Henry did not believe for one moment that Briggs had fled because he loved Corah Lee and the two of them wanted to be together. No, in Henry's view it was more likely that Briggs had got himself involved with Mrs Lee for sheer devilment or perhaps to prove that no one could have authority over him, not even his ersatz boss. They had been found out and both of them been forced to take to the hills before Lee's fury descended upon them. He was not a man to be crossed; interestingly, unlike some of the other Birmingham gangs, he'd shown no interest in gaining territory in the Greater London area. He'd been at pains to consolidate what he had, and mopped up those who over-stretched and failed but, Henry noted from the discussions he had with his one-time colleagues at Central Office, he was not a man given to risky expansion just for the sake of it.

Henry had been touched by the well wishes of his ex-colleagues and their genuine relief that he had been found, if not safe and well, then at least alive.

The private detective Calvin Aims gave him one more piece of information. That a reward had been put on Briggs' head by his one-time boss.

'It seems Sir Eamon put this to his son as evidence of how dangerous his association was. He was trying to warn him that you cannot run with wolves and not get bitten, but Mark Barry did not take it that way. His father said he seemed excited by the idea and even speculated on collecting the reward for himself.'

Mark Barry had been even more out of his depth than he realized, Henry thought. If Briggs even got the slightest hint that this was his intention, he was a dead man.

Mickey took the lead, descending the narrow staircase, lamp in hand. It descended for fifteen steps and then dog-legged for another fifteen. He arrived at a wooden door and it was the smell that first alerted Mickey and the others that they were not going to like what they found. The door was locked from the other side and the space was awkward – no run-up could be taken – but Mickey and Knox, the bigger of the two constables, working together, broke the timber around the lock and pushed it aside.

'Jesus!' Constable Knox whispered.

Mickey shone the torch at the floor to illuminate the debris as they stepped inside and then they all stood within a surprisingly large room. The floor was earth, the wall stone and it was damp and cold. An overflowing bucket of human urine and excrement stood in one corner and accounted for part of the stink. The remainder was from the body of a young woman who lay in one corner.

'Sweet Jesus,' the constable again. 'Is that a baby?'

Mickey moved closer. The woman, a young girl really, lay on her back on the earth floor and illumination from the torch showed that her skirts were pulled up and there were brown stains on her thighs and swollen belly that were probably blood. The baby, tiny and as dead as its mother, lay on the floor, naked and bloodied, the cord uncut.

'She gave birth to it here?' Tibbs sounded shocked.

'She gave birth to him – it was a little boy,' Mickey said very softly. He looked around the room, noting that it had once been occupied by others. There were blankets, mugs, a bucket that still held a small amount of water. Mouldy remnants of a loaf of bread. He fetched one of the blankets, covered the girl and her baby and then led the way to the other door. This too was locked but easily dealt with. This time their torches lit on crates and packages. 'Booze and cigarettes,' Mickey commented. 'Most likely other stuff too.'

He moved forward again and found a short flight of stone steps going up and another door. He had his hand against the door, feeling a draft between the boards and his torch pointing down so that it would not shine out. He ordered the others to do the same. 'This must be the exit from one of the outbuildings,' he said. Despite the chinks between the boards, this door was stronger and, he judged, had been reinforced quite recently.

'Now we know what Briggs and his gang were using the house for, no doubt with Mark Barry's full knowledge and agreement,' he said.

He led the way back through both rooms and up the stairs. When they had reached the library, he took his spirit flask from his pocket and handed it around. Even Tibbs took a swallow. For a few minutes all four men stood there in silence, shocked by what they had seen and horrified by the implication.

'She birthed her child down there,' Constable Knox said. 'Poor little sod.'

'We need to call the police surgeon,' Tibbs said.

'And we will, but we'll do it quietly and discreetly and bring him up under cover of darkness. We cannot remove the body yet.'

Mickey allowed the chorus of protest that followed to run its course and then he said quietly, 'If we wish to catch the men who did this, who left mother and baby to bleed out without a care for either of them, then we need to let them believe it's safe to come back. They'll be after their goods – the vans moving to and fro that the taxi driver told us about are them shifting stuff about. From the direction of the staircase I'm guessing that basement is at the other end of the house from where Henry was staying, but even so he must have inconvenienced them, and I'm now thinking that was Mark Berry's intent. What's the betting he had been taking a cut for himself?'

'How long do you think she's been lying there?' Tibbs asked.

'From the level of decomposition, I would say perhaps two weeks. I saw no evidence of fly strike, but at this time of year that would not be unusual and the cellar is damp and cold. That would have kept the insect life at bay. But the rats have had their fill,' he added and saw Tibbs change colour. The sergeant had not come close enough to see that.

'If you're going to be sick, lad, go and do it elsewhere.' He handed Tibbs the flask and the sergeant took a larger gulp. Slowly, his colour returned.

'Now,' Mickey went on, 'the two of you stay here, patrol around a bit and make yourselves obvious. I'm going to have a word with Sergeant Fox. There'll be pictures of our quarry all over the press tonight and posters put up in as many public places as we have glue to stick them. They'll have to make their move and we'll be ready for them.'

TWENTY-EIGHT

Mickey and Tibbs were in sombre mood as they made their way back along the coast road to Cynthia's.

They had spoken to Fox and he had contacted a local police surgeon and his own superiors. No one liked Mickey's plan to leave the bodies in situ, but all saw the sense in it. The police surgeon would be taken to the house under cover of the normal shift change. Once he had confirmed life extinct and given his judgement, he would be escorted back to the road, through the woods, hopefully unseen, and then driven home.

It was not a very sophisticated plan, Mickey thought, but it would have to do.

'So tomorrow instead of a shift change, the constables pull out and do so in very visible fashion. We arrive on foot, having concealed the car a few hundred yards away. We bring Knox and Cousins with us and we come back armed. The local constabulary can take care of weapons for the two officers and you and I will make use of Albert's collection.' He patted his pocket. 'I've already availed myself of his Mauser and most welcome it's been too. I take it you can shoot, young Tibbs?'

'I . . . I know the basics. Inspector, I'm not the best of shots.'

'Then just make sure you wave your weapon in the direction of the criminals and not the constables and only fire off a shot if you're close enough not to miss,' Mickey told him.

'Inspector, I think that would have to be very close.'

Mickey laughed. Of course, Tibbs was too young to have served in the war, far too young to have come under fire or had to take a life to preserve his own. *Different times*, Mickey thought. When he had been Tibbs' age . . .

'I'm sorry, Inspector Hitchens. I'll do my best.'

'Sorry you've never had to shoot a man? Don't be silly, lad.

Long may that continue to be the case. But just to be sure, I want you armed and as ready as anyone ever can be.'

Monday evening and images of Briggs, the deceased Sean Matthews and Gilbert Baker and Emory Joseph were in every newspaper on the south coast and many of the London editions. Constables had been out with paste and posters and boys employed to distribute leaflets in the busy streets. Mickey pronounced himself satisfied.

The one man they did not have any intelligence about was the one Henry had described as the quiet man – his contrast to Matthews and Josephs pronounced enough that he had stuck firmly in Henry's mind.

This was not a man that Malina had observed and so Tibbs had been unable to produce his likeness. That evening Henry sat with the young sergeant and they tried to pin his memories to paper. It had not been the most successful enterprise, Mickey thought. Henry had glimpsed the man a few times but his brain had been preoccupied with dealing with pain and anger and anxiety, and his image had failed to fix.

Tibbs' visit to Scotland Yard had not yielded a Known Associate that immediately fitted Henry's scant description – small and slim and fair-haired. Gracile, unlike his compatriots.

For the moment the man and whatever role he was supposed to play remained a mystery.

'So now Baker is dead and Matthews too,' Mickey said. 'That suggests Briggs is left with this Yank, Josephs and our mystery man.'

'I wish I could be with you,' Henry told him. He had come downstairs this evening and eaten a light supper by the fire in Cynthia's small sitting room, but the effort had cost him, Mickey could see that.

'I wish it too, but I suspect you'd be a little bit of a liability.' Mickey smiled.

'I suspect so too. How is Sergeant Tibbs shaping up?'

'Well enough. The best of the bunch so far. How long I'll be permitted to keep him is a moot point. I just get them trained up to the point where they are useful and some bugger comes along and claims them for themselves.'

'They know you do a good job,' Henry said. He took a sip of the brandy Mickey had poured for him and winced as the spirit found one of many cuts.

'And what do you plan to do when this is over?' Mickey asked him bluntly. 'There's to be no more prevaricating, Henry. No more hiding yourself away and digging a deeper hole. Those of us that love you will not put up with that.'

Henry nodded. 'I've been foolish,' he agreed. 'But, Mickey, it felt as though there was no purpose to life. It wasn't a dramatic feeling, not even . . . It was as though I looked at my life and I just thought, what is the point?'

'And now?'

'I feel guilt and pain and a degree of self-loathing for what I put you all through. But I will survive this, Mickey, and I will decide what comes next.'

'And Malina? What about her? She loves you, Henry.'

He could see the confusion on his friend's face and wondered if he had overstepped the mark.

'And I think she deserves better than me. Mickey, I have the greatest regard for Malina, but is that enough? Am I capable of loving anyone?'

You did once, Mickey thought. Then he thought, to hell with prevaricating and he said it out loud. 'You did once. You know that you're capable of it.'

Henry's eyes flashed with anger and Mickey waited, sipping his own brandy implacably. He waited some more and then finally the anger died in his friend's eyes and though Mickey was not certain this was because he'd been forgiven, or because Henry was in too poor a shape for his body to sustain it, he was relieved.

'I could say that was different,' Henry said.

'And so it was. But it was love that grew out of friendship and regard. Henry, you are not a man given to sudden passion. I saw Belle for the first time and it was like God had struck me with a lightning bolt. That's not the way of things for you. Perhaps you could just allow that your feelings for Malina might grow into something more than friendship and regard. It's a fine place from which to begin.'

Henry nodded slowly and took another sip of his brandy.

A few minutes later Mickey was easing the glass from the hand of his now sleeping friend. He tucked the blanket more firmly around him and tipped the remaining brandy into his own glass. *Waste not want not*, Mickey told himself, and as for Henry, well, at least he'd moved his thoughts on, if only by a few steps. For the moment that would have to do.

TWENTY-NINE

Early on the Tuesday morning Mickey received a phone call from Central Office at Scotland Yard. A woman had come looking for him late last evening, he was told. She had seen the evening newspapers and had intelligence to pass on.

On being told that Inspector Hitchens was not available, she had been most insistent on speaking to someone in charge who could get a message to him and insisted she wasn't going anywhere until that happened. Eventually she'd been interviewed and the detective sergeant carrying out that task had soon realized that this was not one of the usual 'concerned citizens' that felt they might have something important to say. This woman really did.

'Her name is Mrs Hamblin. She said she spoke to you a few days ago about that odd business over the Carpenter murder. Well, it seems she saw the portrait of our man Briggs in the *London Evening News* and she's insistent that his name wasn't Briggs the last time she set eyes on him. It was Deans. Matthew Deans. The same one that disappeared when Carpenter croaked outside their house.'

'Did she leave her number?' Mickey asked, and it seemed that Mrs Hamblin had. He called her back. Yes, she was certain. There was no mistake about it.

Mickey put down the phone and thought about this. If Corah Lee, aka Mrs Angela Deans, had in fact left in a taxi and the scene staged so that it appeared the family had left the scene at lunchtime, was it possible Briggs had lain in wait for Carpenter? That he'd known he would be coming?

'But why the devil would Carpenter beard Briggs in his lair?' Mickey asked Henry.

'Perhaps he was after the reward. Remember, his cousin was Olds; Briggs took up with him briefly. Maybe Carpenter realized who he was and sought to turn him in.'

'He'd never have been able to take Briggs down.'

'Perhaps he just wanted to be sure he'd got the right man.' Henry shrugged painfully. 'But Briggs was tipped off, knew it was time to move on, dealt with Carpenter.'

'Perhaps Olds betrayed him?' Mickey suggested. 'He turned up dead in the Thames a few months later so—'

'Catch Briggs and you can ask him,' Henry suggested.

Mickey smiled. 'That I will.'

Later that morning the constables were collected from the Barry house and driven away, along with the remaining provisions they had brought with them.

Tibbs and Mickey parked the car and waited for fifteen minutes after the designated time of departure. They had moved along the line of the hedge in the adjoining field to a point Knox had suggested from where the driveway and the little copse could be observed but they could remain out of sight. Tibbs crouched low among the dead and dying remnants of dock and teasel, Mickey beside him, and observed the house through a pair of field glasses borrowed from Albert.

'No children today,' he said.

'Perhaps they have been reported to the truant officer. Perhaps their parents got wind of their absence from school yesterday. The weekend is one thing, but a Monday is something else and a Tuesday definitely a step too far.'

'There is a man in the trees,' Tibbs said. 'He's walking a dog.'

'Keep an eye on him then.'

For a little while they sat in silence. The man walked by with a white terrier on a lead. 'Wait longer,' Mickey told his sergeant.

They waited longer. Tibbs began to fidget and Mickey took back the field glasses. He observed the house and then the trees, watched a burst of rooks breaking from one of the tallest trees, turned his attention back to the path. 'And here he is, back again.'

'The constables mentioned a man taking a short cut through the woods,' Tibbs said. 'They took his name and address. He was just a local man out with his pup, if it's the same man.'

'Apparently so and in all probability he's now still just a local man curious as to what the police have been up to and wanting to take a look. But let's see what he's about.'

Mickey handed the field glasses back to Tibbs and together they watched as the man came to the edge of the trees and stood for a moment before crossing over to the house. The dog was sniffing and poking at the leaves and the man dropped the lead and went to the kitchen door. Turned the handle. The door, locked when the constables had left, remained closed.

'Do we challenge him?'

'No, we keep away,' Mickey said. 'If all he's guilty of is beakiness then showing our hand will work against us. Our presence here will be all around the area before you can say Jack. If he's one of those we're after then he'll be expected to report back, and if he fails to turn up the others will be alerted. So no, we watch and we wait until the whole kit and caboodle come to us.'

The man was now standing beside the window and peering in through the glass. Then he did something that caused Mickey to surmise that this was definitely not an innocent if curious man. He walked around the house to the outbuilding where Mickey and the constables had guessed the cellar steps emerged and he checked the padlock.

Mickey held his breath. He'd had the constables posted at the house check these locks on their regular patrols, just for the look of things, and to complain loudly when off duty that watching an empty house was a waste of their time and public money.

'Not just idle curiosity then,' Tibbs said.

'I would think not, lad. I reckon we've rattled the cage good and proper.'

They waited until the man had gone and then waited again. After about an hour Mickey led the way to the house and they entered through the kitchen door before ascending to the library, which gave a better view over the surrounding landscape.

When Constable Knox and Sergeant Fox arrived that evening it was to find Mickey and Tibbs comfortably ensconced in two armchairs, drinking tea and eating sandwiches brought from Cynthia's.

'Enough for us and enough to share,' Mickey told the newcomers gravely.

'You think they'll come tonight?' Fox asked.

'I'm sure of it,' Mickey told him. 'It's only a matter of time before someone recognizes Briggs or Josephs. The man we spotted today answers the broad description Henry gave us of the one he called the quiet man. Slim, blond, not what you'd call a fighter from the way he's put together. They've got a lot to lose and a lot to gain by acting fast and then getting the hell out of here.'

THIRTY

It was late when Henry tapped on Malina's door. The doctor had encouraged him to move around as much as he could so long as he took it slowly (was there any other way, Henry had wondered) and he had spent a little time downstairs that evening. He had then gone back to bed and slept for an hour then found himself, at eleven o'clock, wide awake and unable to settle.

He knew the obvious cause: Mickey was at the Barry house and he was not. With luck tonight would see the matter reaching a crisis and Henry felt decidedly left out.

Malina opened the door. She was ready for bed and wrapped in a deep blue dressing gown. Her hair was loose; Henry always forgot how long it was, but it fell to her waist in a black as treacle heaviness.

'Are you all right?' she asked. 'You're missing Mickey, you're missing the action.'

'I suppose I am. It's late, I should go, I should not have disturbed you.'

'Come in and sit down before you fall down,' she told him.

Henry sat in the bedroom chair and Malina perched on the bed and studied him thoughtfully. He always felt naked under her scrutiny, as though she saw to the heart of him and there were very few people who did that. Oddly, it did not make him feel vulnerable. He would sometimes wish that his sister did not see so much and occasionally even Mickey probed too deeply, leaving Henry feeling irritable, but somehow he did not mind that Malina looked just as deep and just as thoroughly and knew him just as well.

Was that a good thing? Henry wondered. He had experienced that once before and the love he had felt for that person had been deeper and more significant than anything before or since. If this time he could not feel with that intensity in return, then was he cheating the person he was with?

'I think I've been an idiot,' Henry said.

Malina's laughter was cheerful and unrestrained; there was no mockery in it. It was as though he had told her a really good joke. 'Henry Johnstone, you are often an idiot,' she told him. 'You're the most intelligent man I know, but you don't possess even the wisdom of a child.'

'I know you hoped—'

'Henry, don't. Now listen to me, you are my best friend, an even greater friend than your sister. I will do nothing, you hear me, nothing to risk that. If in time, when you stop being an idiot, that friendship can become something more, then I will welcome it. You know how I feel; I won't push you to declare something you do not. I have more pride in myself than that and more affection for you. Be my friend; we will see what the future brings. Now go to bed. Before you know it Mickey will be back, eager to report, and he'll need you awake.'

Suddenly he was dropping with weariness but he was glad he'd come to see her. He had been terribly afraid that she was disappointed in him, that she wouldn't forgive him. What Malina thought mattered, probably more than anyone else apart from Cynthia and Mickey. Possibly even more than that, he realized with a slight shock.

She helped him out of the chair and then walked him back to his room. 'Now can you manage to get into bed?'

He assured her that he could and then bent and kissed her gently on the cheek. 'Thank you,' he said.

Gently Malina pushed him inside and then closed the door. 'Damned fool,' he heard her say. Henry was smiling through cracked lips when he returned to bed.

THIRTY-ONE

It was almost three o'clock on the Wednesday morning. They had taken it in turns to get rest and Mickey was watching by the window while Tibbs dozed, Fox paced and Constable Knox snored softly. The sound of two vehicles approaching alerted Mickey. Soon Fox joined him by the window, Tibbs had startled into life and Fox nudged Knox into wakefulness.

Quietly they descended to the kitchen and stood in the scullery as the vehicles, a large van and a long, streamlined car, came up the drive and went around the back of the house.

As silently as he could, Mickey opened the kitchen door and stepped outside. They had been so long in the gloom of the unlit library that their eyes were already accustomed to the darkness. The night was cloudy, the moon flitting in and out of sight, but not enough to eliminate them as they crept around the side of the house, weapons drawn. He sidled up to the corner and peered around.

The door to the storeroom was now unlocked, standing wide open. Only one man was visible to Mickey, who presumed the other two must be inside. The man standing guard was not the one they had seen that afternoon – he was taller and more heavily built and wore a plaid Ulster. It was cold in the stable yard and he was stamping his feet and rubbing his hands together. Mickey said that everyone should stay put. He wanted all three men to be visible – he was hoping they were only dealing with the three, and Briggs had not conjured up some reinforcements to make up for those who had been shot.

It seemed to take forever but was probably only minutes before two other figures emerged, bottles chinking in the boxes they carried.

Mickey gave the signal and suddenly there was chaos. Knox blew a whistle to bring reinforcements, Mickey fired a shot into the air and then ordered the men to put the boxes down and to get onto the floor. Josephs pulled a pistol from his pocket and fired in their direction but Mickey and the others were moving, anticipating this, and Josephs was peering into deep shadow. Mickey fired, Josephs fell.

The man he realized must be Briggs dropped the box that he was carrying and then a weapon was in his hand and he was shooting his way out and running towards the car. Mickey fired again, and his shot must have winged him because Briggs was thrown off balance. He found his feet again and was in the car. Constables were running from the woods where they had been concealed and the smaller, blond-haired man that they had seen with the dog stood uncertainly, not knowing what to do. He then set the box down and began to back away, but Mickey realized with a slight shock that he was not backing away from them but from something emerging from the storeroom.

'There's someone else behind the door,' Mickey shouted and another shot rang out, proving his point. Who the devil . . . He was aware of Tibbs beside him and that the young man had fired his own weapon, blindly, into the darkness beyond the door. A cry of pain told Mickey that the sergeant had found his mark, albeit by a lucky shot.

Sergeant Fox and Constable Knox were moving into position now, covering the men, and the constables were in the stable yard. 'Sergeant Tibbs, with me,' Mickey yelled.

Briggs had reached the car and Mickey ran towards him. He swung around in a large arc, turning back down the drive and aiming for Mickey at the same time. He threw himself aside and Tibbs grabbed him and pulled him back to his feet.

'If we can make it to our car, we might be able to catch him or even get ahead of him. There's only one way he can go,' Tibbs yelled in his ear.

They took off at a run across the field towards the track where they had parked the car, under cover of trees. The going was rough and muddy, slippery underfoot and treacherous with brambles and weeds and overgrowth even this late in the season. What had provided them with cover when they had watched the house earlier that day now threatened to break ankles.

They had reached the car. They could hear Briggs' vehicle – he was gunning the engine and the sound carried on the still night air. Mickey started Cynthia's car and floored the accelerator, wishing fervently that this was the Lagonda and not the little Ford. Albert's vehicle was set up for racing starts. They reached the road just as Briggs' car flashed by and then they were on his tail, flat out around the bends and heading down into Rottingdean. For one fervent moment Mickey recalled the congestion at the bottom of the High Street, the jostling for position of buses and trucks and cars and pedestrians, and wished for a little bit of that daytime chaos in the middle of the night. But the way was clear. Briggs hurtled from the end of the High Street and swung right on to the Brighton Road, and for a moment Mickey's spirits rose. Cynthia's little car was capable of up to sixty-five miles per hour on the flat and straight, and though the coast road rose gradually it was mostly straight, the rise not severe. Now they were gaining on Briggs.

And he was turning to fire at them.

Mickey jinked and swerved, losing speed, making himself a more difficult target. He could hear Tibbs muttering and wondered for a moment if he was praying and then realized with shock that he was swearing. Mickey chuckled, not able to help himself, wondering what Tibbs' mother would think.

'Hang on, lad, I think he's about to turn,' Mickey said, reacting more to instinct than any indication that Briggs was giving to them.

Briggs did indeed swing left, taking the road to Ovingdean. For a brief while, the road flattening out, Mickey once more gained on the speeding car. The engine complained and the narrow tyres skipped on the greasy road. And then they were climbing again and more steeply this time.

'Inspector!' Tibbs yelled as the road suddenly disappeared into the darkness, but Mickey, having seen Briggs make a sudden swerve, the headlights of the other car catching what looked like a solid wall, was just enough prepared to make the turn. But he'd had to slow down and that had cost them distance and time. Now they were climbing again and the other car was gaining ground.

They reached a T-junction and Briggs went right. He was well ahead of them now and the road was still climbing. Cynthia's little Ford, though it leapt forward eagerly enough, did not have the power or the pace. And to make it worse, Briggs had doused the lights and there was only a dark shape ahead of them and as he crested the rise even that disappeared.

Mickey stopped the car. They had reached a crossroads, quite literally, and although they could hear the car engine in the distance it was hard to know which direction it had taken.

'Damn and buggary,' Mickey exploded. 'I thought we'd have him.' He sighed and glanced sideways at Tibbs, noticing how pale the young man was, his face white and shocked.

'Best get back to the Barry house, see what's gone on there,' Mickey said. Reluctantly, he turned the car around and headed back down the hill.

Back at the house Sergeant Fox had taken charge. Josephs lay on the floor, and Mickey realized that he was dead. He'd caught the man in the throat and his plaid Ulster was now black with his own blood.

'Anyone hurt?' Mickey asked, concerned only for the policeman he was with. Counting only his colleagues as casualties.

'Remarkably, no. Or at any rate not seriously. Knox has a black eye courtesy of yon blond over there.' He nodded towards the man they had seen walking the dog. 'Seemed to think he had better put on a show of fighting back. Knox flattened him for his trouble. He's been good as gold since.'

'And who was our fourth man, or can I guess?' Mickey asked.

'Guess away,' Fox told him.

'I'm guessing it was Mr Mark Barry.'

'Bull's-eye,' Fox said. 'Your sergeant got him in the arm, but he'll live.'

'And there's you telling me how bad you were with a pistol.' Mickey clapped Tibbs on the back. 'Sergeant Fox, I'm going to leave you and your men to it. I want to get back to where I can have use of the phone and call up further resources. See if we can track Briggs.'

'You're thinking,' Sergeant Fox said, 'that a fast car chase at three o'clock in the morning will have woken a few folk from their beds and there may have been a few complaints.'

'I'm thinking exactly that,' Mickey said. 'I'm thinking we can put out an appeal for anyone who heard two cars being driven recklessly, asking the public to come forward. We'll get a lot of false leads, no doubt, but if we can get the local constabularies to plot the route, according to the witness statements and complaints, we might get an idea of the direction he's taken.'

'It would help if we knew what car it was,' Tibbs added.

'Well, now I've seen it up close and personal,' Mickey said, 'I have a few ideas about that. To my mind it's a Mercedes-Benz. I was fortunate enough to see two of them racing last spring when we went to watch Albert take to the track. So we need to examine copies of the *Police Gazette* circulating over the last month. That car was stolen from somewhere; it's not something Briggs would own.'

'Who gets the job of going through the gazettes?' Tibbs asked. He was clearly hoping it wouldn't be him.

'I think we set Henry on to that one,' Mickey said.

It had been a long night but Mickey had at least set things in motion. The local newspapers would put out an appeal and the BBC was also going to broadcast a bulletin. A last-minute addendum had been added to the *Police Gazette* and this would be circulated along the south coast and in London. Mickey considered there was a good chance of Briggs heading back to the capital where it was easier to get lost.

Beyond that he had spent time with the man they had now identified as Clive Cookson and a call to the Criminal Records Office had identified him as a safebreaker and a previous associate of Briggs. He had not been exactly cooperative and had maintained a calm silence on the journey to the police station and then maintained this in subsequent interviews.

Mark Barry, on the other hand, once he'd been patched up by the police surgeon, seemed unable to stop talking. Briggs had forced him into it – he hadn't wanted to get involved, he was an innocent party here. Mickey had reminded him that he had shot at police officers and remarked that so far as he could make out, no one had been forcing his hand over that.

'So where do you reckon they were holed up for the last few days?' Tibbs asked.

'That will come to light sooner or later. I just hope it was an empty house, but the dog makes me think otherwise. It has to have been within walking distance of the Barry place. Cookson took the dog for a walk in order to keep watch on the house; if he had been driven there we would have heard the car.'

Tibbs nodded. His belly grumbled loudly and Mickey was reminded that since the sandwiches the previous evening neither of them had eaten.

'Breakfast, I think,' he said. This time when they entered the White Horse and asked if the restaurant was open to non-residents for breakfast, Tibbs did not look quite so daunted. The manager remembered them and told them that although this was not usually the case, he would make an exception.

Watching Tibbs devour his meal, Mickey reflected that he seemed to be getting used to frivolity and that his mother would be very disappointed in him.

Tibbs didn't say much after they left the hotel. He looked tired and strained, Mickey thought, and reminded himself that this was the first major enquiry the young sergeant had been involved with in his detective role. While Mickey had taken charge of the interviews, Tibbs had spent half the night at the local constabulary, reporting on what had happened and seeing those reports relayed to other interested parties in London and Birmingham and along the south coast. Patrol cars had been sent out to look for the vehicle but as Mickey expected had come back with nothing to report.

It had been too dark to be certain of the model, but Mickey was now satisfied that it was a Mercedes. He had also been unable to make out the complete number plate as this seemed to have been deliberately obscured by mud, but he thought the first characters had been an A and six and that might in itself prove helpful.

They walked down the promenade to collect Cynthia's car. It was a grey day, waves and clouds matching one another for

drabness, seagulls screeching in protest overhead. The
susurration of waves on stones was loud, and to Mickey's ears
this morning oddly irritating.

Mickey drove in silence along the coast road and Tibbs
seemed disinclined to break it. Both, Mickey realized, were
disheartened despite having two criminals in custody. They
sensed that they had lost the main man, and from what Mickey
had read about Briggs he was not a man you'd want to lose.
He was a man to keep your eyes on.

He turned right towards Ovingdean with less speed than he
had employed the night before; this time all four wheels
remained firmly on the ground. The land here was oddly flat
and was largely agricultural, either side of the road, with a
scatter of older houses and newly built bungalows suggesting
that the town was encroaching into the farmland. Beyond the
cow fields the landscape rose again, quite sharply on both sides,
and it wasn't long before the road itself began to climb. Mickey
entered the village of Ovingdean with more caution than he had
the previous evening, seeing for the first time the track leading
to the ancient church on the left just before the sharp, almost
right-angled bend in the narrowing road ahead.

Driving in daylight between a high stone wall on one side
and a row of houses, frontages butted against the road on the
other, Mickey was amazed they had got through unscathed. A
sharp intake of breath from young Tibbs informed Mickey that
his colleague was enduring similar thoughts. What amazed
Mickey more was that the larger, faster car they had pursued
had made these turns at all. It spoke of skilled driving – or
pure dumb luck.

They came to a narrow crossroads that Mickey hadn't even
been aware of the previous night and then on between high
hedges and up the steepening road, leading to the major
T-junction he did remember. He paused, looking both ways,
getting the lie of the land.

'So, we turn right and we go back to Rottingdean, coming
in the back way past the village pond and the rear end of
Whipping Post Lane.' Not that he'd even think of taking the
car down Whipping Post Lane – he doubted you could even
get a donkey cart down the end of it.

He turned left as he had done the previous night, up the long hill which steepened sharply as it reached the crest and the crossroads at which he lost the other car. Cynthia's vehicle, though trying its best, had just not been powerful enough to keep up.

'Eenie, meenie, miney, mo,' Mickey said.

'Well, forget eenie,' Tibbs told him, 'that's where we are now.'

Mickey grinned, glancing at Tibbs, who had regained a little of his colour and composure and now seemed ready to get on with the job in hand. Amazing what a solid breakfast followed by the reassurance that you'd not actually been killed by your foolhardy inspector did for you.

'And according to the map, mo leads nowhere but a few houses in Woodingdean, though he might have turned back, I suppose. There is a narrow road which loops back to rejoin Falmer Road.'

Mickey shook his head. 'The sound of the engine would have been louder and more distinct. When we reached the crossroads it was growing more distant. So meanie it is then.' Mickey turned left and about fifty yards from the corner pulled the car to the side of the road and tucked it on to the verge. There were no hedges here and the view was largely open across the downs and right out to sea. On the opposite side of the road was a short row of houses and indications of more to be built. Mickey could imagine the builder and the estate agencies exploiting the glories of the view. He could also imagine the viciousness of the winds on dark winter days come January and February, Mickey's least favourite months.

'So, if we continue on this road we find ourselves in Brighton. From there our quarry could hole up, double back along the coast road or turn toward Shoreham and points beyond. Or he could have continued straight on at the crossroads and been in London within a couple of hours.'

'He didn't take the London Road,' Tibbs said with sudden certainty.

'Oh, and why is that?'

Tibbs shrugged as though suddenly losing that resolve.

'No, go on, lad.'

'Because everything that happened was around here, close to the coast. The action has taken place on a narrow strip with the Barry house at one end and the house Inspector Johnstone was watching at the other. Even the house where the bodies were found was within that narrow strip of hinterland, a mile or two inland at most. And he's arrogant. He won't be driven off course, not by this, not by losing his compatriots or by being chased by the police or anything else. Inspector, that car was likely stolen—'

'That is the conclusion, yes.'

'So why take something that flashy and expensive when another would do? Either he thinks he's going to have to make a quick getaway or he just wants something that looks . . . He wants to give a particular impression. That he can do anything he likes, that he's got the money and the power to pull off anything he sets his mind to. Or both.'

Mickey nodded. 'I've reached a similar conclusion,' he agreed. 'If this Briggs is also our Mr Deans, then he's shown a similar pattern before when he got involved with Corah Lee and offended his boss. Then he rented a house in an area where there was money, where there are affluent people. I don't mean toffs, I don't mean people at the top, but well-off and middle class which, for someone like Briggs, dragged up off the streets like he was, probably feels like pretty high up. The car, however, suggests to me that he's overreaching himself. That he wants more. That he has *expectations*, to reference our friend Mr Dickens.'

'Expectations of something at the Barry house. Well, we've scuppered those, so what's he likely to do now?'

'That's the question, isn't it? He's wanted by the police, by his old friends in Birmingham, probably in London too. His portrait is in the newspapers and the word is out. So, does he have a bolt hole we don't know about where he can ride this out? What friends does he have that are not known associates? Or will he have to improvise? That's when he'll be most dangerous, lad, if he has to make up his next moves as he goes along. If he's without a plan. And there's nothing we can do now that's quick or certain. He's going to take time to track down.'

'You think Cookson knows where he might have gone?'

'Possibly, but what incentive does he have to tell us at this juncture? No, there's a man who's holding out for a deal, you mark my words. He'll wait us out, then offer to trade inform-ation for a lesser charge. He fired no weapon and beyond thumping Constable Knox, and I doubt that's the first shiner Knox has received, offered no resistance. He'll want to trade on that.'

'And Mark Barry?'

'Will tell us everything and nothing and likely misdirect because of that.' Mickey started the car and set off down the long hill of Falmer Road.

'Where are we going now?' Tibbs asked.

'Back to Cynthia's to have a bath and a sleep and then more sustenance,' Mickey told him. 'There's nothing more we can do – events must unfold in their own time and we need to be ready for them.'

THIRTY-TWO

Late that afternoon Mickey was summoned by Sergeant Fox. House-to-house enquiries had found the residence where Briggs and his men had been hiding out. The dog, tied to the front gatepost and barking its protest, had attracted the neighbours and they had been unable to rouse the elderly owner, or the 'nephew' who had been staying for the past days.

'The constables broke in and found Mrs Kirk in the cellar. Looks like she's been dead around three or four days,' Fox said.

'So around the time that Briggs shot Matthews and Baker,' Mickey suggested. 'How was she killed?'

'Stabbed and then pushed down the cellar steps. The fall broke her neck so it's moot which action killed her.'

Mickey nodded. 'And the nephew? I'm taking it that was Cookson?'

'The neighbours recognized him from his mugshot, yes. He apparently seemed fond of the dog, said his aunt had been unwell and he was looking after her.'

A little later Mickey returned with Fox to the police station armed with hastily processed crime scene photographs. It made a change, Mickey thought, for him not to have produced them himself – usually in a borrowed bathroom or scullery.

Cookson was brought in. Mickey waited until the man was settled and then pushed the photographs across the table towards him. 'She was seventy-nine years old, so some people might argue she'd had a good innings. If she died of a heart attack, or caught the flu, or something else of a natural manner had finished her, there would be those that said that. But I don't imagine she got up that morning expecting to be stabbed and shoved down the stairs into her own cellar just because three miscreants decided they wanted her house.'

Cookson said nothing. He glanced at the photographs and sat back in his chair as though waiting for Mickey to continue.

'What did she do to deserve this?' Mickey asked.

'What do any of us do to deserve the direction life takes us?' Cookson asked. He looked back at the photographs and this time Mickey sensed he was interested. Interested in the same way that someone might look at pictures in a gallery, not interest in or concern for the dead woman, but in the composition of the image, the light and the shadow. Mickey felt a chill run down his spine.

'Briggs is nothing, is he?' Mickey asked. 'It seems to me you're the brains behind the operation.'

Cookson made no comment. Instead he picked up one of the photographs and examined it even more closely. 'It's likely she was dead before she hit the floor,' he said, his voice flat and almost toneless.

'And none of this touches you, does it? How many people did you keep in that basement at the Barry house? And where are they now? A young woman died down there, giving birth to her child in complete and utter squalor. She bled to death, but none of that matters to you.'

Cookson laid the photograph back on the table. 'I could have killed the dog,' he said, 'but as it happens I like dogs.'

'So what was all that about?' Fox asked. 'You're telling me Briggs isn't pulling the strings. That it's yon little man?'

'I suspect Briggs might argue about that, but I think it's possible,' Mickey said. 'I've seen his type before. Lacking in even the most basic conscience. Sergeant Fox, I suggest when you next have Mark Barry questioned that you ask him about Cookson. My guess is that it is Cookson Barry most fears, not Briggs. Briggs is impulsive and arrogant and undoubtedly violent, but he's also predictable. Cookson, I suspect, is not, but he's possessed of brains and guile and a low cunning and, as I say, not one shred of conscience.'

Intelligence had been trickling in from members of the public who had heard or been woken by the sound of two fast cars racing through the lanes on the Wednesday evening and then by the sound of just one being driven fast and hard. Tibbs had been correct: Briggs had not taken the London Road but had turned left towards Brighton.

Through Thursday and into Friday the evidence mounted. The car had driven fast, turned right at the crossroads and down into Brighton, then regained the coast road.

Witnesses stated it had continued out of town at high speed. Through Hove and on to Shoreham. Only then had he turned inland again, and after some confused reports that seemed to have Briggs turn back on himself, he had been identified again on Mill Hill.

'We are certain it was him?' Mickey questioned as Fox gave him the report.

'Driving like a maniac, but this time we have eyewitness reports and they tally with the car we saw at the Barry House. The irony is if the idiot had slowed down no one would have paid him any mind and he'd have been away.'

'Eyewitnesses?' Mickey asked.

'Agricultural workers. It was just getting light when they spotted him.'

'And where did he go from there?' Mickey wondered.

'Then we lose him. Which most probably means he stopped somewhere. Habitations are widely spread out in that location. So now we trust to the constables canvassing the area or to members of the public spotting the car.'

'He's still armed,' Mickey said anxiously. The newspapers and the radio bulletins and the local police had all warned that Briggs was armed and dangerous, but Mickey knew that in the minds of some that just added to the attraction of finding him.

'I hate waiting,' he told Henry. He and Tibbs had been out all hours joining the search, but it had not satisfied Mickey's need to do something significant.

'We are neither of us good at boredom,' Henry agreed. He was more mobile now and didn't look as though he'd fall down if someone blew on him.

'If nothing happens in the next day or two then Tibbs and I will be heading back to London,' Mickey said. 'We can't stay here waiting for developments, there's enough work to do elsewhere.'

'There always is. Fox and his officers seem capable enough and what is needed at this stage is bodies on the ground, looking and probing and asking questions. It's not a job that can only be carried out by detectives.'

Mickey nodded but he was willing Briggs to make a move. He wanted to be in at the finish of this. Henry shifted uncomfortably and then said, 'Do you think that Fox would allow me to speak to Cookson?'

Mickey was on the point of reminding his friend that he was no longer a serving officer. He bit his tongue. 'For what reason? He's been interrogated thoroughly. Not that he's saying much, but the circumstantial evidence will be enough to lock him away.'

Henry nodded. 'Of course. I'm sorry, Mickey, that was a foolish question. Is anything known about the young woman that was found? About the others that had been kept in that cellar? Mickey, I can't get over the idea that I was there, in the same house, and I knew nothing.'

'Nothing as yet on who was there or where they might have been taken. And the fault is not yours. You could have heard nothing. We're assuming that someone came and left water and food, though from the look of things very little of either. As for the young mother and her baby, there was no form of identification, no idea of where she might be from. Henry, none of this is your fault or your responsibility.'

Mickey looked anxiously at his friend, examining him for signs that the dark mood was returning, but Henry shook his head. 'Mickey, I know what you're thinking. I feel badly, as any person with a conscience would feel badly. But I am not about to sink again.'

'I'm glad to hear it,' Mickey told him. He was about to risk asking how things stood with Malina when Tibbs knocked on the door. Fox had telephoned. The car had been spotted hidden behind a farmworker's cottage, and although there was presently no one living there, lights had been seen inside.

THIRTY-THREE

Constable Grace, who had reported the car, was waiting for them at the end of the lane, his bicycle propped up against the hedge. Other local officers had congregated beside him in the quiet road and though Mickey had seen no traffic for the last mile he was concerned that such a gathering of police might attract attention. How far away was the cottage?

Constable Grace reassured him. There was a farmhouse further down the lane but the cottage they were interested in was almost a quarter-mile away down a muddy track that cut between fields. No one could see them in their present position.

'How did you come to see the car?' Mickey asked.

'I was asking at the farm about hearing anything unusual on the night in question. Mr Benson and his missus was up for the milking, cows don't care if it's winter or summer, they need milking at the same time every day.'

Mickey nodded encouragingly.

'So they was up, and heard the car come screaming along the main road. Road's higher than the farm, sound carries. Then it went quiet, never occurred to him it went quiet because the man was at the cottage. Then they heard the bulletins on the news, and next time I see them, old Benson mentions it. We got to thinking why the engine noise might have stopped and all we can think is the man's parked it somewhere. And only place round here he could have parked it is the old farmworker's cottage.'

'And no one lives there?' Mickey wanted reassurance on that point.

'No.' The constable sounded as though it was a stupid idea and wondered why Mickey was asking. 'Ain't no one lived there last few years. Last family what lived there moved to the village. No one else wants to take it on. Right in the middle of nowhere. That might have been all right before the war, when a farm like this belonged to the big house and had plenty of workers and three or four of the young'uns shared the place. Then the sons got killed and the house got sold off. For a little while the cottage was used for lodging summer pickers and then the family took it on for a time, but it's too far away from everything.'

'So it would take local knowledge to even realize it was there?' Mickey asked.

'I'd reckon so. You'd not come on it by chance.'

Mickey was thoughtful. He turned to Fox and said, 'Briggs is not a local man and is definitely not a rural man. He is much more a city boy. But according to what little we know, Cookson grew up round here.'

'So it's likely Cookson knew where he'd be headed,' Sergeant Fox agreed. 'So why bother concealing that? Cookson might've got a better deal if he cooperated with us and he knew that. Turn Briggs in and the courts would have looked more kindly on him.'

'Loyalty?' Even as he said it, Tibbs looked unconvinced.

'Bloody-mindedness, more like,' Mickey said. He turned back to the constable. 'And am I to understand you went to investigate?'

'I wouldn't say that. I have to say I have more sense than that, if you'll excuse me saying it. Let's just say I got close enough to see that the car was there, and I managed to watch for a bit and there was definitely somebody inside. It was near dusk and there was a light, flickering like a fire in the hearth, though it was too murky to see if the chimney was smoking.'

'Any reports of thefts in the area? The man would need to eat and drink.'

'There's a pump in the garden above a well, spring water filtered through chalk and pure enough to drink so he'd not go short of water. And a mile further on down the lane there's a market garden, close to the road that runs parallel almost to this one here. They've got a little stall with eggs and vegetables, mostly cabbages and leeks this time of year, near the gate with an honesty box. Well, most folk put the cash in the box, good as gold, but Mrs White did complain, when I asked her, that some eggs had gone and no coins put in the box.'

'It's a wonder he didn't make off with the rest of the cash,' Mickey said.

The constable laughed as though that was a great joke. 'Mrs White ain't that daft, Inspector. It's a metal box with a damned great padlock on it and the box is welded to the gatepost. Occasionally produce does walk, but not so often as you might think. But the cash is always safe.'

Mickey nodded. 'This also speaks of local knowledge,' he said. 'So probably more intelligence from Cookson. Constable, I know you said that there were fewer farmworkers around here than there had been, but have you noticed any increase lately? Perhaps people not speaking English?'

The constable shook his head. 'They'd stick out like a sore thumb round here,' he said. 'We hear rumours from time to time of people brought in for work, cheap labour, but they'll be off to the sweatshops in the cities.'

It was a valid point, Mickey thought. 'So how do we proceed?' he said. 'I'm happy to bow to local knowledge here. Constable, you and your colleagues know the lie of the land and I do not. Though I suggest the first thing we do is put a roadblock on the lane at the other end by the market garden and a similar block here in case a man decides to flee.'

The constable's smile spread slowly across his face and he was obviously very pleased with himself.

'You already have something organized, I'm guessing,' Mickey said, deciding that he rather liked this man. He had initiative.

'Got Jeb from the garage to park his breakdown truck at the end of the lane. Jeb recovers lorries and agricultural vehicles when they break down. Damn great vehicle it is, solid as a rock. No one's going to get past that. And as for this end . . .'

The constable signalled to the police van that Mickey had noticed parked just down the lane. The van pulled forward and constables opened the back doors, lowered a ramp and down that ramp two men rolled a tarpaulin-wrapped drum. Once out of the van they set it on its end and carefully unwrapped the tarpaulin to reveal a reel of heavy-duty barbed wire of a type that Mickey had hoped never to see again. The last time he had encountered it the vile stuff had been used as antipersonnel defences at the front. He'd seen men and horses caught up in it, vehicles and even tanks wrapped in its coils.

'Nasty stuff.' The constable must have seen his face, Mickey realized. 'It was left over from when the last of the sea defences were finally dismantled in 1919. Parked in the storage depot all this time and I thought it might be just the thing.'

'So long as none of our lot come a cropper in it,' Fox said, and Mickey could see he was regarding it with similar distaste.

'There's a gap in the hedge that side, big enough for pedestrians to get by,' the constable told them, 'and on the other side of the track there's a stile that leads to the path through that little copse. But if he tries to get away in that posh automobile, he'll have no chance.'

'We're losing the light,' Mickey said. 'Best get set up. And Constable Grace, if you'd be so kind as to direct us to the cottage, I'd like to see what we're up against before we're trying to see in the dark.'

Tibbs, Mickey, Sergeant Fox and Constable Grace made their slow, silent way up the lane until they reached a shallow bend and then Grace directed them through a gap in the hedge and into the adjacent field. Mickey's eyes were growing accustomed to the gathering dusk, but even so he went carefully. A trip or a fall or a false step now and that might make sufficient noise to alert their quarry.

The cottage backed on to the field, the front door facing the track. There had once been a garden surrounding it on three sides but this was now overgrown and neglected. Dropping to the ground, Mickey crawled forward, the others beside him. He could see the car, half concealed among the overgrowth. The cottage itself was low to the ground, the upper floor tucked in beneath the eaves and though it had been disused for so long, Mickey could see that it was still largely in reasonable shape. It would provide quite adequate shelter at least for a short while.

As he watched the darkened windows he saw a shape of greater darkness pass one. Then caught a glimpse of a faint glow as though, as the constable had suggested, a fire had been lit. Then, abruptly, the back door to the cottage opened and Mickey flattened himself against the ground, aware that beside him Tibbs did the same. The sound of water puzzled Mickey for a second and then he realized: Briggs had come outside to relieve himself. The faint but unmistakable tang of urine drifted across the garden and emphasized just how close they were.

Could he make a run at Briggs? Mickey wondered. Could he get to his feet and make it across the garden while the man still had his back turned to them? He began to move. Tibbs grabbed his arm, stilled him.

It was as though Briggs had heard his thoughts. He turned, facing where Mickey and the others lay, their faces now buried in the dirt so he did not glimpse the paleness of their skin in the dimness of fast falling night. In the split second before he pressed his face into the earth, Mickey had seen that Briggs held a pistol in his hand.

Later, when they had re-joined the others at the end of the lane, Mickey berated himself. Had he been able to reach his weapon he could have taken the shot. As it was, Albert's Mauser was stowed in the pocket of his coat and retrieving it would have meant moving and almost certainly being seen. He had felt the shape of it digging into his hip as he flattened his body against the grass and weeds and mud, but for all the chance he'd had of reaching it safely, it might as well have been back in Albert's desk.

'At least we know he's there,' Tibbs said. Then added, 'Why *is* he still there? I can't believe he'll stand it for much longer.'

'No more can I,' Mickey agreed. 'It's been two days since we challenged the gang at the Barry house. My guess is he'll be ready to make a move. This place has the advantage of being remote, and all the disadvantages of that too. No, he'll be preparing to move out and we've got to be ready for him. The next time that man takes a step outside the door, I'm not planning on being flat on my face in a bloody muddy field.'

'We try and flush him tonight, we could lose him in the dark,' Fox said.

'No, we wait until first light. Get everyone in position ahead of that and then we take him down. I'll not risk men getting shot in the dark or risk losing him either. And don't have any doubt about him shooting first. He's already got enough blood on his hands to ensure the hangman's noose; he'll have no qualms about adding to the count.'

Mickey had no wish to risk that their man would take off into the darkness on foot. Again they moved forward, Tibbs and Fox and Grace beside him with two of Grace's handpicked colleagues bringing up the rear. Mickey realized that he'd been fretting about the delay almost without realizing it. He was profoundly relieved to once more see movement in the little cottage. He recalled the advice he had once given to Tibbs as they sat down to wait, about taking a flask of something hot and laced with a tot of spirit when sent out on a night of cold watching. He felt the absence now.

He was aware of the others in position around him. Satisfied that they had taken his direction that they must remain still and silent as the grave. A man like Briggs would quickly have become accustomed to the sounds native to the landscape he was in. Would be in a constant state of alert and listening. Any change to that subtle soundscape would be noted and responded to.

But even the hunted had to sleep.

The faint glow from the fire had diminished as the night drew on and it was, Mickey estimated, more than an hour since there had been any movement from within the cottage. But still he waited. They had discussed the notion of breaking into the cottage, an armed force at both front and back, but Mickey believed fervently that was the way to get his men killed. The cottage was small but it would still provide cover for Briggs, especially as they had no way of knowing if he'd laid traps in the house or what he might have at his disposal to provide himself with barricades from behind which he could fire at them. They also had no idea of how much ammunition he might have.

No, Mickey had affirmed. The man had to be taken outside, there would be no assault on the little cottage. But there was one thing they could do to make escape more difficult for the man.

Another hour passed with no sense of movement from within, and Mickey began to creep forward. He took his time, pausing every few feet, and gradually, very gradually, made his way towards the car. Mauser in one hand, pocketknife in the other, Mickey approached the vehicle. His breath sounded too loud. The brush of his coat against the grass seemed deafening. Drawing a deep breath, telling himself this just had to be done, Mickey plunged the pocketknife into the wall of the front tyre.

The hiss of escaping air was suddenly the brashest and most terrifying noise Mickey had ever encountered. He withdrew the blade and moved rapidly to the back of the car, stabbed the blade into the second tyre.

And then the back door opened and Briggs was firing his gun.

Mickey threw himself behind the car and then came up with the Mauser raised. He fired at Briggs, now a shadow flitting from the darkness of the cottage towards the shadow of the car.

Mickey heard a grunt and knew his shot had hit. A bullet hitting the ground inches from his feet had him skittering for the safety of the side wall of the building, looking for his opportunity to shoot again.

He could hear Tibbs shouting now, Constable Grace yelling at his men. In the confusion of noise and orders, Mickey could not make out what was going on behind him, his focus totally on Briggs, who had just shot at him again.

Panting, Mickey flattened himself against the wall. He braced himself to peer once more around the angle of the building but then an astonishing sound filled the air. Briggs had started the engine and was skidding away, notwithstanding the two rapidly deflating tyres now flapping off the rims.

'What the hell?' Fox was now beside him. Mickey swore roundly. As they gave chase he could see Tibbs running along behind the car, firing his weapon more in hope than expectation. The car, lolling to one side, slewing dangerously back and forth across the narrow track as Briggs fought for control, seemed on the verge of rolling, and Mickey could not help but admire the control that kept it on its four wheels. It was as though Briggs had brought the full power of his will to bear in just keeping it heading in what approximated a straight line. He was heading towards the barricade of wire at the end of the track, headlights blazing, swinging like searchlights as the car drifted and skidded and seemed ready to tip and roll at any moment.

And then a scent carried to Mickey on the night air filled him with horror. One of Tibbs' shots must have found a mark and the smell of petrol leaking from the tank followed the big blue car down the track.

They had reached the bend in the road now and Mickey could just make out the exit on to the lane. He prayed the constables would have the sense to get out of the way and allow the barrier to do its intended job. Though previous knowledge told him that ruptured tanks rarely explode, that it was the petrol vapour and not the fuel itself that posed the greatest danger, he was still horrified by what might happen next.

Tibbs was beside him now. 'I punctured the tank,' he said, and Mickey could, in the dimness, make out the same anxiety in the young man's face.

He could try and shout a warning to those by the barrier, Mickey thought, but he knew any noise he might make would be drowned out by the roaring sound of the over-revving engine. He stood beside Tibbs and watched the drama unfold, knowing that it was now beyond any intervention.

Just too late, Briggs seemed to realize that there was something stretched across the path. The wire glinting in the headlights. He swerved, tipping the balance of an already unstable car, and Mickey saw the vehicle slew violently across the track and then tip and then roll. Momentum carried it to the end of the track, the wire wrapping around it as it crashed through, spiralling tight around the body of the car. There was a moment that seemed to stretch out infinitely when the car flipped, still constrained by the wire, and Briggs was thrown clear. He fell, limbs flailing, head snapped back, into the coils. They seemed, to Mickey's eyes, to be reaching and then closing on the soaring body, pulling it back to earth.

Mickey closed his eyes, momentarily transported back to another time, another place, another battlefield.

Then Tibbs was clutching at his arm and instinctively he began to run towards the car. And then there was silence, and Mickey realized that one of the constables had run to the vehicle, wheels still spinning despite the wire trap, and had cut the engine, dead.

The silence seemed profound. The scent of petrol was now heavy in the air. He could see that Briggs was beyond help and definitely beyond the need for arrest. 'Clear your men out,' Mickey shouted. 'The whole lot could go up.' But already the constables were hurrying back along the narrow road. Mickey turned and ushered those with him back towards the house where, until it grew fully light, they waited for an explosion that never came.

EPILOGUE

I t was late afternoon before Mickey and Tibbs returned to Cynthia's house for welcome baths and clean clothes. Dinner was a quiet affair. Henry picked at his food and was still struggling to eat, but Mickey was just relieved he now had the energy and interest to join the family at dinner.

'So there's only Cookson to carry the can,' Henry said.

'And Mark Barry. He'll not get off scot-free. Both face long prison terms, I suspect. But what saddens me is that we'll likely never know the name of the dead girl or those that must have been brought to the house with her.'

'Talk to your Sergeant Fox,' Cynthia said. 'Tell him we're prepared to pay for a decent burial. I know it won't put things right, but if anyone ever comes looking at least there'll be a proper record of where she is.'

Mickey nodded and thanked her. That, he thought, was so typical of Cynthia.

'So I suppose we know a little more of what happened with the Deans,' Mickey said. 'Mr Deans was Briggs and Mrs Deans was Corah Lee. Though Lord alone knows what became of her, and what about the so-called brother who was living with them? Who the devil was he?'

'I have no doubt if you take the redoubtable neighbour to look at your criminal photographs . . . mugshots, is that right? . . . then she'd be able to solve that one for you,' Albert suggested. 'But enough of this depressing stuff. Has Henry told you about his office? I'm happy to say that I've found him a nice little place above an estate agent's, just off the promenade.'

'Office?' Mickey asked.

'I've not actually seen it yet,' Henry admitted wryly, 'but I trust Albert's judgement.'

'Office for what?'

'Oh, Henry's going to become a private detective,' Albert

said. 'And there's a little flat that comes with the office space, so he'll be well set up there.'

Mickey blinked. Cynthia was looking down at her plate as though her food was particularly fascinating, but he could see the slight twitch of a smile at the corner of her mouth. Malina was just watching Henry as though, Mickey thought, she expected him to tell his ex-sergeant that this was all just one big joke.

Henry did not. 'I've just told Albert that I'll not be handling divorces,' he said. 'Anything else, but definitely not that.'

Mickey raised his glass. 'To the Henry Johnstone Detective Agency,' he said.

Then, to himself, *I give it six months.*

Milton Keynes UK
Ingram Content Group UK Ltd.
UKHW012229181223
434609UK00012B/602